I0587183

Tide Stalker

The Sea Remembers

Patrick Timm

Coastal Tides Press

Copyright © 2025 Patrick Timm

No part of this book may be reproduced or transmitted in any form or by any means, electronic or mechanical, including photocopying, recording, or by any information storage and retrieval system, without the prior written permission of the author, except for brief quotations in reviews or articles.

This is a work of fiction. Names, characters, places, and incidents are either the product of the author's imagination or are used fictitiously. Any resemblance to actual persons, living or dead, or actual events is purely coincidental.

Published by Coastal Tides Press

ISBN 978-0-9910205-1-5

Printed in the United States of America

Cover Design: Patrick Timm

Contents

1. Off to the Beach   1

2. Frank Joins Hayden   19

3. Tide Stalker Returns   29

4. Back in the Day   41

INTERLUDE   55

5. Investigations Begin   59

6. Planning   67

7. Visitor in the Night   77

Hayden's Reflection   85

8. Bandon by the Sea   87

INTERLUDE   95

Frank Alone in Bandon   99

9. Anchors Aweigh   103

10. Echoes and Departure   111

11. Shifting Tides   119

12. Shadows on the Shore   131

13. The Waiting   145

14. The Sand Dollar   153

Miss Scott's Vigil   163

15. Death at Dory Cove   165

16. Plan B   173

17. Showdown   183

18. Oregon or Bust   199

INTERLUDE   209

19. The Ravine's Secret   211

20. Together Again   219

21. Uninvited Guest   229

22. The Ghosts we Carry   239

Interlude   255

23. Memory Overload   259

24. Dark December Days   273

INTERLUDE   285

25. The Winter Crossing   287

INTERLUDE   299

26. Eye of the Storm   301

INTERLUDE 309

27. The Awakening 311

Addy's Private Moment 319

28. Stormy Seas 323

INTERLUDE 331

29. High Tide 333

30. Christmas by the Sea 341

Epilogue 351

Abby's Final Reflection 355

About the Author 357

Chapter One

Off to the Beach

Beneath a bruised October sky

The sky was a bruised purple, the kind of color that promised both rain and remembrance. The wind carried the scent of wet pine and distant sea salt, a ghostly blend of storm and memory. Hayden Lansford moved through his small house like someone closing chapters rather than packing for a short trip. The tattered green duffle sat open on the bed, its faded seams whispering of other journeys. He packed with the slow precision of habit—toothbrush, razor, laptop, notebook, charger—each item a small act of control against the growing unease humming inside him.

The old clock in the hallway ticked like a heartbeat. Outside, the rain threatened, but hadn't yet begun. He stood for a moment at the window, watching the maples lean under the wind. Their red leaves scattered across the yard like embers, catching in the gravel drive.

When he finally shouldered the duffle and headed for the car, the air bit cold and metallic, filled with that pre-storm silence that comes just before the world exhales. The October sun was weak and uncertain behind a gauze of clouds. As he eased the car into the street, tires crunching on wet leaves, Hayden told himself it was only another weekend escape—writing by the ocean, solitude, a chance to breathe. But deep down, beneath the calm surface of routine, he felt the first faint pull of something waiting—something he couldn't yet name.

He drove west, the landscape shifting from dry city streets to mist-wrapped hills that breathed of cedar and moss. Highway 26 unfurled before him like a silver ribbon, vanishing into a wall of fog that thickened with every mile. The wipers scraped a rhythmic protest across the windshield, steady as a heartbeat, as the first drops began to fall.

The forest closed in around him—towering Douglas firs rising on either side, their black trunks slick with rain. Water pooled in the ruts of the road, glinting like shards of glass in the fleeting headlights. The storm had come faster than expected. Hayden gripped the wheel tighter, leaning forward as gusts rocked the car.

For years, this drive had been a kind of pilgrimage—his way of rinsing out the noise of city life. He'd always felt a strange kinship with these storms, the way they stripped the world down to its rawest shape. But tonight, the rain didn't cleanse. It pressed against him, insistent and heavy, as if testing the edges of his resolve.

***

When the first flash of lightning illuminated the winding road ahead, Hayden's pulse jumped. For an instant, he thought he saw something—a pale figure at the roadside, gone as quickly as it appeared. He blinked, shaken. Nothing but rain and shadow.

He exhaled and turned the heater up a notch, convincing himself it was nothing more than exhaustion, tricks of light. Yet the thought lingered like a whisper behind the wiper's beat: something's waiting out there.

A secluded rental cabin overlooking the ocean south of Haystack Beach was his destination. Another fall storm had begun over Highway 26, sending sheets of rain across the northern Oregon coast. Hayden loved these trips—writing by the sea, lost in another world—but the drive through the coastal mountains was treacherous.

Wind whipped against the windshield, and the wipers struggled to keep pace. The white line along the edge of the road vanished under the torrents, and the usual ninety-minute drive stretched toward two hours. Thoughts and phrases for his novel flitted through his mind, interrupted by the rhythmic slap of rain and the roar of the wind.

Then, between a blur of wiper strokes, a massive shadow loomed. Hayden slammed on the brakes. A huge Douglas fir had fallen across the roadway, its roots torn from the earth. His heart jumped. "Dang... what next?" he muttered, gripping the wheel.

Rain pounded the car like a relentless drum. Headlights cut through the sheets of water as an Oregon Highway Department truck pulled up behind him. A sharp rap on the window startled him.

"You holding up okay?" the driver shouted over the wind.

Hayden's knuckles whitened on the steering wheel. "If the tree wasn't there..."

The man pointed toward the back. "Chainsaw's ready. Won't take long."

Hayden exhaled, picturing a warm fire in the cabin, the storm rattling the roof, the scent of rain mingling with cedar. Strange how a fleeting thought of comfort could calm him, even as the storm pressed in from every side.

Minutes stretched like hours as the crew carved a one-lane path through the massive tree. Hayden's pulse thumped in time with the wind and rain. Finally, the opening appeared. He flashed his headlights in thanks and merged back onto the road. The rain still pelted the car, blinding him with sideways sheets driven by fierce ocean winds.

***

South of Haystack Beach, a cluster of vacation homes emerged through the mist. Hayden turned off the highway, following the slick coastal road to the rental office to check in and get the keys to the cliff-side bungalow.

Hayden ran to the slippery wooden porch. The door was locked. A handwritten note read: They'll be back in twenty minutes. Daylight was fleeting, heavy clouds and rain turning the world gray. Hayden waited in the car, windshield wipers slicing the sheets of water. A yellow Volkswagen bug pulled in, and a heavyset woman in a purple raincoat dashed inside. Hayden killed the ignition and ran to the porch.

The door swung open, raindrops dripping from his brow. "Hello, you must be Mr. Lansford?"

"Is the house ready?" he asked, impatient.

She smiled, handing him a handful of papers. "Why yes, Mr. Lansford. May I call you Hayden?"

"You can call me Mr. Lansford—or whatever. Are the keys ready?"

She listed instructions in a rush: extra firewood in the shed, a downdraft might send smoke into the living room, happy hour at Captain's in Haystack Beach. Hayden nodded, signed the papers, and fled back into the rain.

By the time Hayden crested the last hill, the ocean had turned the world to slate and silver. The rain came sideways in thin, needling threads. He pulled into the gravel parking spot above the bluff and killed the engine. For a moment, he just sat there, listening to the tick of cooling metal and the distant thud of waves. Then he grabbed the duffel and his groceries and made the short dash to the door.

The key stuck, then gave with a grudging click. He stepped into a pocket of quiet—the hush of an empty place that had spent all day waiting. The cabin smelled faintly of damp wood and salt. He flicked on a lamp. A cone of amber light pooled across a braided rug, a small couch, a round table with two mismatched chairs. In the far corner, a cast-iron stove crouched like an old dog, flue rattling softly with the wind.

He carried in the rest of his things, shaking water from his jacket at the threshold, and set about his ritual. Duffle by the bed. Laptop on the table, charger coiled to the side. Groceries into unfamiliar cupboards—mug here, tea there, a stubborn corkscrew whose hinge wobbled like a loose tooth. He lit the stove and fed it kindling until the fire took, flames licking the black belly of the iron. The room exhaled a little warmth.

When he drew the curtain back, the window framed only darkness, the glass flexing under the gale. He could hear the ocean now, nearer—long pulls and heavy, dragging releases, as if the sea were breathing through the house itself. He set water to boil and unfolded his notebook, turning to a blank page already creased in the corner. Title at the top: Late Season. He touched the pen to the paper, waited, lifted it again.

A sudden rattle at the back made him pause—the loose latch on the deck door, he told himself. He crossed the room and checked it anyway. On the other side of the glass, the deck was slick with a thin sheen of rain, the railing beaded with cold pearls of water. Beyond that: nothing but the storm.

He poured tea, wrapped both hands around the mug, and sat at the table facing the window. The page lay open, the first line stubbornly refusing him. He looked up. For an instant, lightning strobed the bluff and the heave of the sea below. And just as quickly: dark again, the cabin settling, the stove ticking—his name nowhere in the sound, but something close to it.

Hours passed. The storm waned. Hayden, weary but restless, noticed a light flickering on the far beach below. He froze, watching the swinging glow move slowly toward the cabin. His pulse quickened. Clouds obscured the moon, the wind picked up, and instinct drove him outside to the woodshed. Back inside with axe in hand, he secured the door, propped a chair against it, and waited.

Finally, shivering under a pile of quilts, Hayden drifted into uneasy sleep, the hypnotic glow still dancing in his mind, mingling with the roar of waves.

Hayden woke early, the world hushed but for the faint murmur of waves beyond the windows. He slipped on his robe, shuffled to the kitchen, and set the kettle to boil.

Steam rose, ghostlike, as he leaned against the counter and watched the sea through the wide expanse of glass. The storm had gone.

The sky was clear, brushed with thin wisps of cirrus cloud, and the ocean lay calm, gray-green and glittering. After tea and toast, he showered, dressed, and stepped onto the back deck. The air was sharp and fresh, still heavy with the scent of rain.

He descended the three slick steps to the path, his shoes dampening on moss-slick grass. Halfway down the slope, the hillside opened to a weathered stairway wrapped in ferns. Each wooden step was slick with age.

The last step hung four feet above a tumble of rock. Hayden dropped to the gravel, steadying himself, and made his way toward the open stretch of beach. To his left, a moss-covered bluff jutted into the sea; to his right, the beach unfurled, pale and empty. The air was clean, briny, alive.

He stopped near the surf, noticing a scatter of sand dollars gleaming like coins. They weren't random. Someone had placed them with care, in a loose arc—almost ceremonial. He crouched, studying the arrangement. The tide hadn't reached this far. These were fresh and deliberate.

The wind was cool against his face as he walked north, toward the place where the light had moved the night before. No footprints marked the sand. The tide had erased everything. Or perhaps there had been nothing to erase.

He turned back. The cabin perched above him, small against the cliff, windows catching the morning light. It watched him, somehow— silent, patient.

***

On his way up, the steps slick beneath his feet, a board lifted unexpectedly, striking his shin. He slipped. The world tilted, the sky whirled gray, and then—nothing.

When he opened his eyes again, the light was softer. He was on the couch, a damp cloth cooling his forehead. His head throbbed, his jeans were soaked, and his shoes sat by the door, filled with sand.

He rose unsteadily, the house silent around him. Photos lined the walls—fishermen, waves, the same cliffs he'd just climbed. One photograph caught his eye: a young woman with dark hair smiling on the very same deck, her hands buried in a planter box. The sea behind her looked unchanged, eternal.

He stepped onto the deck, holding the photo up to the view. The match was exact, the railing, the rocks, even the angle of light. He felt a ripple of something between déjà vu and dread.

Who had lived here before? And why did it feel as if they still did?

After changing clothes, Hayden decided to explore the village. His first stop was the rental agency. Inside, the heavyset woman behind the desk was on the phone, but she nodded for him to come in.

"Okay, Margaret, I've got a client here— talk later," she said, hanging up the receiver. "Well, Mr. Lansford, how was your stay last night?"

"Oh, um—pretty good," he replied. "Slept like a log once I finally got to sleep."

"Oh yes, that storm was a doozy," she said with a laugh. "Lightning, thunder, wind all night long. What can I do for you?"

Hayden hesitated a moment, then said, "I'm curious. Can you tell me who owns the cabin?"

She blinked. "Well, that's an unusual question. I don't think anyone's ever asked me that before." She leaned back in her chair. "That property's in kind of a complicated ownership situation. It's held under a land trust."

Hayden frowned slightly. "A trust? That's rather odd. I'd like to learn more about it."

"Afraid that's not easy," she said. "Since it's a legal trust, the records don't show much. I've been here seven years and never met the owners. Suppose you could look it up in the county records, but I doubt it'd list anything beyond the trust name."

He stood, pacing a small circle in front of her desk. "Where would I find those records?"

"Astoria's the county seat for Clatsop County," she said. "About an hour and a half north."

"Yes, I know where Astoria is," he said. "Is there a local newspaper or a library nearby?"

"Seaside has the newspaper office—it covers both Seaside and Haystack Beach. And we do have a small library right here in town."

"Good," he said, nodding. "I'll check them out. Thanks." He paused, then added, "Tell me, have you ever noticed anyt hing... peculiar about that cabin?"

Her eyebrows lifted. "Why, no—not that I can recall."

He smiled faintly. "I find the place interesting. And the view—remarkable."

As he started for the door, she called after him. "Are you doing research for your novel?"

He turned with a half-smile. "You might say that." He reached into his pocket and pulled out the set of keys. "By the way—there are three keys on this ring. Only one opens both the front and back doors. What are the other two for? They look quite old."

She squinted at them. "Hmm. I don't rightly know. Never gave it much thought. I've never used the others. Let me see what I can find out."

Hayden drove north a few miles, turning off the highway into Haystack Beach. The neon sign for Captain's flickered in the mist, its letters half-swallowed by fog. Music and laughter spilled from the weathered cedar shake building, carrying the scent of fried clams and beer. He parked, checked his watch, and stepped inside.

Happy hour was in full swing. A jukebox hummed in the corner, glasses clinked, and the low murmur of conversation filled the room. Hayden found an empty stool at the bar and sat down.

The server, a tall man with tired eyes and a friendly half-smile, approached. "What'll it be? Happy hour specials—drinks and appetizers. Can I start you with a beer or a cocktail?"

"Rum and cola," Hayden said, scanning the small, laminated menu. He settled on steamer clams, garlic bread, and coconut shrimp.

When the drink arrived, Hayden nodded his thanks. "I'm visiting," he said, trying to sound casual. "Can anyone tell me a bit about the area?"

The server laughed softly. "I've only been here about a year, but that white-haired gent at the end of the bar—Old Salty—they say he's been here since the ocean was young. Buy him a drink, and he'll talk your ear off."

Hayden smiled, glanced down the bar, and raised his glass. After finishing most of his meal, he took his drink and slid onto the stool beside the old man. "Hi there. I hear you're the local historian."

The old man's sea-worn face cracked into a grin. "That's what they call me. Name's Salty. Been here all my life—what's left of it, anyway."

"That's saying something," Hayden said. "Can I buy you a drink? Looks like you're due for one."

Salty pushed his empty mug forward. "Sure—being friendly, or fishing for something?"

"Both," Hayden said, shifting closer. "I'm a writer, here to work on a book. Not about the coast, exactly, but I'm curious about the place. Thought I'd soak up a little local color."

Salty chuckled and scratched at his beard. "Born in '36. My father was a fisherman; my mother worked the cannery. I did both. Crab pots, nets, boats, the works. You name it, I've done it. Folks here call me Salty, and at eighty-four, I guess it fits. Crusty old soul and all."

They clinked glasses. "You've seen a lot around here," Hayden said.

"Yep," Salty murmured. "Too much, maybe." He squinted at Hayden. "You look like a man about to ask something I don't wanna answer."

Hayden hesitated, turning his glass in his hand. "Maybe. Have you ever heard of Dory Cove?"

The old man froze. His fingers tightened around the mug. A long silence hung between them before he wiped his brow with the back of his arm.

"I figured someday someone'd wander in here and ask that," he said at last. "Took longer than I expected."

"I don't understand," Hayden said.

"No, you wouldn't. Not your fault. It was years ago—three decades, maybe more. Folks don't talk about it anymore. I suspect you're talkin' about a boat?"

Hayden nodded slowly. "Yes. I'm renting a cabin south of town. There are old photographs on the walls. One shows a boat called Dory Cove."

Salty set down his mug. "That's enough beer for me."

"Come on," Hayden said. "You can't leave me hanging like that."

The old man rose from his stool, joints creaking. "Some things are better left buried. That cove near your cabin? Folks used to call it Dory Cove too. My advice? Go find another place to write your book. The more you dig, the less you'll like what you find. Some stories'll eat you alive."

"Why? What happened there?" Hayden pressed.

Salty's eyes, clouded and gray, met his. "Sad things. Unfortunate things. Leave it be." He cleared his throat and shuffled toward the door. "Good luck to you, feller. You'll need it."

***

Hayden watched him disappear into the fog.

He turned to the server. "You were right— he talked until I asked one question."

"What'd you ask?"

"About a boat. Dory Cove."

The server frowned. "Can't say I've heard of it. I've only been here for a year. These days it's a tourist town—shops, surf, and summer rentals. Not like the old fishing village it used to be. Most of the old-timers are gone."

"I suppose," Hayden said. "But something tells me not everything from the past is gone."

The server shrugged. "Maybe. You coming back tomorrow?"

"Maybe," Hayden said, tossing a few bills on the counter. "You said Salty's a regular?"

"Every afternoon. Creature of habit."

Outside, the air was heavy with salt and drizzle. Hayden drove back along the dark highway, thoughts spiraling. What had shaken the old man so deeply? Why warn him away?

Curiosity, he thought, is a double-edged sword. It can lead to truth—or ruin. It opens doors better left closed. Sometimes it unearths what time itself tried to forget.

Back at the cabin, he built a fire, brewed tea, and settled into the worn armchair. Moonlight shimmered on the restless sea. He stared through the wall of glass, thinking of the strange events of the day—the mystery of the property, the sand dollars arranged like a sign, his fall on the hillside steps, the photographs, the old man's fear.

If this wasn't a mystery, then writing one was only second place.

He checked his watch. Not that late. He picked up his phone and dialed.

After four rings, a familiar voice: "This is Frank. Leave a message."

"Hey, old man, pick up. It's Hayden. I know you're there watching Columbo."

A chuckle came through the line. "How dare you interrupt my lonely solitude? What's up, Hayden? Been a while."

"Too long. I'm writing again or trying to. But something's come up out here—something odd. I'm staying at a cabin south of Haystack Beach."

Frank sighed. "The beach, odd? Sounds like you've been reading too much of your own material. What's going on?"

"Too much to explain over the phone. You free to drive down for a couple days? You'll enjoy the view—and I could use your help."

"You mean drag me away from my thrilling life of yard work and old detective shows?"

Hayden laughed. "Something like that."

"Alright," Frank said. "I'll head out in the morning. Lunch time work for you?"

"Perfect. I've got plenty to tell."

"Well then," Frank said, "You've stumbled onto the story of a lifetime, or you've finally gone stir-crazy. Either way, I'm intrigued."

Hayden smiled. "This is no story on a page, Frank."

"Guess I'll find out soon enough. See you tomorrow, my friend."

Hayden hung up, leaned back, and pulled a blanket from the couch. The fire cracked softly. Outside, the moon drifted through torn clouds over the endless sweep of ocean. The waves whispered their secrets against the shore.

Peaceful—at least for the moment.

Chapter Two

Frank Joins Hayden

The cabin beyond the storm

Morning light filled the cabin, chasing the shadows from corners and waking Hayden from a restless doze in the overstuffed chair. He blinked against the brightness and sat up, bones stiff from sleep. On the back deck railing, several seagulls perched like sentries, their sharp eyes peering through the glass. Whether they were expecting a handout or simply watching the solitary writer, he couldn't tell.

Hayden stood at the window with a cup of tea, gazing at the endless ocean below. The storm had stripped the beach clean. Logs lay scattered like bones, their bark torn and slick. Seaweed coiled in dark ropes along the tide line. He could hear the waves long before he could see them—an endless, breathing pulse against the shore.

Another rare, sunny October day had arrived—mild and deceptive in its calm. The horizon was seamless, the blue of sea and sky blending into one vast, oblivious plane. He opened his phone's notes app and began typing fragments about the coast—small impressions he didn't want to lose before Frank arrived. He became so focused that he didn't notice the gulls still lined up outside, waiting.

Hayden remained for a long moment at the window, tea cooling in his hands. The world outside looked deceptively peaceful. The ocean had that early morning sheen, silver where the sun broke through and dull gray everywhere else. He could still smell last night's storm— salt and ozone and something metallic, like wet iron. For a second he thought he saw movement far out on the beach, a darker shape shifting near the drift logs, but when he blinked, it was gone.

He rubbed his eyes, reminding himself that solitude sometimes invented company. "Storm ghosts," he muttered, forcing a dry laugh.

***

The phone rang. Frank was twenty minutes away. Hayden set it down and looked back at the gulls. "Stupid birds," he muttered. Opening the door, he waved them off. "Shoo, shoo, go away!"

They erupted in a clatter of wings, circling above the deck. But as soon as he turned to go back inside, two settled right back on the railing, cawing defiantly. He frowned. "Fine. Stay there. I'm not feeding you."

A knock at the front door startled him. "That must be Frank," he said, striding to open it.

It wasn't. The woman from the rental office stood smiling on the porch.

"Mr. Lansford! I thought I'd drop by to clear something up—oh, were you expecting someone?"

Hayden sighed, irritation flickering across his face. "Yes, a friend. What's this about?"

"You mentioned two extra keys on your keyring yesterday," she said brightly. "I asked around and checked the old records, but no one seems to know what they're for. They're quite old—might've gone to an outbuilding that isn't there anymore."

"Doesn't matter," he said, shifting his weight.

"I can take them if you'd like—"

"No," he cut in. "I'll hang on to them till I leave."

Her smile faltered for a moment. "Of course. Didn't want you worrying. Enjoy your stay."

Hayden watched her yellow Volkswagen bump up the gravel drive, shaking his head. As her car disappeared, another pulled in—

Frank's.

***

He exhaled, tension releasing from his shoulders. The sound of tires crunching gravel had never felt so reassuring. Until that moment, he hadn't realized how uneasy the woman's visit had left him. The idea of two old keys, once belonging to some vanished outbuilding, had unsettled him more than he wanted to admit. What doors had they opened? And why did he feel, irrationally, that something still waited behind one of them?

Relief swept over him. He stepped outside, waving. "Frank! You made it!"

The two men met halfway, exchanging a quick hug and back pat. "I nearly hit that yellow car leaving your driveway," Frank said. "Traffic even out here, huh? How's life at the beach treating you?"

"Eventful," Hayden said dryly. "Come in." Frank set his bag down in the spare room. "Bunks or double bed?"

"I think my bunk bed days are over," Frank said with a laugh. "I'll take the double."

"Come see the view." Hayden led him to the window. The ocean shimmered beyond the glass, sunlight glancing off the waves. "Not bad, right?"

Frank gave a low whistle. "You sure know how to pick a writing spot."

Outside on the deck, the gulls had returned. Hayden waved them off again. "Persistent things."

Frank grinned. "They're part of the package. Salt air, gulls, and visions of fishermen past."

After showing Frank the photos on the wall, Hayden grabbed the keys. "Let's grab lunch. I'll fill you in on everything."

Over bowls of clam chowder and steaming bread at a seaside café, Hayden recounted his strange arrival—the storm, the mysterious light on the beach, the fall, and his encounter with old Salty. When he finished, he leaned back, frustrated. "It doesn't add up, Frank. You can't even walk along that cove at high tide. Whoever was out there had to come from somewhere. And the way Salty reacted—he was terrified. Over a simple name: Dory Cove." Frank steepled his fingers, studying him.

"Maybe there's less to it than you think, Hayden. You've spent your life turning shadows into stories. Could be your imagination filling the gaps."

"You think I'm chasing ghosts?"

"I think your gut's chasing something. And maybe it's right." Frank smiled faintly. "Let's check into this Tide Stalker of yours."

"Tide Stalker?" Hayden laughed.

"Well, someone wandering beaches at night deserves a title," Frank said, grinning.

"Has a ring to it, doesn't it?"

"Actually, yes," Hayden said. "It fits."

***

They agreed to return to Captains for happy hour. "We'll talk to Salty again," Frank said. "Maybe he'll be more talkative with two of us."

Before then, they drove the coastline— past the sea-stacked cliffs, through stands of wind-twisted spruce, down to Hug Point. The tide was halfway out, revealing smooth, water polished stones. "No wonder it's called Dory Cove," Frank said. "A cove you could row into—once."

Hayden nodded, eyes fixed on the sea. "It's beautiful—and dangerous. Just like everything else here."

By late afternoon, Captains was buzzing again. They took a quiet table near the wall, ordered drinks, and waited. No sign of Salty. After half an hour, the same young server appeared, his expression subdued.

"Hey," Hayden said. "We were hoping to see old Salty tonight."

The server hesitated, lowering his voice.

"You haven't heard?"

Hayden tensed. "Heard what?"

"He's gone," the server said quietly. "Found this morning down by the pier. Head crushed. Sheriff thinks a sneaker wave got him."

For a long moment, neither Hayden nor Frank spoke. Hayden's stomach dropped.

"What?" he said finally. "That's impossible. He was fine last night."

"Yeah. I was at the station giving my statement. Told them you'd talked to him before he left. They might want to talk to you too."

Hayden sat rigid. "I only asked about a boat. That's all."

The server nodded uneasily. "Dory Cove, right? You should tell the police everything. Just in case."

After he left, Frank leaned forward. "An accident, maybe. The ocean's unforgiving."

"On a calm morning?" Hayden said. "He lived his whole life by the sea."

"People slip," Frank said. "Or maybe something else weighed on him."

Hayden exhaled. "You think I pushed him too far? With one question?"

"Maybe the question wasn't the problem," Frank said quietly. "Maybe the memories were."

At the Haystack Beach police station, they were ushered into a small conference room. Chief Dixon, gray-mustached and square shouldered, looked up from a pile of papers. "You're the writer who spoke with Salty?"

"Yes," Hayden said. "He seemed upset when I asked about Dory Cove, but that's all."

The Chief frowned. "Odd thing to get worked up about."

Frank spoke smoothly. "Writers have a way of asking the wrong right questions. I'm Frank Thompson—retired detective, Portland PD."

The Chief's face brightened. "I know that name. The Smith family cold case up at Klootchy Creek wasn't it? You cracked that one."

Frank nodded. "Long time ago."

"Well, this one's simpler. Looks like a tragic accident. Sneaker wave, skull fracture, no sign of struggle. The old man was stubborn about getting close to the surf. We'll file it as accidental unless the coroner says otherwise."

Frank handed him his card. "Understood. Still—mind if we stay in touch?"

"Of course." The Chief gave Hayden a measured look. "You staying around long?"

"A few days," Hayden said.

As they left, the Chief called after them, "You said you're north of Arch Cape?"

Hayden nodded, uneasy. "That's right."

Back at the cabin, the fire crackled softly. Hayden sat with a blanket draped across his legs, staring into the flames. Frank jotted notes in a small yellow pad.

"Well," Frank said at last, "You're not a suspect, but it's strange timing."

"Everything about this place feels strange," Hayden murmured. "Salty knew something, and now he's dead."

Frank tapped his pen. "Then we'll find out what it was."

***

Hayden stared into the fire, its orange glow painting shadows on the walls. The house creaked again—timber expanding, air shifting—but in his tired state, every sound felt deliberate, purposeful. "You ever notice," he said softly, "how a place seems to remember?"

Frank looked up from his notes. "You mean apparitions?"

Hayden shrugged. "Call it what you want. The sea, the cliffs, the old cabins... they hold stories. Not all of them end clean."

Frank smiled faintly, closing his pad. "You're a writer, my friend. You see stories where most people see weather."

Hayden met his eyes across the flickering firelight. "And you? You see crimes where most people see accidents."

"Fair enough," Frank said. "Maybe that's why we make a good team."

The wind rose outside, brushing against the cabin walls like a passing hand.

Outside, the moon spilled silver light over the restless sea. Inside, the fire whispered and the house settled around them, holding its breath.

Chapter Three

Tide Stalker Returns

The stranger by the sea

They both retired to bed. The night was quiet, almost unnaturally so. Hayden awoke at two o'clock and crept into the living room. He placed another log in the woodstove and moved to the windows. The moon had nearly vanished below the horizon, and a light flickered on the beach—slow, deliberate, almost purposeful.

The glass of the window breathed faintly with the pulse of the surf, each wave dimming and brightening the reflection of his own face. For a moment he thought the light was a boat offshore—but it moved too smoothly, too human. Back and forth, as if someone were combing the sand for a lost soul.

Hayden focused and watched the light swing back and forth along the sand. He raced down the hall and shook Frank awake. "The beach walker is back—come see!"

Frank jumped out of bed and followed him. Together they observed the moving light.

"I'm going to get my night vision binoculars from the car," Frank said. He returned moments later, peering through the lenses. "Hayden... I see a man in a long raincoat, boots, and a wide-brimmed hat. His face is lost in shadow, but he's holding a double-mantle lantern—kerosene or white gas. You don't see those anymore. He's raising and lowering it, scanning the water's edge."

Hayden took the binoculars. "Wow... almost too bright to stare at with these." He studied the figure a few minutes before handing them back. "What do you make of him?"

Frank exhaled. "His stature and gear... reminds me of an old fisherman on a vintage fish-stick package. Ghostly, almost. And that lantern... it's like he's searching for something he lost decades ago."

Hayden chuckled, though uneasily. "Humor aside... how did he even get there? The tide is way up past the north cove."

Frank shrugged. "Good question. And one of many. I guess I believe you now—I thought your writing had gotten the better of you."

Hayden smiled. "I was just kidding, you know."

"So was I."

The light paused, then swung once—almost a signal—before turning toward the distant rocks. A faint breeze whispered against the glass, and Hayden shivered though the fire was still burning. The whole beach seemed to breathe with him.

"The only way to find out who he is... is to go down there," Frank said.

"Not a good idea," Hayden warned. "Moon's gone, it's dark, and those slimy steps down the hill are treacherous even in daylight. I speak from experience."

Frank put down the binoculars. "Yeah, I thought so. He'd vanish the minute he saw flashlights moving toward him."

They watched as the 'Tide Stalker' made his way across the beach to the sand dollar area and then returned north, sweeping the lantern sideways along the water's edge.

"Odd night gear for a calm evening," Hayden said.

"Maybe he's waiting for something—or someone. Like eagles hunting along the northern Washington coast," Frank offered. "They stalk the tide for their prey. Maybe this one is looking for secrets hidden in the sand—or memories someone wanted buried."

"What now?" Hayden asked.

"Go back to bed and regroup in the morning," Frank said.

"About all we can do. As old Salty warned, don't let this consume you," Hayden replied.

***

Hayden lingered a moment longer, staring out at the water. The lantern glow had vanished, but its afterimage burned in his vision—a ghost light that pulsed behind his eyelids. He closed the curtain, but the reflection of the sea still shimmered faintly across the glass, like a living thing that would not sleep.

They retreated to their rooms. Outside, darkness ruled. Stars struggled to illuminate the sea. A soft breeze stirred the trees. The mystery of years past lingered—now pulled into motion by a writer and his detective companion. Old Salty was gone, but the ocean kept its secrets. Beneath the serene surface lurked danger, the restless dead, and stories untold.

By dawn, a low fog pressed against the house like a living wall. Hayden dreamed of the lantern's circle of light, moving endlessly along the sand, and woke with the sound of waves in his ears. He brewed tea and stood by the stove, watching the gray smear of surf through the window. Every creak of the cabin seemed amplified, every shadow alive. The air smelled of brine and woodsmoke and something faintly metallic—like rust, or old lantern oil.

Overcast skies greeted the two men the next morning. Hayden sipped his tea, reflecting on the previous night.

"So much for a peaceful week of writing," he said.

Frank stood at the window, watching gulls flit overhead. "Your birds are back. Those three on the railing—seems they want to read our lips."

"I don't know why they're here. Maybe someone used to feed them. Puzzling," Hayden said.

"We should check in with the Chief about Salty's death, find the beach house owner, and figure out this land trust," Frank said.

At the police station, Chief Dixon greeted them.

"Salty's coroner report?" Frank asked.

"Blunt force trauma to the head, likely from a sneaker wave," the Chief replied. "No signs of struggle. Mr. Lansford, did he seem upset to you?"

"No, other than avoiding a question about Dory Cove," Hayden said.

The Chief nodded. "Then I'd classify it as a freak accident unless the coroner's revises his report. You two should keep me posted if you discover anything. Small towns have long memories... sometimes things surface decades later."

***

When they left the station, drizzle stitched the air, turning the coastline silver-gray. Frank's windshield wipers swept rhythmically as they drove back toward the cabin. The beach looked empty now, but Hayden couldn't shake the impression that someone—or something—was still out there watching, just beyond sight.

Back at the house, Hayden scoured the internet while Frank made inquiries.

Trip Advisor reviews hinted at previous guests noticing the beach walker, isolating the house, and seagull troubles. "Hey Frank, listen to this review. One from 2014 read: 'Spooky at night, with someone walking back and forth along the beach with a light. We cut our stay short.' How about that?"

"Deja vu," Frank muttered. "Tide Stalker has been at it for years, apparently."

"Looks like our Tide Stalker has a history," Hayden said.

They began searching the house. Hayden sifted through books and photos; Frank explored drawers and cubbies. A bookmark with never enough and a photo labeled Abby, 1978 emerged—a small clue hinting at someone's long-forgotten life here.

Frank found a note: "Charlie" with a phone number.

They called. A woman at Coastal Antiques said, "Charles—he goes by Charles to most, only dear friends call him Charlie. I'll inquire and get back to you," she said.

***

Meanwhile, property searches revealed little beyond a land trust and a law firm refusing to release information.

Hayden frowned at the ocean. "No recourse, it seems."

"Not without a lawsuit," Frank said. "For now, we follow the clues. Photos, names, old letters, the seagulls, Salty's warning... it's all connected. Something's lurking in the history of this house."

Dark clouds rolled in. Frank received a call from Coastal Antiques: Charles Lookingglass would see them in person.

Hayden and Frank exchanged a puzzled look. "Lookingglass?" Hayden muttered.

Frank's brow furrowed. "Rockaway's only about an hour south. We'll pay him a visit tomorrow."

That night, they watched the beach through the wide front windows. The wind was calm, the moon low and silver on the horizon. Then, just past eleven, a figure appeared again—a faint moving light on the wet sand, swinging like a lantern.

"There," whispered Hayden.

Frank reached for his camera, but the figure vanished into the mist.

"The Tide Stalker," Hayden murmured.

Neither man spoke again until the fire had burned low.

***

The next morning dawned crisp, with low clouds rolling in from the sea. After lunch they grabbed their jackets and headed south along Highway 101 toward Rockaway Beach, the ocean wind whispering secrets across the waves.

On the way, Hayden asked, "What do you expect when talking with Mr. Lookingglass?"

Frank shrugged. "We ease in, show him the note, and see where it leads. Could be nothing—or it could open the door to everything. If we mention Dory Cove—just the name—we might stir something."

Hayden smiled faintly. "And if it leads nowhere?"

"Then you go back to writing your novel, and I go home to rake leaves."

"Remind me to ask for a few more days at the rental office," Hayden said. "Something tells me we'll need them."

They passed Nehalem Bay under a restless sky, the road twisting between forested cliffs and glimpses of gray ocean. Soon the town of Rockaway Beach appeared—quiet, windblown, and scattered with empty cottages.

"There it is," said Hayden.

Frank parked in front of a weathered white building. The sign above the door read Coastal Antiques. The salt-streaked windows gave the place a ghostly pallor.

"Well," Frank said, cutting the engine, "shall we?"

The antique shop appeared weathered but charming, salt-stained windows and old white wood giving it character.

Inside, the air smelled of time and dust. Rows of shelves overflowed with relics of the past—ship lanterns, maps, model boats, photographs, glass bottles clouded with age.

An older woman in a gray wool sweater greeted them. "Mr. Thompson—and associate, I presume?" Her British accent gave her words a precise edge.

"Yes, this is my friend Hayden," Frank replied.

"Very well then," she said, leading them into the dim, cluttered aisles. Outside, a squall pelted the windows.

They arrived at a room with overstuffed red leather chairs facing an enormous desk. Bookshelves lined every wall, stacks of yellowed papers cluttered tables. A grandfather clock ticked steadily. A nameplate on the desk read C.W. Lookingglass.

From a small squeaky door behind the desk, a wiry man emerged. White, messy hair, half-lens glasses perched on his nose, wearing a vest and gold pocket watch chain glinting faintly in the lamplight. He regarded them from his high-backed chair.

"Who am I conversing with today?" he asked.

"I'm Frank Thompson, retired detective, and this is Hayden Lansford, mystery novelist," Frank replied.

"Ah, the infamous cold case detective? Here to solve another?"

"It's complicated," Frank said.

Hayden leaned forward. "We found a note in the cabin nightstand with your name— 'Charlie'—and this phone number. We hoped it might explain some things."

"Only a handful have ever called me Charlie," Lookingglass mused. "Even my mother called me Charles. Tell me, what's so odd about that cabin?"

So, Hayden told him everything—from the storm and the beach walker to Salty's cryptic warning and his sudden death. He spoke until he was breathless.

Lookingglass lit a pipe, puffing quietly as he listened. The smoke curled above him like a thin ghost. Finally, he poured three glasses of brandy from a crystal decanter and raised his own.

"To the Tide Stalker," he said.

Hayden and Frank hesitated, then clinked their glasses.

Outside, wind howled. The office lights flickered as the grandfather clock struck half past seven.

Lookingglass leaned forward. "I'm sorry about Salty. His time had come, I suppose. A wise man, though—he knew when to stay clear. His real name was Wendell Smith. Born and raised in Haystack Beach. After a serious encounter years ago, he became a recluse. He trusted no one."

Hayden's curiosity sharpened. "What kind of encounter?"

Lookingglass's eyes glimmered. "Ah, Mr. Lansford—eager to turn the page, are we? This story is long, and it has no last chapter. You and your friend may have to write it yourselves."

Frank shifted in his chair. "We're not looking to write any chapters, Mr. Lookingglass. Only to understand what's been happening."

The old man smiled faintly. "The only difference between life and fiction is that you can't rewrite the beginning—but the ending is always within reach. How you finish it, though—that's up to you."

He stood and walked to the grand father clock, resting his hand on the brass pendulum. "Lives were lost. Some never left this earth in peace. Their stories remain unfinished. Gentlemen, would you like to hear the rest?"

Hayden looked at Frank. "We've come this far," he said softly. "Might as well."

Lookingglass nodded. "Then pour yourselves another drink. It's going to be a long night."

Chapter Four

Back in the Day

Lookingglass and the forgotten truth

The storm pressed its palms against the windows, a steady percussion of wind and sea. Inside, the room seemed to breathe in rhythm with the pendulum of the great clock, a slow and solemn heartbeat. The scent of pipe smoke and old paper thickened in the air as Mr. Lookingglass settled deeper into his chair. The lamplight caught the brass rims of his glasses, flashing once before dimming again.

The old man's words filled the room like a tide rising slow and deliberate. Outside, rain streaked down the window in long silver lines, and the steady drum of wind pressed against the glass as if urging him on. Hayden could smell the faint salt dampness even through the walls. Every creak of the building seemed to echo the pulse of the ocean beyond.

"Before the darkness," he began, his voice low and unhurried, "there was light. There was laughter along that cove you call Dory—though none have called it that in decades. It was a small community once. Fishermen, a few families, a girl who could out-row any man in the village. And a storm that changed everything."

Hayden leaned forward, elbows on knees, the brandy untouched in his hand. Frank stayed still beside him, only the faint creak of leather marking his breath.

The old man leaned back, eyes half-closed, letting memory steer the room.

"It was 1980 when a skinny young man entered the antique shop seeking employment," he said. "He introduced himself as Jeremy Stayton, a drifter of sorts, with sand in his shoes and the sea in his eyes. He loved the ocean—the way it revealed and reclaimed, how it left behind bits of wreckage, old stories disguised as driftwood.

"Jeremy was born and raised in the lower Nehalem River Valley. After high school, he hustled for a living—buying and selling whatever he could find, working crab pots in Nehalem Bay, and combing beaches for flotsam and jetsam. When he stepped into Coastal Antiques—with its worn shiplap floors, salt-streaked windows, and the faint smell of brass and varnish—it was like walking into a dream.

"He and I—Charles Lookingglass—hit it off from the start," he said. "I saw something in him: a hunger for meaning, a quiet endurance. He became my apprentice, though I never called him that. His duties were... as one might say, 'other assigned tasks'—fetching, restoring, and rescuing forgotten relics from the tide.

"Before long, Jeremy was driving the shop's old white Econoline van up and down the coast. Estate sales, fishing villages, abandoned canneries—he found treasures in places most folks overlooked. He had an instinct for it. After winter storms, he'd be the first on the beach at dawn, combing through what the sea had surrendered overnight.

"His story wasn't without loss. His parents died the year he graduated high school—an auto accident with a logging truck on Highway 53. With no family left, I suppose I became his surrogate father, though neither of us ever said so aloud. I let him live in a small cottage I owned in Rockaway Beach. He was grateful—and in time, I came to depend on him far more than I expected.

"Over the years, I taught him how to restore old furniture, how to handle fine china, and even a bit of etiquette—he always laughed at that. I was raised an Englishman, after all, and couldn't bear to see him sign a letter without a proper salutation. He worked hard and never complained. I once told him, 'You've earned your knighthood, lad.' From that day on, he called me Charlie.

"His travels expanded, and so did his reputation. From the Long Beach Peninsula down to Gold Beach, everyone knew the antique hunter in the white van. He brought back vanloads of forgotten history—sometimes towing a trailer piled high with driftwood and relics wrapped in burlap.

"It was on one of those southern trips that he met her—Abby Scott, a young woman from Bandon. Her aunt owned a weathered trading store on a hill above the old harbor. Abby was five years younger, with raven-black hair that fell to her waist and a smile that could stop the rain. She was gentle but sure of herself—a rare combination.

"When Jeremy returned from that trip, he couldn't stop talking about her. I remember the way he said her name—as though it were a song. Abby. There was no doubt in my mind that he was in love. I called him into my office and gave him my blessing.

"Her aunt didn't want her to marry," he said. "She feared losing her only help at the store. But love, as it often does, wore down her resistance. In June of 1985, they married in a small chapel in Garibaldi, with the sound of the ocean rolling in through the windows.

"Jeremy had saved every penny since he started working for me. With a bit of help from my end, they found a charming cabin overlooking a five-acre private cove just north of the Arch Cape tunnel. It was the kind of place where time seemed to slow down. The two of them called it Dory Cove.

"Abby transformed the place. She filled the deck with pots of flowers, hung seashell chimes that tinkled in the wind, and befriended a small flock of seagulls who visited daily for treats.

I can still see her in my mind—barefoot, feeding the gulls, her laughter echoing against the cliffside.

"Jeremy had a different dream: to buy a dory boat and fish the coast. He learned from the old-timers in Haystack Beach, but his closest mentor was Salty—you might remember him, the same man who befriended you, Mr. Lansford. He taught Jeremy everything—how to read the tides, how to launch from the beach, how to survive a sudden squall.

"Together, Jeremy and Abby became inseparable. He'd haul crab pots while she steered the dory, her hair whipping in the salt wind. After their catches, they'd sell to the cannery, then share supper with Salty before heading home to their cove.

"Those were golden years. Their laughter, their love—it was something to behold. But the sea... the sea always keeps its due."

***

As Lookingglass spoke of the storm, Hayden closed his eyes for a moment and pictured it—the pale light over the gray sea, Abby's hair streaming behind her as she reached for the line, Jeremy's call torn away by the wind. The old man's voice softened when he said her name, like a prayer.

Frank sat motionless, his detective's face unreadable, but Hayden saw the flicker of something human—grief, maybe recognition—in the older man's eyes. For a moment they weren't investigator and writer; they were witnesses at a kind of memorial service conducted by a survivor who had never truly survived.

"It was a fine morning that dawned in early October of 1990," Lookingglass continued. "The air was calm, the horizon clear, and the sea glistened like beaten silver. Jeremy and Abby gathered their crab pots and gear, working together with the familiar rhythm of old hands. The dory boat, their pride and joy, slid into the surf as it had a hundred times before.

"They set their pots, marking each with a bright red float. The water was gentle, the pull steady. When the work was done, they headed to Haystack Beach, where Salty was bent over his boat, patching a net.

"There was laughter on the pier—the easy kind that comes when the morning is still young and the sea seems friendly. Salty cracked jokes about their catch, and Abby brushed a strand of hair from her face, smiling in that way Jeremy always remembered. After lunch at Chief's, they returned to find the sky darkening. Along the horizon, clouds were piling high and bruised, and the breeze had turned sharp and cold.

"By the time they reached the cove, whitecaps had begun to roll in. Jeremy decided to haul the pots early, not wanting to risk the worsening weather. Salty, ever the fisherman, offered to come along and lend a hand.

"Two miles out, the waves rose higher, and the horizon disappeared in a curtain of gray. The boat pitched and rolled as Salty hauled in the lines. Abby worked the pots, steadying them as water slapped over the gunwales. The wind howled through the rigging.

"'Two more!' Jeremy shouted." Salty nodded and pointed. 'There—they're close!' he shouted back.

"The boat rocked violently. The swell lifted and dropped them like a toy. Abby reached with the harpoon pole, trying to hook the last float. Salty leaned over to grab the line, his cap whipping away into the sea. Jeremy fought the tiller, keeping the bow into the waves. But a sudden crosswind caught them broadside, and the dory twisted hard.

"The next moment came like a hammer blow—an immense wall of water struck the hull and flung them into chaos. The boat overturned. Cold, roaring water swallowed everything.

"Jeremy surfaced, gasping, clinging to the side of the boat as it righted itself. 'Abby!' he shouted." Salty's voice came faint and ragged through the wind. 'I can't see her!' "Another wave rolled over them, and for an instant Jeremy saw her—a flash of her arm, her hair—then she was gone again among the white peaks." 'Grab her! She's there!' Jeremy yelled. But his arm throbbed in agony, useless, maybe broken. He watched as Salty, wearing the only life vest, struck out toward her, fighting the surge. Another breaker hit, and both vanished from sight.

"Then silence—except for the wind and the hiss of rain.

"When the sea finally relented, Jeremy found himself and the boat washed up on the sand, shivering and half-conscious. Salty lay farther down the beach, sprawled and coughing. Jeremy stumbled toward him, his voice hoarse. "Where's Abby? Where is she?' "Salty shook his head, dazed and hollow-eyed. 'I—I couldn't reach her...' "Jeremy stared out into the gray emptiness, then began to run, shouting her name over and over until his voice broke. The tide was coming in. Every wave looked like it might bring her back, but none did. They searched the beach for hours, long after dark. Only the sound of the surf answered."

Lookingglass stopped speaking for a long moment, staring into the amber glow of his brandy glass. The fire crackled softly in the grate, and the light flickered over the deep lines in his face.

"When the Coast Guard finally came," he said, his voice low and deliberate, "they searched three days. They never found her. Not a trace. The sea keeps what it wants." He swirled the glass slowly, then took a sip. "Never forgave himself. Or Salty. The two men never spoke again after that day. He stayed on at Dory Cove for a while, kept the boat up on its rig, though he never took her out again. Every day he walked the beach. At night he walked the beach with a lantern, looking for his bride. One can only imagine how he felt. Then one morning he was just... gone. Vanished, like Abby. Left everything behind—his clothes, his tools, even his boots by the door."

***

Lookingglass's eyes drifted toward the window, though the view was only of rain streaking down the glass. "I went up there myself a week later. The sea was calm that day, flat as glass. Abby's flower pots were still on the deck, tipped over, the soil dry and hard. There was a single gull on the railing, waiting. I sat with Jeremy for a long spell, a friendly talk and tears as well. I gave him our new phone number. That was the note in the nightstand.

"That gull," he continued quietly, "never moved from the railing the entire time I was there. Just watched me with one black, steady eye. When I left, it followed me up the path to the road. Strange thing, isn't it, how animals sometimes guard the places we abandon?"

Hayden felt a chill at that. He thought of the gulls at his own railing that morning—the same unblinking stare, the same stillness. It was as if the birds themselves were keeping vigil for a story not yet finished.

He sighed and leaned back, setting the empty glass on the table. "That was the last time I saw Dory Cove."

Frank cleared his throat softly, not wanting to break the silence. "And you never learned what happened to him?"

Lookingglass shook his head. "No. Some said he walked into the sea. Others thought he left for Alaska. I don't believe either. He wasn't a man to run. But after losing Abby..." He paused, the words catching. "There wasn't much left of him to stay."

For a time, no one spoke. The only sound was the steady rhythm of the grandfather clock—tick, tock, like the heartbeat of the past refusing to die. Hayden rubbed a thumb along the rim of his glass, thinking how much of what he'd heard could belong to one of his novels.

Yet it felt real, achingly so. He thought of Abby's laughter echoing across the cliffs, of Jeremy's shadow on the sand with his lantern raised against the wind. Somewhere between legend and fact, their lives had become the very ghost story he'd come to write.

Hayden sat forward, elbows on his knees, studying the old man's face. "So that's the cabin I'm in now. The one they called Dory Cove."

Lookingglass nodded slowly. "Yes. That place carries the weight of their story. I always felt... something lingered there. Not a ghost, exactly. More like an unfinished breath."

The room fell quiet except for the ticking of the clock. Outside, the wind stirred the trees, and the sound of the surf rolled faintly up from the beach below.

Finally, Hayden spoke again. "Do you believe he's really gone?"

Lookingglass stared into the flames. "Gone?" He smiled faintly, though it wasn't a smile of comfort. "Perhaps. Or perhaps the sea just keeps its promises longer than we do."

"Wow," said Hayden.

"What about the beach house? I see it's in a land trust," said Frank.

"Yes. I arranged that in case he returned. I always thought he would."

"And Abby's aunt in Bandon? Did she know? Did she say anything?" asked Hayden.

Lookingglass glanced at his pocket watch. The grandfather clock struck midnight—gong, gong. At the last stroke, he snapped it closed. "Right on time tonight. I sent a messenger to Bandon to share the news with her. Her business had been sold, no phone. Upon arrival, her driveway was gated and locked."

"She never found out about Abby?" asked Frank.

"She made it to the gate. My messenger waited in his car for a day and a half. At gunpoint, she accepted my letter, warning him never to return. My letter explained everything I knew and gave my number. She never contacted me."

"I wonder why she was so mean?" asked Hayden.

"She resented Jeremy for taking her niece in marriage. She never liked him."

"Let me get this straight. You have the house in a trust in case he shows up. How do you know he isn't dead? Nearly thirty years have passed. And the Tide Stalker on the beach at night—couldn't that be him?" asked Frank.

Lookingglass leaned forward. "Interesting. After all this time, no sightings of Jeremy... how could that be him? This walking on the beach at night is the first I've heard of it."

Hayden glared. "Do you believe in ghosts, Mr. Lookingglass?"

The old man's face turned pale. He handed Frank a piece of paper.

"What's this?" asked Frank.

"The name and address of her aunt in Bandon. It may help your search."

"Our search?" Frank looked at Hayden, puzzled.

"Yes. We now know Salty's surmise. We must put to rest Jeremy and Abby," said Lookingglass.

Frank shook his head. "Don't you think Abby lies at the bottom of the sea? And Jeremy... he may have given up on life. Or both are lost forever."

Lookingglass leaned back, exhausted. "I understand. But some souls need closure. I believe Abby and Jeremy are alive—and need to reunite."

Frank wiped his brow. "This is crazy. Way beyond a cold case, Mr. Lookingglass."

"Perhaps," the old man said slowly. "But if the Tide Stalker is a ghost, shouldn't his soul rest, so he won't haunt the beach forever?"

Frank and Hayden rose. "We'll go to the beach house, sleep on it, and let you know tomorrow," Frank said.

Lookingglass handed Frank a thick sealed envelope. "Open only if your search reaches a dead end."

He led them to the front door and opened it, letting in the chilly night breeze.

"Thank you for the information. Bittersweet story. Good-night," said Frank.

Hayden nodded. They climbed into Frank's SUV and head-ed north. In the rearview mirror, Frank watched the darkened building fade behind them.

"That was the strangest encounter I've ever had. Write the last chapter, huh? I love writing the last chapter in my novels—it's the climax, beyond the end of the book. But I wouldn't know where to start with this one," Hayden said.

Frank nodded. "Let's get some sleep. We'll talk in the morn-ing. Feeling a chill in here, Hayden?"

Hayden gazed down the highway. "Yes. It's going to be a long, quiet twenty-two-mile ride under dark skies and howling winds."

A sudden shadow flickered across the rearview mirror, and Hayden's stomach tightened.

Somewhere along the darkened coastline, someone—or something—was still watching.

The SUV cut through the night like a slow-moving vessel in fog. The road unwound ahead, empty except for the white flicker of surf glimpsed between trees.

"Why do I feel like we just left the Twilight Zone?" Frank said.

"Because we did," Hayden replied softly.

"Only this one's real."

Frank chuckled once, but there was no humor in it. They drove in silence, headlights slicing the mist. The sea fol-lowed them north, whispering along the cliffs. Once, Hayden thought he saw a faint glow far below on the sand—a light moving slowly, rhythmically, back and forth. But when he blinked, it was gone.

Hayden glanced into the darkness where land met sea. "Or maybe it's waiting for us to finish what we started."

Neither man spoke again until the cabin lights appeared ahead, small and pale against the vast black ocean.

INTERLUDE

Lookingglass's Journal

The sea does not forget. Men think it does, because it moves—because it changes its face from calm to fury, from mirror to storm. But the sea is memory itself. Every wave that falls upon the sand remembers what it has touched, who it has taken, and who it will someday return.

I have spent a lifetime listening to the voices of the shore. You must be very quiet to hear them. The wind speaks the names first— a whisper across the dunes—then the water answers. The language is older than words, older than light.

People say spirits haunt the living. I say the living haunt the sea. When grief is too heavy to carry, the ocean takes it, folds it into its tides, and sends it back in smaller pieces—driftwood, shells, the cry of gulls at dawn.

I have known the tide to bring back more than memories. Once, in my youth, I saw a drowned fisherman walk from the surf at twilight, his eyes as calm as the moon. He looked upon the cliffs as if deciding whether to climb or vanish. When I called out, he smiled—not in joy, but in recognition. Then he stepped backward into the water and was gone.

They called it a ghost. I called it unfinished love.

Every haunting, I have learned, begins with an unfinished story. The tide does not take what is whole. Only what is fractured.

This is why I keep my records, why I study what others dismiss as superstition. Not because I believe in specters—but because I believe in echoes. The human heart, once broken, reverberates forever. And sometimes, when the right person comes along, those echoes find a voice.

There is a place on the Oregon coast—a house above Dory Cove—where the veil between worlds thins with each passing storm. I have walked its porch. I have felt the pulse beneath its boards. I have heard the wind call a woman's name there.

The man who built it never understood what he awakened. He thought he had built a refuge from the world, but the sea never allows such arrogance. You can't keep the sea out; you can only invite it in politely and hope it leaves the door half open.

The woman who lived there loved the ocean too much to fear it. That is why it claimed her—not as punishment, but as return. I think she is still there, between tides, waiting for her name to be spoken again.

The sea does not forget. Men think it does, because it moves—because it changes its face from calm to fury, from mirror to storm. But the sea is memory itself. Every wave that falls upon the sand remembers what it has touched, who it has taken, and who it will someday return.

I have spent a lifetime listening to the voices of the shore. You must be very quiet to hear them. When it is, the sea will stir. The past will rise. And those who hear its call must decide: to remember—or to drown in forgetting.

–Charles Lookingglass

(Undated entry, found with a wax-sealed envelope bearing no recipient's name.)

Chapter Five

Investigations Begin

The ledger of lost days

Hayden stumbled out of bed late the next morning while Frank had been up early, going over his notes. He sat in the armchair by the front picture windows. With clear skies overnight, the fog had moved in—so thick that one could not see the ocean or the cove. The world beyond the glass looked erased, just a pale, shifting wall of white where the Pacific should have been. The kind of fog that made sounds flatten, thoughts echo.

"Good morning," said Hayden. He walked into the kitchen for toast and a cup of hot tea.

"You slept in this morning," said Frank.

"Must have been that long conversation with Lookingglass last night. Looks like you're working on your notes. What words of wisdom do you have today, Frank?" Hayden brought his toast and tea and sat next to him. A pleasant fire glowed in the wood stove.

"Well, I have several questions to ask Mr. Lookingglass, except there's one problem."

Hayden sipped his tea. "And what would that be?"

"I called his number a few minutes ago and got a recording. The line is no longer in service."

Hayden set down his teacup. "What? How could that be? Are you sure you dialed the correct number?"

"Yep, I went to my phone log yesterday and hit redial. Tried it many times. I even did a web search for antique shops in Rockaway Beach, and it doesn't list Coastal Antiques."

"It puzzles me," said Hayden. "How can that be? Why, we were there yesterday and even had a couple of phone calls with Helen."

Frank stood dazed, looking out the window. "We need to drive down there pronto."

"Sure, let me get dressed quick." Hayden dashed down the hall to his bedroom.

Frank, notepad in one hand and coffee cup in the other, still gazed out at the fog. A small flock of seagulls perched on the deck railing, nodding their heads back and forth. They seemed almost expectant, like witnesses waiting for the next strange thing to unfold. The fog pressed close against the glass, a soft, silent audience.

Moments later, they were in Frank's SUV, heading south toward Rockaway Beach. The fog was so dense that visibility was near zero as they approached the Arch Cape tunnel. The tunnel's mouth loomed ahead like an open throat swallowing light. Hayden gripped the seat, feeling the hum of the tires beneath them and the faint, rhythmic pulse of the wipers as if matching his heartbeat.

"Oh, that reminds me," said Hayden. "We need to stop at the rental office on the way back and either renew my stay or something."

"I think after a second visit to Mr. Lookingglass we'll have our answer to that," Frank replied.

Hayden smiled. "When you said 'leave pronto,' that reminded me of something lighter. Did you know the corn dog originated here in Rockaway Beach in the 1930s? Pronto Pup!"

Frank chuckled as he navigated around Nehalem Bay. "I always wondered who thought of those. Not that I care for one."

Hayden glanced out the window. The fog was lifting, revealing the bay. The sunlight broke through in thin shafts, like light filtering down into deep water. For a moment, Hayden imagined Lookingglass's voice still hanging in the mist—calm, deliberate, unfinished.

Soon they entered Rockaway Beach and pulled up in front of the old white building. They got out and walked toward the front door.

"That's odd," said Frank. "Look at the whitewashed windows. You can't see through them. A sign on the front door says business closed."

Hayden looked in disbelief. "What the heck? We were just here a few hours ago." The paint looked brittle, years old. Even the sign was warped by sun and rain. A spiderweb ran across the handle, trembling faintly in the breeze.

Frank glanced around. "Let's go next door to the café and ask about it."

***

Inside the café, a middle-aged woman, busy with breakfast plates in her arms, approached them. The smell of bacon and coffee felt jarringly normal. People laughed softly in the corner booth, as if the world hadn't just shifted on its axis.

"Hello," Frank said. "We were wondering about the antique store next door. When did it close?"

"Well," she said, setting down the plates, "it's been closed for seven years, I think."

"Seven years?" Frank repeated.

"Yep, at least," she said, calling to the cook. "Skip, when did the old shop next door close?" "Seven years ago, at least!" the cook called back.

She laughed. "So there you go."

"Why, that can't be," said Frank. "We were just talking with Mr. Lookingglass last evening."

"Well, I don't know who you were talking to," the server said with a laugh, "but it wasn't him. If it was, it was his ghost."

Hayden and Frank exchanged confused glances. Hayden felt the air shift—thin, unreal. Ghost. The word lingered like smoke.

"Can you tell us where to find him?" Frank asked.

"Sure, but you won't get much from visiting," she said. "He's at the cemetery in Tillamook. Walk around and you'll find his tombstone. Can't miss it. About five feet tall."

The two men shook their heads in disbelief. Frank thanked her for the information.

***

Back in the SUV, Hayden leaned against the vehicle. "What in the heck is going on, Frank? How can that be?"

"I don't know," Frank admitted. "We know the shop has been closed for some time. He is dead. Let's drive to Tillamook and see his grave."

The drive south was silent, the only sounds a little road noise. The silence wasn't empty— it was thick with questions, with the hum of the tires and the weight of what they'd seen. Every few miles, Hayden caught himself glancing in the side mirror, half expecting to see the white van of Lookingglass following them down the coast road.

* * *

Upon arrival at the cemetery, the sun was shining through clear skies. They left the vehicle and walked among the graves.

"You go that way," Frank said. "I'll take the other side."

After twenty minutes, Frank waved. "Here! Hayden, look!"

Hayden hurried over. "Here is our Mr. Lookingglass. Born 1925, died 2013. Eighty eight years old."

They were quiet for a moment. The headstone gleamed faintly in the sun, polished by salt air and time. Hayden brushed his fingers across the carved letters as if touching the proof of something he shouldn't have doubted—or perhaps shouldn't have believed.

"I think we know what we need to do, don't we?" Hayden asked.

"Yep. Investigate and write that last chapter. No way around it," Frank said.

Hayden read the epitaph aloud:

"In all the great mysteries of life, there only becomes one inevitable strife.

Our time on this earth is but a short distance between birth and death.

Others wander through time with no closure. Helpless souls that will never enjoy the fullness of life.

Untold stories worthful of redeeming and expressed by others with a warm heart.

My story began on my birthday and ended upon my death.

My story comprises many pages, many chapters over the expanse of time.

I guess the last chapter lies before you beneath your feet.

But in my soul, that elusive last chapter carries on for eternity.

I wait for the last chapter composed so I may rest in blissful peace."

Frank stepped back from the tombstone. "Reminds you of some phrases he was communicating last night?"

Hayden nodded. "I've never written a last chapter to a story I never composed,". Somewhere, unseen, the sea was whispering against the rocks—steady, patient, waiting for the rest of the story to be told.

Chapter Six

Planning

Whispers through the fog

Upon arrival back at the beach cabin, Frank and Hayden sat at the kitchen table. It was an old table with chrome legs and a yellow plaid Formica top, surrounded by matching chrome chairs with yellow plaid vinyl-plastic seats The surface still carried faint coffee rings and a cigarette burn or two—signs of past tenants who had watched the same storms crawl across the sea.

"Okay, we need to investigate this chain of events. We know Abby and Jeremy lived here, they had an accident in their boat with old Salty some thirty years ago. According to the ghastly conversation with Lookingglass last night, Abby's body is missing, and disappeared," said Frank.

"We solve what happened to the two lovebirds and solve the mystery, right?" asked Hayden.

"Well, sort of. Here's what we need to do. I'll drive down to Bandon to seek her aunt and search the town for anyone who may have known the aunt and Abby. You search here in the old newspapers at the library and newspaper office for any stories about the incident. Also, renew your lease here for, let's say, two weeks."

"What about talking with the police chief to see if there's a police report file?" asked Hayden.

"Hold off on that until you find the incident documented elsewhere. Meander around downtown and see if you can find any old-timers who might talk," Frank replied.

"Are you sure I shouldn't come with you?" Hayden asked.

"No, we need to tackle this from both ends. You hold down the home base, so to speak."

"Maybe I'll explore the beach once again and see if I can make my way through the brush and pine trees in the cove," Hayden said.

"Sounds like a plan. I'm grabbing my stuff and heading out. I should make it a good share down the coast before dark and arrive in Bandon by noon tomorrow."

"Okay, I'll head over and renew my rent for two weeks," Hayden replied.

Frank threw his bag in the SUV, got in, and told Hayden through the open window to be cautious, keep notes, take pictures with his phone, and act as inconspicuously as possible.

He would call Hayden later that night. Then he drove out of the driveway and headed south on Highway 101.

The taillights faded into the white-gray mist until they looked like the eyes of a creature swallowed by fog.

***

Hayden grabbed his notebook, got in his car, and drove to the rental agency by the tunnel. He planned to be friendly and see what he could learn. Walking up the steps, he noticed Diane's yellow Bug outside.

"Why, hello Mr. Lansford," said Diane.

"Well, hello Diane. How are you this fine day?" Hayden replied, taking a seat in front of her desk.

"How's the writing coming along?"

Hayden thought for a moment. "Not too bad. I'm working on a last chapter now."

"Wow, you must have been working quite hard. Last chapter, that's impressive. So you're almost through with your novel, then?" asked Diane.

"Oh, the last chapter always takes the longest—tying in all the other chapters and making a good ending. Then there's the editing process, which can be tedious." His mind was swirling, thinking about the last chapter he and Frank had to write: the mystery of Dory Cove. He smiled faintly, but part of his mind drifted to the other "last chapter"—the one that wasn't fiction at all.

"Well, nice. Can I help you in any other way? I see you're scheduled to depart tomorrow."

"Yes, yes. That's why I came to see you. I'd like to extend my stay for two weeks, if possible."

Diane pulled up the rental schedule on the computer. "Let's see… it looks like it's only available for six more days."

"Six days?" asked Hayden.

"Yes, we have a Mr. Owen coming then."

"If I may ask, for how long has he rented the house?"

"For one week," said Diane.

Hayden leaned back in his chair. "Well, keep me for the time prior to his arrival. If he cancels or delays, please let me know."

"Okay, I have you down. I'll be so eager to read the novel and that last chapter—it sounds exciting."

Hayden repositioned himself. "Tell me, I thought you told me when I arrived the beach house was vacant."

"Yes, that's true in the off-season months of fall and winter. He just called this morning and booked it. Had I known you wanted it longer, I could have—"

"Oh, no worry. I should have talked to you sooner. Is this Mr. Owen coming in from the valley?"

"Oh no, he's traveling from the East Coast."

"The East Coast is a considerable way. May I ask where on the East Coast?"

"New York City," he said. Just himself."

Hayden stood. "Diane, how long have you worked here at the rental agency?"

She stood as well. "Seven years ago, I moved down here. I've loved every minute, even in the dark winter months. I like visiting the shops and chatting with the tourists and locals."

"Do you ever look around in the secondhand shops and antique stores?" asked Hayden.

"Oh, yes. I could look for hours, but this job ties me down."

"How far north and south do you go?"

"I've traveled from Tillamook to Seaside," she answered.

"Any good shops in Rockaway Beach?" asked Hayden.

"Yes, there are several. The largest closed down just after I arrived here. Let's see—"

"Coastal Antiques?" said Hayden.

"Why, yes. I only had the chance to go there once. I guess the owner passed away. Have you been there?"

Hayden smiled. "I went by earlier today and saw it was closed. Too bad—I bet they had loads of stuff."

Diane smiled and nodded.

"Did you ever purchase anything there or meet the owner?" asked Hayden.

"Funny you ask. Just the other day, when it was so windy, my anchor fell off the front porch."

"Your anchor?"

"Yes. That was my one and only purchase from Coastal Antiques. I wouldn't have bought it, but the owner gave me a long story about the anchor and how it would look great on my front porch. He was quite persuasive. He said it came from Bandon and that his employee found it several years before."

"His employee?"

"Yes, I don't recall the name, but the owner's name I will always remember—Mr. Lookingglass. Odd name, don't you think?"

Hayden chuckled. "Quite odd. Did he give you any other words of wisdom?"

"We had quite a chat. I told him I'd just moved here and such. Not much more I can remember," Diane replied.

"Okay, guess I'll be off and get back to work." Hayden walked out the door and down the steps to his car. Diane stood in the doorway, waving and shouting something inaudible.

Hayden stepped back from his car. "What was that?"

"You know, there was something Mr. Lookingglass said that I remember and thought was unusual. He asked me how things were at Dory Cove."

Hayden looked surprised. "Dory Cove? Uh... what is that?"

"Why, I don't know. I asked him the same question. I told him I was new here and worked at the rental agency but hadn't heard of Dory Cove. He paused for a moment and told me that one day someone would come asking about Dory Cove. And you know what? The police chief came by yesterday and asked me about Dory Cove."

"Did you mention your conversation with Mr. Looking-glass years ago?" asked Hayden.

"No, I forgot about that until you and I talked. Think there's anything to this?"

Hayden thought to himself. "Nah, a coincidence. I wouldn't give it a second thought. Authorities always ask strange questions. Like you said, Mr. Lookingglass was an odd fellow."

"Yes, yes, I suppose," said Diane.

***

As she spoke, Hayden noticed how the light through the office window turned her hair pale gold, the same color as the sand when the fog thinned. For a fleeting second, he felt caught between two worlds—the ordinary rhythm of her office and the deep, waiting hush of the coast.

Hayden waved goodbye to Diane and started the engine. As he drove back toward the beach house, the wind rattled the car windows and the fog rolled in again along the coastline. The headlights cut through the mist in thin beams, illuminating the dark shapes of pine trees and brush along the road.

He turned on the wipers, more from habit than need. The rhythm matched the faint pounding of the waves below. Everything seemed connected now—the sea, the road, the mystery—all leading him toward something inevitable.

***

Dory Cove. The name kept echoing in his mind. Why would Mr. Lookingglass—or anyone, for that matter—mention it so specifically, if it was just a coincidence? And why would the police chief suddenly show interest? Hayden shook his head. Probably just a strange local name, he told himself, but the uneasy feeling in his stomach didn't go away.

He glanced at the ocean beyond the fog, dark and restless, imagining the swells thirty years ago that had taken Abby. The cove's hidden waters seemed to whisper secrets he wasn't yet ready to hear. If anyone could uncover what really happened, it would be us, he thought. But the idea that Dory Cove held answers— and perhaps dangers—made him grip the steering wheel a little tighter.

The winding road back to the beach house seemed longer than usual. Every curve revealed shadows that might have been driftwood—or something watching from the mist. Hayden reminded himself to stay focused: notes, pictures, observations. Keep it methodical. Still, the thought of the 'last chapter' lingered in the back of his mind. This wasn't just a mystery to solve—it felt like walking into a story that had been waiting for him all along.

By the time the beach house came into view, the sun was dipping low, casting a warm glow through the morning fog.

Hayden parked the car, grabbed his notebook, and stepped out, the smell of salt and damp pine filling the air. Somewhere down along the beach, the surf whispered, and he could swear he heard the faint echo of a lantern clinking against the sand.

He stood on the deck for a long time, listening, the fog wrapping around him like breath. Somewhere beyond it lay Dory Cove—half memory, half myth—and it was waiting.

Dory Cove is out there, he thought, and sooner or later, it's going to tell us its story.

Chapter Seven

Visitor in the Night

The house that watched the sea

Back at the beach house, Hayden fixed himself a simple dinner while waiting for Frank's phone call. He stoked the wood stove and settled onto the couch. The cozy warmth contrasted sharply with the gray drizzle outside.

The wind sighed through the cedar boards, and every now and then, a wave broke with a low boom that seemed to shake the glass panes. The old house creaked like it was breathing with him, waiting.

His phone rang.

"Hi Frank, how's it going?"

"Hi Hayden. Going well. I'm in Florence for the night and will head to Bandon first thing in the morning. How are things on your end?"

"Not too bad. I managed to secure the beach house for six more days."

"Six days? I thought we were aiming for two weeks."

"Someone just booked it this morning for one week—a guy from New York."

Frank whistled. "New York? What are the odds? Did Diane give any details?"

"She said a week. And yes, I got to talk with her. Friendly chat. She mentioned that she'd visited Coastal Antiques years ago and had spoken with Mr. Lookingglass."

"That's interesting," Frank murmured.

"She thought he was... odd. But here's the thing: he told her that one day someone would come asking about Dory Cove."

"Dory Cove?"

"Yes. And the police chief apparently spoke with her just yesterday, asking if she'd ever heard of it."

"Did she tell him anything?"

"No, she had forgotten about Lookingglass until we spoke today. I told her not to worry; authorities always ask strange questions."

"Good enough," Frank said, a hint of tension in his voice. "We'll see what we uncover. Keep digging tomorrow. And... if you had a chat with his ghost, well, that's a story in itself."

Hayden chuckled nervously. "I hope I don't have nightmares tonight. One thing at a time—I'm not chasing the Tide Stalker tonight."

"Fair enough," Frank replied. "I'll call you after my day in Bandon. Take care tonight."

After hanging up, Hayden carried his dinner to the couch with a cup of hot tea. Outside, clouds thickened, a steady drizzle began, and a southeast breeze whispered along the cliffs. The rhythm of the waves blended with the ticking stove and the soft hiss of rain—nature's metronome keeping time with his pulse. He ate slowly, lost in thought, before drifting off.

***

A little after midnight, a soft knock rapped against the back door. Hayden stirred, rubbing his eyes. Another knock, slightly louder. Heart racing, he rose and moved toward the door. The house seemed to listen with him, every creak amplified by the silence. The rain had stopped. Even the sea had gone still. A tall figure in a black hooded raincoat peeked in. Hesitation gripped him, adrenaline pulsing.

He flicked on the porch light. Hayden took a deep breath. "Who are you? What can I do for you?"

She motioned urgently to come inside. Hayden unlocked the door, stepping back as she entered. A chill passed him. He closed the door behind her. The young woman's face emerged from the shadow, water dripping from her coat onto the rug.

"Thank you," she said, her voice trembling slightly. She removed her black hooded long raincoat and allowed Hayden to guide her to the warmth of the wood stove.

He handed her a dish towel and gestured for her to sit. "Would you like some tea?"

"Yes... clover honey, if you have it."

The ordinary request unsettled him more than anything. Something about the way she said it—gentle, familiar—stirred recognition he couldn't place.

Hayden brought over a tray of tea and crackers, watching her. There was something familiar about her face, her presence. She wore a black V-neck sweater that clung damply to her shoulders, dark jeans streaked with rain, and boots that left faint prints on the wood floor. Her hair, coal-black and tangled with mist, caught the light as she looked up.

"Who are you?" he asked again, quietly.

"My name is Abby," she said, calm but insistent.

Hayden felt his pulse quicken. "Abby? How... how can this be? Thirty years have passed. You're still so young."

She reached for his hand, icy cold yet strangely warm at the same time. "I am here in spirit. My body is elsewhere, though I do not know where. Somewhere out there, I am alive but unknowing who I am."

"Why now?" Hayden asked.

"I waited for the right moment—after you knew my story. You must open the realm of possibilities and seek the answers."

Hayden shook his head in disbelief. "How long have you been here?"

"Since the accident. I have remained in this cove, waiting for someone to release me. I was with you when you walked on the beach, helping you back to the house after you fell." "That was you?" She nodded.

"And the figure walking along the beach at night?"

She shook her head," That is not me."

Hayden frowned. "We believe that is your husband, still searching for you. Why haven't you reached out before?"

Abby held both his hands. "It is an illusion that taunts my soul. We exist in parallel worlds. So close... yet millennia apart. I cannot see him, and I cannot see myself. I need your help."

"I will do my best," Hayden promised. "Frank and I will uncover the truth, put you and your husband at peace. This... is the last chapter commissioned by Mr. Lookingglass. If you and your spirit exist here, there is no one better than us to resolve it."

Abby's lips curved into a faint smile. "Why now, after all these years, do I reach out? We go through life, meeting many souls, but some are chosen. I have waited for you in the realm of time. Please... come find me," she said.

Her voice softened, fading almost to a whisper, yet it filled the room as though the sea itself had spoken through her.

Hayden helped her to her feet, holding her close. "I'll find a way," he whispered.

"I have a few questions first," he said, gently.

She nodded.

"Why are the seagulls here every day?"

"They are my friends. They sense my presence, waiting for my return."

"And the sand dollars on the beach?"

"That was me. I needed you here until the right moment—to speak, for you to find me."

"Will you stay here at the house?" asked Hayden.

"I will return to the darkness, waiting to reunite with my soul. But when you look at the sea, I am there. When you walk on the sand, I am there. When the birds rest on the deck, I am here."

A draft rippled through the room. The tea on the table trembled in its cup.

She donned her raincoat, producing a sand dollar from her pocket, placing it on the kitchen table. Hayden escorted her to the back door. She kissed him lightly on the cheek.

"I give you my love and thanks. Be careful—dark, evil dangers await you and your friend."

"We will be careful," Hayden promised.

Abby descended the deck stairs into the mist. The drizzle eased, moonlight pierced the clouds, glinting across the wet ground. Her figure seemed to dissolve with the mist, like breath fading from glass. Only the faint scent of salt and clover honey lingered.

***

Hayden closed the door, added more wood to the stove, and lay back on the couch. The sand dollar rested on the table—a tangible link to the mysterious, lost love he had just met.

As he drifted toward sleep, Hayden couldn't shake the faint impression that someone—someone tall, carrying a lantern—was walking along the beach. The dim glow flickered briefly in the mist, vanishing as quickly as it appeared.

The faint shimmer in the air dissolved, leaving only the echo of her voice—and the weight of silence that followed. Outside, the sea returned to its steady breathing, as though it had swallowed her secret again.

Hayden's Reflection

The house had gone still. Not the stillness of peace, but the hollow kind that follows after something unexplainable leaves the room. Hayden stood in the doorway, staring at the empty space where Abby's spirit had lingered moments ago. The air still shimmered faintly, as if the light itself remembered her.

He sank into the chair by the window, his hands trembling in his lap. The fire had burned low, the embers pulsing like a slow heartbeat. For a long while, he said nothing. The storm outside had drifted inland, leaving only the quiet roll of waves against the rocks—the sound of a world returning to itself.

How do you make sense of something like that? He had come here chasing stories, the kind that earned polite nods from editors and side glances from skeptics. But this was no story. He had seen her—felt her warmth, heard her voice, the plea in her eyes. She was real. And she was lost.

He rose and crossed to the fireplace. On the kitchen table sat the seashell Abby had left glistening faintly in the firelight. He turned it over in his hand, tracing its spiral with his thumb, listening to the faint echo inside. It sounded like the ocean remembering her name.

"Where are you now?" he whispered to the quiet room.

The clock on the wall ticked softly, steady as a heartbeat. Somewhere in another room a floorboard creaked—old wood shifting in its sleep. Hayden smiled faintly at the sound. The house wasn't haunted, not in the way people feared. It was waiting—holding its breath like the tide before it returns.

He placed the shell back on the table and stood by the window. The rain had stopped. A thin ribbon of moonlight shimmered across the sea, silver and fragile. In the distance, he thought he saw a shape move across the bluff—maybe a trick of the wind, or maybe something else entirely.

He didn't turn away. He just watched, and listened, and waited for the next sign.

Chapter Eight

Bandon by the Sea

Through the veil of time

Frank left Florence early and arrived in Bandon mid-morning. The address Lookingglass had given him led to an overgrown driveway, the gate wide open and half swallowed by blackberry vines. If there had ever been a "No Trespassing" sign, it was long since weathered away or buried under the bramble. It looked like no one had been down this road in years.

The road itself seemed forgotten by time— mud ruts swallowed by weeds, the air thick with the metallic scent of ocean damp and decay. Somewhere offshore, a foghorn moaned, low and mournful, like the sea clearing its throat.

He eased his SUV over the potholes until an old, faded white two-story house appeared ahead. He jotted a few notes, snapped a couple of photos, and studied the place. The shutters hung crooked, one dangling from a single hinge. A rocking chair lay toppled on the porch. Everything about the property whispered neglect.

Frank's instincts prickled. Empty houses had their own pulse—this one felt like it still remembered its owners, holding its breath as he approached.

***

Frank instinctively felt for the pistol at his side before stepping up the creaking porch steps. Lace curtains covered the windows. He checked behind him out of habit, then used the heavy brass nautical knocker on the front door.

No answer. He knocked again. This time he thought he heard movement inside. Then— crack!—a gunshot split the quiet air. Frank dropped flat, drawing his weapon.

"Stand up, you fool!" a voice barked— from behind his SUV.

He twisted, spotting only the long barrel of a rifle aimed in his direction.

"Put the rifle down and show yourself," Frank called. "Then I'll stand up."

"If you don't stand up and drop your gun, I'll shoot you where you lie."

Frank didn't like being on the wrong end of a standoff. "Okay, okay," he said. "I'm dropping it." He pushed his gun out ahead of him, stood slowly, and raised his hands. "All right. Let's see you."

A frail figure stepped into view—a woman, maybe in her eighties, wiry gray hair blowing in the wind. The rifle looked almost too big for her.

"You're trespassing," she said sharply. "Whatever you're selling, I'm not buying."

Frank kept his hands up. "I mean no harm. I'm looking for someone."

"Well, there's someone living here, and you've no business being on this porch."

"I'm looking for Abby's aunt," Frank said carefully. "I was told she lived here."

The woman frowned, lowering the rifle a few inches. "Abby? What do you know about Abby?"

"Can we sit and talk? There's a lot to explain."

"Who are you?"

"Frank Thompson. I'm a private investigator, looking into Abby Stayton's disappearance."

She scowled. "I ought to shoot you dead right now and be done with it."

"Hey now," Frank said, hands raised again. "I'm not here to harm anyone. I'm trying to find Abby."

Her lined face softened slightly. "Did that scoundrel send you?"

"No, ma'am. I don't even know if he's alive. Have you seen Abby in the last thirty years?"

She climbed the steps and settled into the fallen rocker, the rifle across her lap. "That man took my niece away back in '1990."

Frank eased into a rickety chair nearby.

"They must've loved each other, didn't they?"

"Love?" she spat. "She was too young to know love. He lured her off and left me alone."

Frank showed her his PI badge. "I don't take sides, Mrs....?"

"Lawson," she said, staring past him.

"Mrs. Lawson. I'm just trying to solve what happened. Both she and Jeremy vanished thirty years ago."

Mrs. Lawson rocked slowly, the old chair creaking under her weight. Her eyes seemed to glaze over.

A strange quiet fell. The gulls outside stopped crying. Even the wind seemed to hold its breath.

"Ma'am? You all right?"

No response. Her eyes fixed straight ahead. Frank moved closer, removed the rifle from her lap, and checked her pulse—slow, but there. Her skin felt cold.

Then the sound of a car crunching over gravel made him turn. A woman in medical scrubs rushed toward the porch.

"Have you seen an elderly lady walk by?"

"Yes, she's right here. I think she needs medical help."

The woman—her badge read Susie—checked Mrs. Lawson's pulse and eyes. "What happened?"

"She fired a shot at me," Frank said. "Swore she'd kill me if I didn't leave."

Susie frowned. "That's impossible. There aren't any bullets in that gun."

"Well, I heard one. Clear as day."

Susie sighed. "I'm her caregiver from the senior home up the road. She wandered off again. She's been diagnosed with dementia— this happens when she gets agitated. I need to get her back."

***

"I'll help," Frank said. Together they got the old woman into Susie's car. Frank retrieved the rifle, sniffing the barrel—no smell of powder. He examined the chamber. The firing pin was missing. So where had the shot come from?

For a moment he stood there, holding the useless weapon, the wind fluttering through the open porch door. Somewhere far off, another crack echoed faintly—but this time, it was just thunder rolling over the Pacific. Or so he hoped.

He followed Susie to the care center a few blocks away. Once Mrs. Lawson was settled, Susie invited him into her office.

"Why were you at her house?" she asked.

Frank told her the truth: "I'm looking for her niece, Abby Scott—later Abby Stayton. She disappeared in a boating accident around 1990. Her husband survived but later vanished. There's reason to believe she might still be alive."

Susie listened, eyebrows raised. "We never knew she had a niece. She never listed family."

"Any other relatives? Maybe a sibling?"

"Not that we know of," Susie said. "She used to run a secondhand shop in Old Town before her health declined."

Frank thanked her and handed over his card. "If anything about her past comes up, call me. And you might want to lock this up."

"Yes," she said, taking the rifle. "She's always been oddly attached to it."

Back in his SUV, Frank stared out at the fog rolling in from the sea. Judy Lawson. Abby's aunt. A phantom gunshot. It didn't add up.

He'd handled hundreds of strange cases, but this felt different—like the line between memory and haunting had blurred. The gun had no firing pin, yet he could still feel the shock of the shot vibrating through his bones.

He drove into Old Town and stopped for lunch, jotting notes between bites of sandwich. The streets were dotted with antique stores and curio shops, the salty air thick with the smell of fish and kelp. After asking around, he learned little—until he stepped into Claire's Collectables, a tidy shop filled with brass lamps, ship wheels, and seashell clocks.

A small bell jingled as he entered, releasing the smell of lemon oil and old rope. It was a comforting scent—the scent of honest work and better times.

A cheerful woman approached. "Welcome! Looking for something in particular?"

"Just browsing," Frank said. "You've got a lot of nautical pieces here."

"Well, this is Bandon by the sea," she said, laughing.

Frank smiled. "You wouldn't happen to know if this shop used to belong to a Mrs. Lawson?"

The woman blinked. "Yes, actually. I bought it from her about seven years ago."

"I just saw her at the care home," Frank said.

"Poor thing," she said softly. "She had to sell when the dementia got worse. I worked here for years before that."

Frank showed his credentials. "I'm looking for her niece, Abby Stayton. Know anything about her?"

She shook her head. "Never heard of her. Mrs. Lawson never talked about family. The only person she ever mentioned was a sister back east—sent her boxes of nautical items to sell."

"Do you remember the sister's name?"

"No, but she once told me the sister's family owned a foundry up in Maine. Made bells, anchors, boat ornaments—things like that."

"That's helpful," Frank said. "Do any of those pieces remain?"

"Not anymore. The last one she got was a brass bell, maybe nine or ten years ago."

Frank handed her a card. "If anything comes to mind, call me."

"I will," she said with a smile. "Good luck, Mr. Thompson."

Back in his SUV near the marina, Frank stared at the gray water and jotted in his notebook:

Judy Lawson—Abby's aunt. Sister in Maine. Foundry. Possible lead.

The pen hovered for a moment before he underlined the word "foundry." Metal, bells, echoes—something about it struck him as important, though he couldn't yet say why.

Frank started the engine, the wipers swiping away the first drops of rain. As he pulled back onto the highway, he made a call to Hayden, but the call crackled, the signal fading with the fog—and the chapter of their search took another strange turn.

The last thing he heard before the line died was the faint cry of a seagull over the radio static, thin and distant, as though it were calling from another time.

INTERLUDE

The House Remembers

The wind rose off the Pacific with a low, mournful hum, threading through the cedar boards and hollow spaces of the old house. The walls shivered, as if listening. For thirty years the tide had come and gone, licking at the base of the bluff, leaving its silver scars on the stones below. The salt had worked its way into every nail and hinge, into the grain of the porch railing, into the very bones of the place.

The house remembered when laughter lived here. It remembered the sound of a piano through open windows, the warmth of sunlight spilling across the floorboards. It remembered the scent of sea lavender drying on the table and the woman's voice humming softly as she moved through the rooms.

Now it remembered silence.

Gulls wheeled overhead, their cries echoing like old arguments fading on the wind. The house had watched the man return once, years ago, alone and broken, sitting on the porch through a long gray afternoon until the rain came. It had listened to his voice whispering to no one. Then it had watched him walk away for good.

Sometimes, when the storms rolled in and lightning cracked across the horizon, the house swore it could still hear her footsteps—the light, quick pattern of bare feet on wood, running toward laughter that never answered. The air would thicken with the smell of salt and something older, something like memory. The walls would creak in reply, and the sea would pound the cliffs in time, as if trying to wake what was buried.

In winter, the fog would come. It slid through broken shingles and warped sills, curling down the hallway like breath. The house welcomed it; fog was company, a soft hand tracing its weary frame.

Then one autumn morning, footsteps again—different this time. Hesitant. A man's tread, cautious, respectful. The floor groaned beneath his weight. The house stirred, recognizing something in the way he paused in the doorway, how he touched the frame with his fingertips, as if greeting an old friend.

The stranger whispered her name.

For the first time in years, the air in the room changed. Dust lifted, motes swirling in a narrow beam of light. The floorboards, swollen with time, settled as if easing into awareness. Outside, the sea quieted for a breath.

The house did not know who this man was, but it knew his sorrow. It knew the way grief bends the spine, how it hollows out the heart like rot beneath paint. And it knew—somehow—that this man carried her memory like a lantern through darkness.

The wind shifted, rattling the shutters, and the sea answered with a long, low sigh. The tide was coming in again. The house felt it in its bones. Something long kept beneath the waves was stirring, rising, ready to return.

Frank Alone in Bandon

The wind off the Pacific hadn't let up all evening. Frank leaned against the warped window frame of his small second-floor room at the Bandon Inn and watched the storm push inland. The sign out front flickered half-lit, half-dead—its reflection shivering across the wet pavement below.

He loosened his shirt, poured a splash of bourbon into a paper cup, and listened to the rain drum against the glass. It wasn't the kind of storm that made you feel alive—it was the kind that reminded you how small you were. Somewhere down the street, a loose sign banged against its chain. The sound came and went, regular as a heartbeat.

Frank pulled the worn chair closer to the window and sat, elbows on knees, eyes half closed. He'd seen plenty of strange cases over the years—things that didn't fit the usual mold of reason, but this one was getting under his skin. A missing. Woman who wasn't truly missing. A man haunted by tides and time. And a story that seemed to shift every time he tried to hold it still.

He reached for his notebook and flipped it open, pages damp from the sea air. His handwriting—always neat—had started to lean, a little shaky around the edges. He wrote: "There's something about this place. The way the fog moves like it remembers. The way the sea never lets go. Hayden thinks it's about finding Abby, but maybe it's about finding what's left of himself."

He stared at the words until the ink blurred.

Somewhere outside, the foghorn let out a low, mournful call. The sound seemed to rise straight from the water, rolling over the rooftops and through the narrow streets. It wasn't hard to imagine the ocean speaking through it—old voices carried on salt and mist.

Frank rubbed his eyes and leaned back, listening. He thought of Abby—not as she was in Hayden's stories, but as he pictured her now: a woman suspended between worlds, caught in a memory the sea refused to surrender. He wondered if she could hear the same foghorn wherever she was, if the sound might reach her across the years.

The clock on the nightstand ticked toward midnight. The light from the window dimmed as fog pressed harder against the glass, muting everything but the pulse of rain. Frank finished his drink, set the cup down carefully beside the lamp, and murmured to no one, "We're in deep, girl. Real deep."

He let the words hang there, soft and uncertain, before reaching over to turn off the light. The storm answered him with another hard gust against the windowpane, as if to say yes—you are.

Chapter Nine

Anchors Aweigh

A room of forgotten questions

Hayden woke before dawn to the low hum of the surf and the faint crackle of dying embers in the stove. The sand dollar still lay on the table—pale, perfect, its five-pointed star catching the first gray light creeping through the windows.

For a moment, he thought it had all been a dream—the knock at the door, the girl in the raincoat, her hand cold in his. But the sand dollar told him otherwise.

It shimmered faintly in the dim light, as if holding its own quiet pulse—something between a keepsake and a promise.

He rose quietly, pulled on his coat, and stepped onto the deck. The air was damp and cool, carrying the mingled scents of salt and pine. Beyond the bluff, the beach stretched in silver and shadow, the tide whispering secrets across the sand.

The morning felt older than the day itself—like a leftover piece of another time, folded into this one.

Something moved near the edge of the surf. A tall, solitary figure walking with deliberate steps.

Hayden squinted. It wasn't the casual stroll of a beachcomber—it was searching, tracing the tide line like someone hunting for something... or someone.

He reached for the binoculars on the table and focused. The man's raincoat gleamed wet in the dawn light. In one hand he held a lantern that swung gently with each step.

Hayden's chest tightened. The man stopped, turned toward the cove, and lifted the lantern slightly—as if acknowledging someone unseen. Then the light went out.

Hayden lowered the binoculars, heart pounding. The figure had vanished. Only the soft hiss of waves remained.

***

He stood there for a long time, listening, trying to convince himself it was just an early fisherman—or his imagination, haunted by what Abby had said.

But deep down, he could feel that same electric weight in the air—the sense of being watched by something that remembered him.

He knew. Jeremy had returned as the Tide Stalker.

When Frank called, Hayden answered on the first ring. "Hey, Frank. How's it going down Bandon way?"

"Oh, so-so," Frank replied. "I get close to a clue and then it slips away. IT was quite an experience." He told Hayden about the old woman, the rifle that couldn't fire, and his strange visit to the senior home.

Hayden exhaled slowly. "Boy, it's a good thing that rifle didn't work. I had a pretty unnerving night myself."

"Bad dreams, huh?" Frank asked.

"I thought so—until I got up this morning. I could swear Abby visited me after midnight. She knocked on the back door. I let her in, and we talked... for quite a while."

Frank let out a low whistle. "You're serious?"

"She looked twenty-five, maybe twenty-six. Not the fifty-something she'd be now. It was like her spirit was standing right there, asking us to find her real self. Could she still be alive?"

Frank hesitated. "You're sure it wasn't a dream, Hayden?"

"I thought it was—until I saw the sand dollar on the table. It wasn't there last night."

"Maybe you picked it up on the beach?"

"No. Abby said she'd left sand dollars on the shore as signs. When she came in, it was raining hard—her coat was soaked. This morning, the rug by the door was still wet."

There was silence. "Frank? You there?"

"Yeah, still here," Frank said. "Spirits, ghosts, Tide Stalker... what's next? We've crossed into another world, my friend."

"You can say that again—no, wait— don't," Hayden muttered.

Frank chuckled, then grew serious. "Well, my only real lead is that Abby's aunt, Nancy Lawson, had a sister on the East Coast. The family ran a foundry somewhere in Maine."

"A foundry? What kind?" Hayden asked.

"Nautical stuff—bells, anchors, that sort of thing."

Hayden paused. "Frank, remember I told you Diane met Lookingglass once? He talked her into buying an anchor for her porch. Said Jeremy brought it back from Bandon."

Frank perked up. "You're thinking what I'm thinking?"

"Yep. If we're lucky, that anchor has the foundry's name stamped on it."

"When can you check?"

"Right now," Hayden said. "I'll call her, take some pictures, and send them your way."

***

Diane didn't answer her phone, so Hayden decided to try her usual haunt—the Crab Pot. Sure enough, he spotted her in a back booth with a friend.

He knew from his conversations with her that she favored the corner booth with the fogged-up window overlooking the docks—a spot where she could gossip and keep half an eye on the world outside.

"Why, Hayden Lansford!" she said with surprise. "Trying happy hour?"

"First time," he said with a grin. "Sorry to interrupt, but I need a quick word if you've got a minute."

Her friend excused herself, and Hayden slid into the booth. He ordered rum and Coke, popcorn shrimp, and offered some to Diane. "You remember that anchor you bought years ago—the one Lookingglass convinced you to get?"

"Of course," she laughed. "Why?"

Hayden hesitated. "I was thinking about using an anchor in a story I'm working on. Thought if I could see it, maybe it'd spark something."

She smiled. "Writers and their inspirations. Sure, you can take a look. It's a little heavy though—I had my neighbor hang it for me."

"I'll manage," Hayden said. "Tonight work?"

"It's dark, but my porch light's good enough. Follow me up."

They drove up a narrow, private road called Sand Dollar Lane—the name caught Hayden's attention—and stopped before a small yellow house overlooking the dunes.

The fog was rolling back in, low and slow, giving the houses an otherworldly glow beneath the streetlamps. The name of the lane, somehow, didn't feel like coincidence.

"There she is," Diane said, pointing to the porch.

The anchor hung beside the door, rusty and pitted, streaks of orange running down the post below it. Hayden shone his phone's flashlight on the metal.

"Well," he murmured, "she's a beauty." He turned it slightly. "Do you mind if I check the other side?"

"Go ahead," Diane said, amused. "It all looks the same to me."

Hayden carefully lifted the anchor and leaned it against the column. His light swept the shank, and there—barely visible under years of corrosion—were faint stamped letters.

He leaned closer. "Castle Rock Foundry, South Harbor, Maine." His breath caught.

"Did you find what you were looking for?" Diane asked.

"Yes," he said quietly. "I did." He offered to buy it on the spot, and after some friendly back-and-forth, they settled on a price. Diane seemed both surprised and pleased.

When she invited him in for coffee, he declined. "Maybe next time. I should get this back to the cabin."

She laughed softly. "You writers—always chasing spirits."

He smiled at that. "You have no idea."

Back at the bungalow, Hayden set the anchor by the fireplace and called Frank.

"Did you get the photos?"

"I did," Frank said. "That's amazing—'Castle Rock Foundry, South Harbor, Maine.' We've got a real lead now."

"Think the aunt's sister might still be there?"

"Hard to say. But it's something. We can trace the foundry, maybe find a family name."

Hayden hesitated. "Frank... Abby told me her real self doesn't remember who she is. If she's alive, she might not even know her own name."

Frank sighed. "Then we'll just have to remind her. I'll see you tomorrow around noon. Watch out for any midnight visitors."

"Ha-ha, yeah. I'm hoping for a quiet night," Hayden said. "Might even take a tranquilizer."

"Sweet dreams," Frank replied.

Hayden hung up the phone and placed the anchor beside the fireplace, its rusted metal cold and heavy. He glanced at the sand dollar on the table, its pale star catching the last rays of twilight filtering through the windows. For a moment, he let the quiet of the beach house settle over him—the crackle of the wood stove, the distant hum of surf, the faint scent of salt and pine lingering in the air.

The anchor and sand dollar seemed to mirror each other—one born of fire, the other of sea—tethered by a story that refused to rest.

And then, just for an instant, he felt it: a subtle brush against his hand, as if someone unseen had leaned close, whispering across the years and the tide. Hayden shivered, uncertain if it was the imagination of a tired mind—or something more.

The cove was still, but the mystery of Abby and stretched before him like the endless horizon. Tomorrow, he and Frank would take another step, uncover another clue—but tonight, he let the waves and the wind carry the questions, waiting patiently for answers that had been long in coming.

Outside, the sea breathed against the shore, steady and unbroken—the same rhythm it had kept on the night Abby vanished. Somewhere between those tides, he knew, the truth was still moving.

Chapter Ten

Echoes and Departure

Haunting by the sea

Morning came slow and gray, the kind of light that felt unsure of itself. A thin veil of fog drifted in from the ocean and pressed against the windows. Hayden sat at the kitchen table, tea steaming beside the rusty anchor. He'd cleaned off the surface rust where the words were: Castle Rock Foundry, South Harbor, Maine.

The name alone carried weight, a new thread in the tangle of Abby's mystery. He traced the letters with his fingertip, half expecting them to warm beneath his touch, to hum with the same strange energy that seemed to hover over Dory Cove.

Everything in this house seemed to hum lately—low and distant, like the murmur of the tide beneath the floorboards.

Frank would be arriving by noon. Together they would trace the foundry, follow the trail east, and—if fate allowed—find out what had really happened to Abby. Yet even as the sun fought its way through the mist, Hayden couldn't shake the unease that settled in him overnight. The air itself seemed alive, the surf whispering with a tone that felt almost deliberate.

It was the same whisper he'd heard since Abby's visit—half comfort, half warning.

He rose, crossed to the window, and watched the tide roll in. For the briefest moment, he thought he saw someone standing at the edge of the cove—still and solitary, like before. But when he blinked, there was nothing but fog.

Only the shifting white curtain, breathing against the glass, as though the sea itself was thinking.

He exhaled, slow and uncertain. Whatever lay ahead, the tide was shifting.

***

As in any mystery—twists, turns, and dead ends abound. Sometimes it goes full circle. It is a game of clues and happenstance, light and darkness bordering on the edge of reality.

Jeremy and Abby's existence, given the circumstances after thirty years, was most intriguing. An admission into the realm of paranormal characters might be pseudoscience to many, but

Hayden and Frank had entered the ordeal through the talents they possessed.

The story had stopped belonging entirely to them—it had taken on its own current, pulling them deeper, further from the safety of reason.

At this point in the story, they could give up and return to their daily lives—or could they?

But what was their destiny? Could they manage the moral compass? Where would that compass lead them? Writing that last chapter might consume them in the darkness of night. The events along the Pacific coast will now led them to the opposite end of the country—to another ocean, the Atlantic. The last chapter might be a long one—with or without a happy ending.

The sand dollar still sat where she'd left it, pale and silent, as if waiting. He picked it up, tracing the star with his thumb. "Find me," she had said. her words lingered like a promise carried on the salt air. He slipped it into his coat pocket just as Frank's car turned down the gravel drive.

***

The twosome sat and chatted about their adventures, shared notes, and made plans for the next step.

"This is a long shot," Frank began, "but one of us needs to go back to Maine and track down Abby's other aunt. I don't understand how Abby could have survived being tossed into the ocean."

"Yes, and if she survived, how did she make it away from this area? What about hypothermia? Did she somehow get back to her aunt in Bandon with amnesia? I didn't think so until the other night, with her visit here," said Hayden.

"All good thoughts," said Frank. "It's unfortunate that her aunt has dementia. I couldn't get anything solid out of her. But it was strange—she responded when I mentioned Abby. For a moment, she was alert. Then— bang—back into that fog of memory loss. I jogged her mind for a few minutes and almost got shot—if there'd been a bullet in the rifle. Crazy."

"Well, should we both go back east? I think if only one of us goes, that should be you since you're the expert detective," said Hayden.

"You said a guest from New York would be here in a few days?" asked Frank.

"Yep. And I think that's weird. Why would a person from New York find this little secluded beach house in the off season and want to spend a week? Something's up with that. Haven't had time to think about it but—"

"Well, this whole thing is crazy," said Frank. "Look how far we've come since I got here—and all the unfathomable events that have occurred. Did you ever search any news about the event or obituaries for Abby or ?"

"In town I went through old issues of the weekly paper—nothing. Asked a few long-time residents—nothing. Checked old obituaries online—nothing at all came up."

"Perhaps that's a sign," said Frank, leaning back, his brow furrowed. "Maybe old Lookingglass was right—that his hunch they both were alive wasn't just superstition. I've never been keen on paranormal talk, but after your visit from Abby—well..." He rubbed the back of his neck, thinking. "You know, I've seen things on the force that never made sense. Maybe this'll be another one of those cases where the evidence looks impossible—until it isn't."

Hayden smiled faintly. "Maybe this isn't about solving a case, Frank. Maybe it's about giving someone their ending."

He didn't say aloud that he felt part of that ending himself—as if he'd been written into their story without knowing when or why.

Frank nodded slowly. "I hope you're taking notes, Hayden. When this is done, you'll not only write the last chapter—you'll have the makings of a whole mystery novel."

"That's for sure," Hayden said.

"I think we both should go back east. It'll be an adventure, and we could use a change of scenery. Besides, Maine's beautiful—fresh lobsters, too."

"Okay. I'll let my friend Diane know I'll be leaving. Should I make another reservation after the other guy leaves?"

"Sure," said Frank. "Our search continues—we'll be back after our trip to Maine. Even if we find Abby or discover her whereabouts, we still need to track down Jeremy.

"Are you sure you have time to go on this hunt?" asked Hayden.

"When we get back to Portland, I'll stop and pack a bag more fitting for the Atlantic," said Frank. "We can meet at your place and take an Uber to the airport."

"Okay, I'll call about the house now. If I stop by, she'll think I'm making a move on her," Hayden said, chuckling.

"I'll go online and get us tickets to the other Portland. We can rent a car there and drive north along the coast to the foundry. And begin the search for Abby and her family."

"Frank, make sure they're round-trip tickets."

"No worries there. We'll research the foundry and town on the flight, see what we can dig up. We came into this ordeal three decades later—plenty of catching up to do."

***

That evening, as Hayden packed, he noticed the back door latch he was sure he'd locked standing slightly open. The rug by the door—the same one still faintly damp from that strange night—had shifted a few inches, as if brushed by a passing breeze. He hesitated, then smiled faintly to himself.

The quiet was almost companionable now; even the empty spaces seemed to breathe with memory.

"Goodnight, Abby," he whispered, closing the door softly behind him.

They drove back to Portland, Oregon— then onward to Portland, Maine the next morning.

Two Portland's, two oceans, and a single unfinished story threading between them.

Chapter Eleven

Shifting Tides

Shadows on the water

A long flight—three thousand miles of inky blackness, broken only by the faint glow of the wing lights—stretched between coasts. With thoughts of their adventure weighing heavily, Hayden and Frank dozed, woke, and dozed again. Every journey begins and ends, though sometimes the road between is longer than expected. Their story still had chapters left to write—each one filled with suspense, action, and the slow burn of a mystery yet unsolved.

***

Hayden rested his forehead against the window, watching the faint reflection of his own tired eyes. Down below, the country was a scatter of tiny constellations—farm towns, truck stops, someone's kitchen light still burning at 3 a.m. He thought of Oregon's coastline, the damp air, the gulls crying over Dory Cove. Now that they were leaving it behind, the whole place felt like a dream he hadn't quite woken from. The anchor sat wrapped in his luggage beneath the plane, a silent weight pulling him east. He wondered if the mystery waiting in Maine would unravel anything—or simply tangle them deeper.

***

Somewhere over the heartland, the cabin lights dimmed and the two Portland's—one left behind, one ahead—felt like bookends on a single, unfinished page. Different oceans, he thought, but the same tide.

The pilot's calm voice came over the speaker, announcing their arrival in Portland, Maine, just as the sun was rising over the cold October landscape. Hayden stirred, rubbing his eyes as the plane began its descent. The engines rumbled, the fuse-lage creaked, and light spilled through the small oval windows.

A flight attendant passed with a pot of stale coffee, the scent mingling with metal and carpet cleaner. Through the window, Hayden caught his first glimpse of Maine's jagged coast—dark spruce against pewter water, a scatter of fishing boats moored in calm inlets. The horizon flared pale gold, the kind of light that made you pull your jacket tighter and breathe deeper.

Hayden squinted toward the horizon. "Looks like a sunny day ahead, eh Frank?"

Frank yawned. "Man, I had the weirdest dreams on that flight. Feels like I didn't sleep at all. Guess that's why they call it the red-eye." He grinned. "If I start talking to phantoms at breakfast, just nod and hand me coffee."

Hayden smiled. "Deal. But if you start answering questions no one asked, I'm switching seats next time."

Frank smirked. "You're the one who writes mysteries for a living—don't blame me if I get possessed by plot twists."

Once off the plane, they collected their luggage, picked up a rental SUV, and set out toward South Harbor—a three-hour drive along U.S. Highway 1. Frank had ruled out the faster interstate. "If we're coming this far, we're going to see the real coast," he said.

Cold air hit them as soon as they stepped outside—sharp, briny, alive. The SUV smelled faintly of pine air freshener and old vinyl, but the window cracked open brought in the crisp scent of seaweed and woodsmoke. Hayden settled into the passenger seat and watched the flat gray Atlantic blink in and out between stands of spruce.

The road threaded through spruce and salt marsh; lobster pots blinked red and blue along the shoulders like low constel-

lations. The route was pure postcard: pine forests, salt marsh-
es, weathered cottages, and rocky beaches lashed by the tide.

They passed a hand-painted sign for The Driftwood Grill,
where steam rose from a vent into the morning air. A lobster-
man in yellow slicks waved from the back of a truck, its bed
stacked with traps. On a bend, a church steeple rose over a
village green dotted with carved pumpkins. Hayden cracked
the window further and inhaled deeply. The Atlantic smelled
colder than the Pacific, somehow more metallic. "It's like the
same sea with an older memory," Hayden murmured.

Frank glanced over. "You poets always get sentimental when
you're jet-lagged."

"What do you think we'll find when we get there?" Hayden
asked.

Frank sighed. "Could be a run-down foundry boarded up
for decades, or maybe more questions than answers. The inscription on that anchor is all we've got. If anyone remembers
the place, we'll have to tread carefully—small towns don't take
kindly to strangers digging into their past. Especially strangers
asking about old grief," he said, watching fog lift from a cove.

Hayden studied him for a moment. There was something
in Frank's voice—an undertone of fatigue that had nothing to
do with the flight. He wondered what ghosts his friend carried
and whether they ever spoke his name when he was alone.

Hayden gazed out the window at the waves hammering the
rocks. "Sounds good to me. Let's just hope we don't stumble
into another paranormal mess like Oregon."

Frank laughed. "At this point, I'd expect anything. Watch out for black cats, Hayden."

They shared a chuckle as the sign for Welcome to South Harbor came into view. Frank pulled into a small gas station to refuel and ask directions to their B&B.

***

"Hi there," he said to the clerk, "how do we get to the Swift Inn?"

The clerk chuckled. "You can see it from here—across that swale of mudflats. That's the town proper. When the tide's out, you can drive across. When it's in, you wait six hours."

Frank raised an eyebrow. "So, you just drive across that?"

"Yep. Hardpan and rock. Locals have done it forever. Just don't park down there when the tide's due, or you'll be swimming home. Smithy's Dock'll tow you out—for a fee."

Hayden caught the tang of fuel and salt through the cracked door. A calendar curled on the wall behind the clerk, marked with tide tables and moon phases. A bulletin board beside it was crowded with missing-dog flyers and handwritten ads for firewood. The whole place smelled faintly of oil and rain.

Frank grinned as he returned to the SUV. "Well, add that to our list of oddities."

"A town on a hinge," Hayden said. "Opens and closes with the moon."

They crossed the tidal slough, the SUV splashing lightly through puddles and seaweed as boats rested tilted on their keels beside the marina. On the far side, an archway greeted them: Welcome to South Harbor. The town looked like it belonged on a postcard—white clapboard buildings, shuttered shops, and gulls circling overhead.

A row of lobster buoys hung like ornaments outside a bait shop. Somewhere a screen door slammed. Hayden saw the word SCOTT faintly painted across a boarded-up storefront—letters nearly lost beneath years of salt and sun. He blinked and almost dismissed it, but the echo of the name followed him down the street.

A buoy bell tolled once, low and hollow, as if clearing its throat.

At the Swift Inn, an older woman with a warm smile greeted them. Her gray hair was piled high in a bun that reminded Hayden of Aunt Bee from Mayberry.

The place smelled of lemon polish and old cedar. A grandfather clock ticked near the staircase, and the sound of wind sighed faintly in the eaves. A kettle whistled somewhere down the hall, sharp and comforting all at once.

"Welcome, gentlemen I'm Harriet," she said. "You must be Mr. Thompson and—oh!—a writer, I see?"

Hayden smiled. "Fiction. Mysteries mostly."

"My goodness! We don't get many writers, though plenty of painters come to capture the storms. I do love a good mystery novel on a stormy night."

She led them upstairs to a cozy room overlooking the sea, complete with twin beds, a window seat, and the faint scent of cedar. "Breakfast at nine, and there's tea, coffee, and our famous cookie jar in the den. Help yourselves."

She lowered her voice, conspiratorial. "Just don't let the gulls see you with a cookie on the porch. They'll charge you rent."

Hayden chuckled. "We'll keep the blinds drawn." As she left, he watched her go, thinking of how kindness seemed to find them in the most remote corners. It reminded him of a truth he'd written once in a story—how people carried light without realizing it.

***

They unpacked and then headed into town for lunch.

At The Chowder Shack, Frank tackled a seafood platter while Hayden savored a bowl of clam chowder.

The windows fogged from steam, and the air was thick with butter and brine. A radio played old rock songs under the chatter of locals. Through the glass, a man in a yellow cap mended nets beside the dock. Hayden overheard a fragment of conversation from the next table—something about "the foundry road" and "the old Scott place." He pretended not to listen but tucked the words away.

"I'm surprised you didn't quiz the hostess about the foundry," Hayden said.

Frank dabbed his mouth with a napkin. "Didn't want to spook anyone. Let's start slow." He took the bill up front. "By the way," he said to the server, "is Castle Rock Foundry nearby?"

The young man smiled cautiously. "Sure. About a quarter mile east, then left at the fork. It's been closed for decades—just an old stone building. You folks collectors or something?"

"Not exactly," Frank said easily. "We've got an old anchor back home with the foundry's mark. Thought we'd see where it came from."

The man nodded slowly. "Scotts ran it for generations. Family closed it down years ago. Folks here like their privacy—best to remember that."

His eyes flicked to the window, to the bell buoy beyond the breakwater. "Tide brings things back you don't expect."

Frank smiled thinly. "Understood. Thanks."

A faint chill prickled the back of Hayden's neck. For a heartbeat, he thought he heard the same hollow note the Oregon wind used to make against the cabin's gutters. He met Frank's eye; neither spoke.

Back in the SUV, Hayden murmured, "He got tense fast."

"Yeah," Frank said, starting the engine. "Means we're on the right track."

The foundry stood alone on the edge of the island, its faded sign reading Castle Rock Foundry—Established 1890. The stone walls were mottled with lichen, windows broken, a single chimney jutting like a watchtower against the gray sky.

***

Gravel crunched beneath their boots. The place smelled of rust and seaweed, the air thick with the hiss of surf striking rock. Hayden shaded his eyes and peered through a broken pane. Inside, dust floated in angled shafts of light. An overturned chair, a set of rusted calipers, and a wall map gone brittle with age clung to the far wall. Faded letters—R.D. Scott & Sons—ghosted across a beam, half lost to salt. Somewhere inside, a loose shutter tapped lazily in the wind, as though the place was breathing. Hayden peered through the dusty glass. "Looks like old drafting tables inside. Nobody's been here for years," Hayden said.

On a wall, a ghost of a stenciled name— SCOTT—half-peeled and salt-burned.

They walked along the ocean side, where waves crashed against the riprap, sending salt spray into the air.

"Let's head back before dark," Hayden said.

Frank nodded, but curiosity tugged him toward a narrow side road. "Let's see where this goes."

The road wound along the coast until pavement gave way to gravel. At its end stood a large white house facing the sea, a garage beside it, one window glowing with lamplight. The gate was rusted but open, beach grass bending in the wind.

For a moment they didn't speak. The headlights swept the porch, catching on a set of wind chimes that clinked softly in the cold. The surf rolled in and out below the bluff like the slow breathing of something asleep. Hayden felt the familiar weight of anticipation—the sense that they'd arrived somewhere that didn't want visitors.

"End of the line," Frank murmured. Then he saw it. "Wait—look at that mailbox."

Hayden leaned forward. "R.D.S."

"That's the same inscription as the rifle Mrs. Lawson had in Bandon," Frank said quietly.

Hayden stared. "You think—?"

"I think we just found the owner of the foundry."

The lamplit window glowed steadily, unbothered by the dark. Whoever lived there, they weren't afraid of what might come calling after dusk.

"Do we go up?" Hayden asked.

Frank shook his head. "Not tonight. We'll visit in the morning. Questions in the dark never end well."

"And answers after dark come with a surcharge," Hayden said.

As he spoke, a curtain shifted just slightly, as if stirred by wind—or by someone standing close behind it. Hayden swallowed. "Let's get back," he said softly.

As they drove back, Hayden chuckled.

"You don't smoke a pipe, do you, Frank?"

Frank looked over, puzzled. "No—why?"

"I just keep waiting for Sherlock Holmes to show up."

Frank laughed, shaking his head. "Let's stick to cookies and coffee."

They entered the warm glow of the inn as wind rattled the shutters. The scent of baking chocolate drifted through the hall. Over mugs of coffee and tea, the two men sat by the crackling fire, wondering what answers or shadows the morning tide might bring.

***

Harriet drifted through, carrying a tray of cookies. "Storm rolling in tonight," she said cheerfully. "The tides always act up before one. Best sleep while the sea's still calm."

Hayden smiled. "You sound like someone who's seen her share of tempests."

Oh, honey," she said, tapping the tray, "around here, it's not the storms you see coming that trouble you."

She left them with that thought, the bell buoy tolling faintly beyond the window.

Hayden and Frank sat for a long while without speaking, listening to the wind rattle the shutters and the faint creak of the inn settling.

"Quite a day," Hayden said finally. "Anchors, old inns, mysterious coastlines... feels like we've stepped into one of my own plots."

Frank nodded. "Except this one doesn't have an ending yet."

The fire crackled low in the hearth. Outside, the Atlantic whispered in waves, carrying a faint hint of mystery and a promise that the past wasn't done with them yet.

Hayden leaned back, eyes half on the fire, half on the dark window beyond. Some stories, he thought, don't end. They just change coastlines and start again.

Tomorrow, the search would continue—and the secrets of the Scott family might finally begin to surface.

Chapter Twelve

Shadows on the Shore

The man who followed shadows

The wind off the ocean rattled the window shutters. The thermostat on the wall functioned erratically—first too warm, then too cold, as if it had chosen to argue with the weather. The two men tossed and turned all night. At seven-thirty, the alarm clock chimed, thin and insistent. Hayden was first to rise while Frank groaned under the covers and pulled the quilt closer.

After Hayden showered and dressed, Frank finally rolled out of bed. "Good morning, Hayden. Rough night with the heater—and everything swirling in my head. How about you?"

"I was freezing or throwing the covers off all night. That window leaks cold air, and the thermostat... well, it has a mind of its own. I'll mention it at breakfast."

They went downstairs to the dining room where five place settings were arranged. A picture window faced the harbor, its glass filmed with salt. An older couple and a single woman joined them, trading polite smiles. Harriet appeared with a tray of grapefruit.

"Good morning, everyone. We start with grapefruit and a little tangy sauce. Next, pear puffed pancakes and sausage. Coffee, tea, and orange juice are on the buffet behind you. Help yourselves."

The fruit was chilled and bright, the sauce puckering the mouth pleasantly. Steam lifted from the coffee urn in a steady ghost. Guests exchanged small talk about where they were from. Harriet offered maps and directions, laughing softly at a joke no one quite heard. Frank and Hayden excused themselves, returning briefly to their room to grab coats and notebooks.

***

Dawn broke pale and cold over South Harbor. The wind had calmed, leaving only the muted rhythm of waves against the rocky coast. Hayden and Frank stood in the driveway, staring down the narrow road that led to the white two-story house at the island's edge. Skies remained gray, a few flurries drifting in the breeze.

"Looks like winter arrived overnight," Hayden said, shivering slightly.

The light revealed what darkness had hidden—peeling paint on shutters, beach grass standing like sentinels, and the faint smell of salt and pine.

Frank adjusted the rearview mirror and exhaled. "Here we go. No turning back now."

Hayden nodded, chest tight. "Let's hope whoever's inside is welcoming. And if they're not..."

Frank smiled. "...we adapt. That's what we do."

They drove the short distance, tires whispering over damp gravel. The mailbox— RDS—gleamed softly where a patch of sun broke through. When they stepped from the SUV, each crunch of gravel underfoot amplified the tension. The house seemed to watch them, silent and imposing, holding the answers for decades. Somewhere inside, the Scott family history waited—along with secrets that refused to stay buried.

Hayden swallowed and glanced at Frank. "You ready?"

"As ready as I'll ever be," Frank said. Together they reached for the gate, its latch cold against the skin.

***

On the covered porch, Frank pressed the doorbell. No response. He tried again. Still nothing. Knocking, he heard a German Shepherd erupt into barking—deep, protective.

The door creaked, and an elderly woman wearing a dark dress and apron appeared behind a screen door, gray hair braided and looped like a crown. She kept one hand on the dog's collar.

"Hello," she said evenly. "How may I help you?"

Frank held up his PI badge. "My friend and I have come a long way seeking information from long ago. We believe you may have an interest in what we have to say."

Her eyes flicked to the badge, then to Hayden. "Is this a legal matter?"

The dog barked again, paws up at the screen. "Tenet," she murmured, "enough." Then to them: "Wait here; I'll put him in another room."

They listened to claws on hardwood, a door click, then silence. Hayden felt his shoulders drop an inch.

When she returned, she unlatched the door. The living room smelled faintly of baking bread. A fire crackled in the brick fireplace, its light reflecting on framed photos—sepia faces, men in work coats, a girl with wind-tangled hair beside a skiff.

"Please excuse my dog," she said, smoothing her apron. "He's protective. Barking is his way of warning strangers."

Frank smiled. "I'm Frank Thompson, a private detective, and this is Hayden Lansford, a novelist. We traveled here from Portland—Oregon."

She motioned to the sofa. The rocker near the hearth creaked as she sat. "I'm Marilyn," she said. "And the dog is Tenet. I may need to excuse myself; I have bread in the oven." A faint ding sounded from the kitchen. "What brings you here?"

"I assume you are Mrs. Scott," Frank said, "of Castle Rock Foundry?"

"Yes," she said, chin lifting. "The foundry's been in the family for generations. Is that why you're here?"

Frank nodded. "The foundry led us. Do you have a sister in Bandon, Oregon?"

Her hands trembled as she drew a handkerchief from her apron. "Yes, but I haven't heard from her in years. I don't know if she's alive."

"She is," Frank said gently. "I visited her recently at a senior home in Bandon. She has dementia, but otherwise good health."

Tears brimmed. "I was so worried. She never had a phone... letters went unanswered. So, she's... all right?"

"Yes," Frank said softly.

"Does she know you came?"

"No. She drifted off before I could tell her."

Marilyn folded the handkerchief. "How did you find me? And what does the foundry have to do with this?"

"We discovered an anchor," Frank said. "We believe it came from your sister's antique shop. It bore the foundry's name, so we traced it here."

Marilyn rose. "Pardon me—the bread." She disappeared into the kitchen.

Hayden leaned toward Frank. "How are we doing?"

Frank shrugged. "We're past the porch."

Marilyn returned, composed, and set a timer on the mantel clock. "I'm relieved she's alive," she said. "How did you find my home?"

"We drove to the foundry last night," Frank said. "At the end of the road, we saw your driveway. The mailbox—RDS—gave us the clue."

"My sister's married name is Lawson," she said. "How did you know Scott?"

Frank hesitated. Hayden stepped in. "The initials matched a rifle found with your sister in Bandon."

Marilyn's face drained. "You mean... she has my father's rifle? They let her keep it?"

"It's inoperative," Frank said. "Locked up, but calming for her."

Marilyn stirred the fire, embers blooming like tiny suns. "You came all this way just to tell me about my sister?"

"Yes," Frank said, "and because we're looking for Abby Scott. Is she your daughter?"

The rocker stilled. "No," she said quietly. "She's my brother's daughter. My father, Richard Dale Scott, owned this house and the foundry. Three children: myself, Nancy in Bandon, and my older brother Jim."

"Does your brother live nearby?"

"About three miles north," she said, "at the pit."

"The pit?"

"The old mining site for the foundry. My grandfather built his house there—three stories, overlooking the pit and the ocean. It's like a castle."

"Is he still there?"

"Yes." She folded her hands. "Why do you ask about Abby? How much do you know?"

Frank glanced at Hayden. "We think she may be alive."

Marilyn's eyes narrowed. "Of course she is alive, but Abby's father is extremely protective. You must tread carefully. And there are things about this place—about my family—that outsiders shouldn't know."

The room seemed to grow heavier as Hayden and Frank raised their eyebrows. The dog gave a soft warning from the next room. The fire popped. Hayden's pen hovered over his closed notebook.

***

Frank cleared his throat. "We know she married Jeremy Stayton in 1985 against Nancy's wishes. They lived near Haystack Beach, Oregon."

"I know that," Marilyn said. "Nancy told me before she stopped writing. Is he still around?"

"We aren't sure," Frank said. "He may have moved on, or perhaps he's deceased."

Marilyn's mouth tightened. "The person to look for is him; he committed the crime."

Frank blinked. "What crime?"

"For attempted murder, of course."

"Attempted murder?" Frank sat forward. "Why do you say that?"

"I don't know what you know," she said sharply. "Why investigate now, thirty years later?"

"We're only trying to piece together the mystery," Frank said. "Before assumptions are made, please share your side."

Marilyn twisted the handkerchief. "I don't know if I can trust you. My sister can't speak wisely, and if my brother intervenes, all hell could break loose."

Silence. Waves pounded the rocks; sleet ticked against the window.

Finally, she stood. "Okay," she said, as if to herself. "I'll take a chance if you tell the truth. Awakening these memories is difficult." She touched a tall bookcase. "The saga of Abby and Jeremy began at my sister's shop in Bandon. She was only nineteen—head over heels in love."

"They married in 1985 against our wishes," she said, resuming her seat. "Abby visited once in those years. Then a missionary couple found her lying on the beach—cold, soaked, barely breathing. They rushed her to the hospital in Tillamook. She remembered nothing, only said 'aunt in Bandon.' Police assisted and took her to Nancy. My sister assumed he tried to strangle her and throw her into the sea. Abby never recovered her memory."

Frank and Hayden exchanged a stunned glance.

"After the incident," Marilyn continued, "Abby knew nothing of her marriage or her life on the coast. We told her she had fallen and hit her head. She didn't recognize her father or me. Doctors tried everything—MRIs, CT scans— nothing wrong, they said. Yet the first twenty five years were gone."

"It was horrific," Frank said gently. "We didn't know she survived."

She sighed. you call it that?"

"Because that's what it was," Frank said. "Abby and Jeremy went crabbing. A storm capsized the boat. Everyone went overboard. and a friend survived; Abby was caught in the lines. The rope likely left the marks on her neck. There was no attempt on her life."

Marilyn stared, disbelief etched deep. "A boating accident? You want me to believe that?"

"Yes," Frank said. "They loved each other"

Nancy assumed the worst, but it wasn't true. "How do you explain the marks on her neck?" she said.

"Desperation and survival. Rope burns. Cold water. We're not here to defend—only to get the facts right. You've heard one story for thirty years. We're asking you to consider another," Frank said.

The mantel clock ticked. In the kitchen, the oven pinged again. Marilyn returned with a loaf on a cooling rack. The smell of yeast filled the room.

"If what you say is true," she asked, "why are you here if her husband isn't around?"

"First, he may still be alive," Hayden said. "If you cherish your niece, wouldn't you want her memory back? To know the life she lost?"

"Happy ever after," Marilyn said with a tired smile, "is for fairy tales, Mr. Lansford. Even writers should know that."

"Maybe," Hayden said, "but a true memory is better than a false story. We didn't come this far to destroy her. Sometimes a single detail opens a door."

She looked down at the loaf. "I want what's best for Abby. I love her dearly, but I worry about her mind. I've spent decades keeping winter storms off her porch."

"Keeping care of her is noble," Hayden said softly, "but sometimes you shut a door against spring."

Marilyn said nothing for a moment. "My brother won't like any of this. He sees dangers most people don't—and he has influence here."

"We'll tread lightly," Frank said. He placed a card on the table. "We're at the Swift B&B. Please call once you've decided."

Marilyn stared at the card. "If you go to the pit, don't go after dark," she said. "The fog comes off the water and you can't see the cliff until you feel the air drop."

"We won't," Frank said.

Tenet gave a low chuff from the other room, as if to end the conversation. Marilyn straightened. "I'll think," she said. "I promise only that."

"That's all we can ask," Hayden replied.

***

They thanked her and stepped onto the porch. The sleet had thickened to a fine white dust drifting sideways. The ocean wind cut their cheeks and brought tears to their eyes. On the drive back toward the tidal slough, neither spoke. The bell buoy tolled once, flattening against the low sky.

"Well," Frank said finally, turning the heater on, "we didn't get thrown off the property."

"And we didn't get invited to tea," Hayden said.

"Give it a day," Frank replied. "She's moving pieces around on the board."

"The brother at the pit," Hayden said. "Castle on the cliff."

Frank kept his eyes on the slick road. "We'll need a plan for him. People who build castles tend to think gravity is a suggestion."

***

At the inn, the parlor fire still glowed. Harriet looked up from a ledger as they entered, her expression sharpening—the way a harbor pilot reads water. "Cold out there," she said, not asking but somehow asking everything.

"Colder than it looks," Hayden said.

"Well." She closed the book. "The sea keeps its own books. Coffee and tea?"

They nodded. She poured and left them by the window. Outside, the Atlantic lay slate-gray and unbroken. Inside, the clock ticked them gently forward. Frank turned the business card face-up on the table, as if to remind fate of its next move.

"What now?" Hayden asked.

"Now," Frank said, "we wait—and we prepare." He tapped his notebook. "Write down every detail. Bread baking. Photos on the mantel. Tenet's reaction. The way she said attempted murder like it was the only shape those words could take."

"And if she calls?"

"We go back," Frank said. "Carefully."

"And if she doesn't?"

Frank looked toward the gray horizon where sea met sky without a seam. "Then we drive to the pit," he said. "And meet the man who followed shadows."

Chapter Thirteen

The Waiting

The breath between worlds

Frank and Hayden were up against a stone wall, both figuratively and literally. Convincing someone with a twenty-five-year gap in memory that her life was built on a forgotten love wouldn't be easy. Abby might question everything—why her aunt and father hid her marriage, why no one ever told her what really happened on the Oregon coast.

Still, their task was clear: reach Abby face-to-face and show her the truth. Hayden had brought photographs from the beach house— the ones of Abby and Jeremy together, the gulls on the deck rail, even the faded snapshots from Haystack Beach. He hoped that something, a color or a familiar shape, might pry open the door of memory and let the light spill in. Their second challenge was Abby's father, Jim Scott. No one could predict how he'd react when two strangers came asking questions about a past he'd spent decades trying to bury

They crossed the hardpan toward town as the tide withdrew, revealing dark seams of rock strewn with weed. A pair of gulls paced the flats like white-robed inspectors.

After driving three miles north of South Harbor, they stopped to observe the castle-like house perched on the cliff. Gray and cold against the sea, it stood as if guarding its secrets. The structure loomed above the pines like a sentinel of another age—stone chimneys, dark windows, and a slate roof glistening with sleet. Even from the road, Hayden could feel the weight of it, as if the house itself exhaled sorrow.

Sleet spattered against the windshield, running in crooked lines. Inside the car, silence pressed close.

"Will Miss Scott call her brother?" Frank asked finally.

"Or will she even let us near Abby?" Hayden added.

A narrow roadway climbed from the main highway toward the house. A rusted black iron gate blocked the entrance, its bars curled in a medieval design, mottled with age and salt. Behind it, the gravel drive disappeared into a tunnel of trees.

They sat in silence, the hum of the engine low, the wipers clicking like a clock.

"How depressing," Hayden murmured. "A woman like Abby, living here tending her father, surrounded by all this gray."

Frank studied the house through the sleet. "We'll have to tread carefully. Words alone might not reach through walls this thick."

Hayden rubbed his hands together for warmth, watching the dark glass of the upstairs windows. "If she's in there, she's probably never had a reason to doubt the life she knows."

"Until now," Frank said. "And we're the reason."

They both knew what was at stake. Convincing Abby's family to let her travel back to Oregon—to the place she nearly died—would take faith, compassion, and proof. And even then, how could they explain the impossible— the waiting spirit on the beach, the voice on the wind? No, that part would stay unspoken. For now.

The sleet intensified, streaking sideways in the wind. They turned back toward town, stopping at a roadside market for sandwiches and coffee instead of finding a restaurant. Inside, fluorescent lights buzzed faintly. A teenage clerk bagged their sandwiches with a distracted smile.

Back in the SUV, the smell of coffee filled the small space, comforting against the chill. They climbed a rocky overlook just off the road. From there, the dark outline of the house stood against the churning sea, the cliffs below streaked with snow and ice.

"This place," Hayden said quietly, "it feels wrong. Like the storm's been sitting here for years, waiting for someone to notice."

Frank followed his gaze. "Maybe it has. But we can't turn back now. If Miss Scott won't help us, we'll go to the castle ourselves."

Hayden nodded slowly, "I hope it doesn't come to that."

***

They drove on through the storm. As the land flattened toward the harbor, the gray daylight thinned to pewter. Hayden's thoughts circled restlessly.

They both thought of the brief backstory that Miss Scott had told them about her brother. Jim Scott had never made peace with himself. When Abby was three, her mother, Violet, died in a foundry accident. Jim had been working the overhead chute that day, his temper short, his patience shorter. He'd been shouting across the factory floor—one hand still on the control lever—when a slip, a shout, and a hiss of molten metal ended Violet's life in an instant.

Her body had been found encased in cooling iron before anyone could reach her. The men who worked there said the sound that followed—the scream of steel cooling—haunted them for years.

Jim left the foundry after that. He lived at the pit, drinking and driving trucks, his guilt rusting inside him like a forgotten machine. He was harsh, unpredictable, and dangerous when he drank. The mere sight of Abby reminded him of what he'd lost—and what he'd done. His father, Richard, and his sister Marilyn took her in as much as they could, but it was never enough.

When Abby was eight, they sent her west to Bandon to live with her aunt Nancy, hoping a new life by the sea might heal what Maine had broken. Abby went willingly, clinging to the promise of blue water and the soft sound of waves at night.

The years that followed were a mystery to everyone—until now.

***

By late afternoon, the tide had come in, cutting off the access road to the island where their B&B stood. They parked on the shoulder to wait. Sleet turned to snow, and the windshield wipers thudded a steady rhythm. The radio hissed faint static before Hayden shut it off.

"Well," Hayden said, "we've got two things to wait for now—the tide and Miss Scott."

Frank gave a thin smile. "One of them's predictable."

They sat in silence, both men watching the gray horizon darken to night. The heater hummed weakly. Frank's hands tightened on the steering wheel as if he could will time forward. "We didn't come all this way to fail," he said. "If Miss

Scott closes the door, we'll find another way in. Abby deserves the truth. Maybe she's the key to finding Jeremy—if he's still alive."

Outside, snow drifted over the road like sand over a forgotten trail. The world had gone quiet, except for the ocean and the occasional hiss of ice against glass.

Then the phone rang. Frank's hand shot to his coat pocket. "Thompson."

It was Miss Scott. Her voice, thin but steady, came through the static. "Mr. Thompson, I will proceed in a discussion with Abby. I've asked her to come by tomorrow at eleven. I have mixed feelings about this, but it's time she knows. Her father and I are old, and this truth shouldn't die with us."

Frank exhaled, relief and tension colliding. "Thank you, Miss Scott. Truly. Did you speak with your brother?"

"No," she said after a pause. "That will come later. I'd rather Abby hear from me first. She may be angry that we hid it so long, but perhaps she'll find peace in the truth. I only hope it doesn't harm her more than it helps."

Hayden leaned closer. "You're doing the right thing, Miss Scott. The truth has waited long enough. We'll be kind, and careful."

After she hung up, Hayden stared out the window at the dark water. The tide was still high, moonlight glinting on the surface. "Tomorrow," he said quietly. "We'll finally meet her."

***

They drove back across the swale once the tide had ebbed and parked outside the B&B. Inside, the fire in the sitting room was down to coals, glowing like watchful eyes. Harriet greeted them warmly and mentioned her handyman, Hank, would be coming by to replace a broken thermostat upstairs.

Tall and narrow-shouldered, with hollow cheeks and mismatched eyes, Hank moved with a ghostly precision. He'd worked for Harriet for years—fixing, cleaning, listening more than talking. His father had once worked at the foundry beside Jim Scott. The two men, locals said, had been close in their youth before the accident changed everything.

Upstairs, Hank replaced the thermostat and tested it, humming softly to himself. As he turned to leave, a few sheets of paper caught his eye—Frank's notes, left open on the dresser. He leaned closer, squinting at the names scrawled across the page: Abby, Miss Scott, Jim Scott, South Harbor. His eyes darted back and forth like dice tumbling in a cup.

He took off his cap, scratched his head, and quietly slipped from the room.

Downstairs, Harriet was in the kitchen preparing for the next morning's breakfast. Hank chatted with her for a few minutes—pleasant, harmless words about weather and supplies.

His tone never wavered, but there was a flicker behind his mismatched eyes that Harriet couldn't quite place. Then, without another word, he went out the back door into the sleet.

The night swallowed him whole.

***

Outside, the streetlight shimmered in halos of frost. Their SUV sat quietly in the driveway, sleet pattering softly on the windshield, mingling with the distant rhythm of the tide.

Inside the B&B, Frank and Hayden sat by the dying fire, their mugs steaming in the lamplight. Neither spoke for a while. Each was lost in his own web of thoughts—Abby, the Scotts, and the dark house on the cliff.

"Feels like we're standing in the breath between worlds," Hayden said finally.

Frank nodded. "Tomorrow, the tide goes out."

"Let's hope it takes the lies with it," Hayden murmured.

The coals shifted in the hearth, a quiet sigh that sounded almost human. Somewhere out in the night, a bell buoy tolled once, its echo rolling in over the snow.

And still, the two men waited—for the tide to recede, for Miss Scott's courage to hold, and for Abby to step into the story that had been waiting for her all along.

Chapter Fourteen

The Sand Dollar

The token from the past bridges a lost life

Hayden and Frank had a peaceful night, and with the thermostat replaced, there were no extremes of temperature to disturb their rest. Frank slept deeply, occasionally letting out a soft snore, while Hayden remained in a lighter sleep, anxiety twisting in his stomach. The cold outside was sharp but not biting, the air crisp, and the light winds kept the window shutters still. Morning sunlight, pale and filtered, crept through the curtains, painting patterns on the wooden floor.

The faint hum of the heater mixed with the faraway sound of surf. Somewhere beyond the glass, a gull cried, its voice drifting through the gray. Hayden blinked, half caught between dream and waking, disoriented for a moment by how quiet everything seemed. The scent of salt in the air pulled him back to where he was—not Oregon anymore, but a coast that felt like its mirror image.

By the time they were ready for breakfast, Hayden's nerves had settled just enough to allow him to function. They joined a couple of other guests in the kitchen, where Harriet chattered away as usual. Today, Hank leaned against the beverage buffet, his tall, thin frame unusually still.

The kitchen smelled of toast and citrus. Sunlight caught the steam rising off a fresh pot of coffee. Hank's posture was stiff, his shadow thin against the beadboard wall. His mismatched eyes moved constantly, never quite landing anywhere for long.

Harriet hummed as she poured coffee, her bright chatter smoothing over the edges of the morning. "I always say a day begun with good company and hot coffee can't go too wrong," she said, her laughter like a quick burst of wind through leaves.

"How was your room last night, Frank and Hayden?" Harriet asked.

Frank smiled. "Great. Thank you for installing the new thermostat."

Harriet turned to Hank. "Pour some orange juice, won't you?"

Hank filled small glasses and handed them to the other guests first, saving Frank and Hayden for last. Hayden studied Hank as he moved, trying to hide the unease he felt at the rapid, almost uncontrollable motion of Hank's eyes. Frank took the glass, nodded in thanks, and gave Hayden a knowing smile.

After breakfast, Frank gathered his sachet of notes and walked to the foyer with Hayden. They took their jackets from the hall tree and stepped onto the porch. "Well, today is showtime. Are you ready?"

Hayden took a deep breath. "My stomach is still uneasy, even after a solid breakfast. I slept, but my insides are still restless. Meeting Abby... after the encounter at the beach house... I'm not sure how I'll handle it."

He rubbed his hands together, breath clouding in the chill air. The cold morning smelled faintly of pine and wood smoke. Somewhere down the road, a gull cried and the sound echoed through the fog like a question

* * *

As they stepped off the porch, both froze. Their SUV was gone. "What the heck?" Frank muttered. The empty space where it had been made the gravel look wrong—as if something vital had been torn out of the morning itself. Tire tracks led toward the road, already softening under a dusting of sleet. Hayden stared, his pulse quickening. He'd seen a lot of strange things in his life, but vanishing cars weren't on the list.

Hayden's stomach flipped. "Our SUV vanished in thin air! Frank, we must be at the Scott house in twenty minutes."

Frank hurried to the parking area. Tire tracks in the gravel led toward the paved road. No sign of the white SUV. He turned back toward the B&B, frowning. Hayden stayed by the porch stairs, staring after him.

"I'll get Harriet," Frank said, gesturing. "You dash upstairs to our room. Check if the keys are on the dresser or dropped on the floor. They aren't in my jacket pocket."

Frank returned with Harriet. "Our SUV is gone. How is that possible?"

Harriet frowned. "I don't know. No surveillance cameras out here, and... nothing much ever happens."

She glanced toward the driveway as if expecting the car to reappear. Her hands twisted the edge of her apron. "Folks around here don't steal," she said softly. "But sometimes things... go missing. Happens after a storm."

"Well, it certainly didn't drive itself away. How far to the nearest police?" Frank asked.

Harriet's expression hardened slightly. "There are no local police on the island. You'd need to drive thirty miles north to Hancock to reach the sheriff's office. A deputy swings by daily, maybe they could help."

Hank leaned against a porch pillar, hands in his pockets, eyes oscillating nervously. The wind tugged at his jacket. He didn't look alarmed—just watchful, as if this were something he had expected all along.

Frank, frustrated, turned to Harriet. "Do you have a vehicle we can borrow? We need to leave immediately."

Harriet offered her green Ford Taurus. "I must go into town for supplies, but I can wait. How long will you need it?"

Frank hesitated. "I don't know exactly. We're not going far—just to the end of the road—but we may be gone for hours."

Hank silently moved the car around to the front, leaving the driver's door open.

Inside the car, Hayden finally spoke. "I didn't see any keys upstairs, Frank. And Hank... those eyes..."

Frank nodded grimly. "Something is off. Remember, he installed the thermostat last night and today seemed relaxed, yet his eyes were moving like lightning. I'll have a talk with him when we return."

Hayden kept glancing into the side mirror as they pulled away, half expecting to see Hank standing in the middle of the road watching them. But the drive behind them stayed empty—just gray sleet and the faint shimmer of Harriet's porch light.

***

They pulled up to the Scott house. Hayden's eyes widened at the shiny red F150 super cab pickup in the driveway. "Is Abby driving that monster?"

"What did you expect, a Subaru?" Frank teased.

Hayden smiled wryly. "Doesn't seem to fit her personality, that's all."

The truck gleamed even under the overcast sky, a bright scar of color against the stone and gray clapboard. It felt out of place—alive, defiant, like something from another world.

They knocked. The large dog from yesterday remained absent. Miss Scott opened the door. "Make yourself comfortable. Abby will be here in a few minutes. She's letting Tenet out back."

Frank offered an apology. "Sorry we're a bit late—car trouble."

Marilyn glanced outside. "Traded the Explorer for a Taurus, did you? Looks like Harriet's car."

Frank sat, saying nothing. Abby entered shortly after, and Hayden felt his stomach twist again at the sight of her.

The air seemed to shift when she stepped in—a small gust of cold following her from the door. She was simpler than he'd imagined, no makeup, hair tied loosely back, yet there was something striking about her presence, like a song half-remembered. For a moment, Hayden forgot why he was there at all.

"I am so happy to meet both of you—the two mystery men," she said, shaking their hands warmly.

"So, you're the writer from Oregon?" Abby asked Hayden.

"Yes. Mystery and thrillers," he replied, feeling like a sixth grader meeting a crush for the first time.

Her laugh came easily, warm enough to dissolve the tension in the room. "I love a good mystery," she said. "Real life's full of them if you know where to look."

Abby smiled, crossing her legs in well-worn jeans. "I enjoy mystery thrillers. I guess I'm a bookworm. Read, read, read."

Hayden gestured toward her truck. "I really like it."

She beamed. "I love it. Comes in handy for hauling things and especially during winter storms."

Abby turned to Frank. "And you? The brilliant detective? What are you investigating here on Mount Desert Island?"

Frank began explaining, and Abby interrupted him. "Auntie told me you came to talk about a few things. She won't tell me why, so get to it."

Frank carefully filled in her past: the accident in Bandon, her memory loss, and her life until twenty-six. Abby's aunt fidgeted, listening closely.

As Frank spoke, Hayden watched Abby's expression change—curiosity giving way to confusion, then to something deeper, almost grief. It was like watching someone try to remember a language they'd once spoken fluently.

"You lived with your aunt, helped run her antique shop, went to school, met Jeremy, and married in 1985," Frank continued.

Abby's eyes widened. "Married? That's correct, Marilyn?" Her aunt nodded, and the two women sobbed, embracing. Hayden and Frank sat quietly, moved by the emotion.

***

Hayden's phone rang. Diane from the Oregon rental agency. He silenced it after a few rings, only to receive a text: 'Hayden, please call me. Something terrible happened at the beach house. Urgent.'

The words on the screen made his throat tighten. "I'm sorry, Frank. I need to take this call," Hayden whispered, leaving the room. Frank continued explaining her relationship with Jeremy.

He stepped quietly into the foyer, the sound of wind against the windows following him like a whisper. When Diane answered, her voice shook: "The attorney's dead, Hayden. Found near the rocks. Just up and died, maybe foul play," she said. Hayden's mind raced, connecting it to Salty's similar demise. Hayden stared at the phone long after the call ended, the cold from the window glass biting into his palm.

Back in the living room, Frank asked Hayden if he would show Abby the photos. Hayden pulled out his phone, scrolling through images of her younger self and the beach house. Abby shook her head in disbelief.

Then Hayden handed her a sand dollar from Dory Cove. Her tears slowed, a small smile forming. "Is that... from my spirit?" Frank mouthed. Hayden nodded. Silence filled the room.

Abby turned it over in her hand, tracing the delicate pattern with her thumb. "It feels... alive," she whispered. "Like something listening." She held it to her chest, her breathing slowing as if the rhythm of the sea were inside her now.

"All your care, your words, the pictures... it's foreign to me. But this... this brings me peace."

Hayden explained the story of the spirit, the sand dollar, and its connection. Abby laughed, brokenly. "All these years, something was missing. Now, I hold this sand dollar bridging my reality."

She knelt before her aunt. "I forgive you sincerely. You only did what you knew. I'm thankful."

Marilyn covered her mouth, nodding through tears. The fire popped softly. Outside, the faint sound of waves reached through the window—the same steady rhythm that had always been waiting for her.

The room felt lighter, free from sorrow. Abby stood, resolved. "I have faith to follow you both to Oregon and seek answers. First, I'll deal with my father. There's much to resolve before I can leave."

Aunt Marilyn invited everyone to lunch, sandwiches, and fresh pie, as Abby clutched the sand dollar, ready to face her past and future.

Hayden looked out the window. The snow was easing, the tide beginning its slow turn. Somewhere far away, in the pull of that tide, he imagined the spirit of Dory Cove stirring—the story coming full circle, waiting to be finished.

Miss Scott's Vigil

The old house was quiet again. Miss Scott sat at the kitchen table with the lamp turned low, watching the rain bead down the windowpane and trace crooked paths into the sill. The storm had passed hours ago, but the wind still prowled the eaves, carrying the far-off sound of surf from beyond the headland.

Her tea had gone cold. She held the cup anyway, fingers wrapped around it for the comfort of habit. The fire in the stove had burned down to embers. In the glow, the room looked like an old photograph—sepia and fading.

On the table lay Hayden's notebook, left behind in his hurry. She traced her finger over the worn leather cover, hesitant to open it but unable to resist. His handwriting filled the pages in careful lines—sketches of the coast, fragmented thoughts, questions written in the margins like someone arguing with himself.

She sighed, eyes drifting toward the window again. Out past the dunes, the horizon was a soft blur, sea and sky bleeding into one. There was something about that view—the loneliness of it—that pulled at her heart the way music sometimes did.

For a long while she sat without moving, listening to the rain's soft whisper. Finally, she stood, placed the notebook gently inside her desk drawer, and turned the lamp off. The room fell into shadow.

"Good luck, Hayden," she murmured to the empty house. "And may the sea be kind to you."

Outside, the last raindrops slid from the eaves, one by one, vanishing into the dark.

Chapter Fifteen

Death at Dory Cove

The call from Astoria

The Coast Guard helicopter lifted the basket with the body and veered north toward Astoria, where the county coroner waited. Chief Dixon and Deputy Ron Morgan of the Haystack Beach Police thanked the state troopers and Clatsop County sheriff for their help, then trudged up the wet hillside toward the old beach house.

The rain had turned to mist, drifting in sheets across the slope. The downwash from the helicopter still stirred the air, carrying the sharp tang of jet fuel and salt. A single gull circled above, its cry thin against the wind.

Inside, Dixon told his deputy to gather the attorney's belongings and bring them to the kitchen table. He stood by the picture window, watching the gray surf pound the cove below.

The glass was streaked with sea spray, blurring the horizon so the sky and ocean seemed to merge. The rhythmic crash of the waves sounded almost like breathing—slow, endless, patient.

"I've got everything," Ron said, setting a few items down. "Poor guy didn't even unpack—suitcase, briefcase, small carry-on. Nothing touched. Briefcase's locked."

The Chief picked it up, spun the combination lock absently. "Here's his business card— law firm back east. I'll call them. Makes you wonder what a professional like him was doing out here alone. Booked for a week, according to Diane."

The Chief found Miller's wallet, keys, and cell phone. "Guess I'll make the call."

He phoned the law firm, explained what had happened, and asked if Miller's trip was business or personal. When he hung up, his frown had deepened.

"They want his belongings delivered to Diane," he said. "They'll contact next of kin and handle arrangements. Didn't say why he was here—just that it was part work, part personal time. We'll see about that once the coroner's report comes in."

Ron nodded. "What about the rental car outside?"

"Take everything down there for now. I'll call later if the firm changes their mind."

As Ron gathered the bags, Dixon scrolled through the phone's call log. Several calls last night to an Astoria number—the last at 10:30 p.m.—followed by missed calls from that same number. He dialed it, listened to a few rings, then hung up when no one answered.

The ring tone echoed faintly in the quiet house, hollow and distant, as though it were calling into the sea itself.

Ron reappeared in the doorway. "Car's packed, Chief."

"Good. Here are the keys. Drop the car with Diane and tell her the firm will be in touch about returning his things. I'll follow in a bit."

When Ron left, Dixon jotted down a few other numbers from the phone. The texts were mostly to that Astoria contact. "Mr. Miller," he murmured, "who were you talking to? Sounds like a girlfriend—maybe one you'd never met."

He turned the phone over in his hand, seeing his own reflection ghosted on the dark screen. For an instant, he thought he saw movement behind his reflection—a pale flicker of light, gone as soon as he blinked.

He flipped through the photos: scenery, receipts, nothing suspicious. Outside, the wind pressed against the windows, carrying the hiss of distant surf.

Something's off here, he thought. Why would a man walk that slippery hillside in the dark—fresh off a flight, suitcase still zipped?

He sighed, chuckled softly. "Maybe buried treasure. Maybe spooks. Maybe just rain and bad luck." Then he grabbed his coat and headed for the car.

***

The air outside hit him like a cold slap. The gulls had vanished; only the sound of the tide remained, whispering low against the rocks. He locked the house behind him and felt, for reasons he couldn't explain, that he was being watched.

At the rental office, Diane stood on the porch with Ron. Dixon stepped from the cruiser and joined them.

"Did Ron fill you in, Diane?"

"He did. I'll call the firm shortly. Such a sad thing. You think it was an accident?"

"Appears that way. Aside from those two hikers' footprints that found him, there were no signs of a struggle. Wallet, watch, phone— still on him. Everything else untouched in the house. What puzzles me is why he'd go down there at all. No flashlight, no reason. Maybe the coroner'll find a medical issue, but I don't like the timing."

He paused, glancing toward the ocean. Even from here, he could hear the dull roar of surf against the cove—a steady pulse, as if the sea were keeping time with something unseen.

He handed her the wallet, watch, and phone. "Get a receipt when you send these off."

As he and Ron turned to leave, Dixon called back, "When's that writer fellow due back?"

"Next week—right after this reservation ends."

The Chief nodded and drove off. Diane watched the tail-lights fade, then went inside, shaking her head.

She lingered by the window for a moment, staring toward the cliffs. The light there looked wrong—not quite sun, not quite reflection.

Then it was gone.

***

Back at the station, Dixon settled at his desk and reviewed his notes. He called the Astoria number again. This time, a woman answered quickly.

"Hello?"

"Miss Kellerman? This is Chief Dixon with the Haystack Beach Police. Do you know a Mr. Dwayne Miller?"

A pause. "Yes—yes, I do. Is he all right? I've been trying to reach him."

"I'm afraid not, ma'am. He had an accident last night on the beach. He didn't make it."

Silence filled the line, broken only by soft sobbing. When she finally spoke again, her voice was thin and raw. "What happened?"

"That's what we're still trying to determine. I see you spoke with him last night between nine-thirty and ten-thirty. Can you tell me what about?"

"He called after he arrived from New York. We talked a while, then he said he saw someone on the beach with a light—swinging it back and forth, like they were searching for something. He thought someone might be in trouble and said he was going down to check. I told him not to—it was dark, he didn't know the place—but he went anyway. He said he'd call me back once he got down there. He never did."

Dixon scribbled notes, his pen hesitating on the words: "light on the beach." He'd heard stories about that cove—fishermen seeing lanterns that bobbed on the waves, lights that led people toward the surf and vanished when they followed. He'd always dismissed them. Until now.

"Did you think about calling the police?"

"I should have, but... we'd never met in person. I thought he'd just gone to bed. We met on an online dating site—talked for three months, mostly calls and messages. He said he had court business in Astoria and thought it'd be a good time for us to finally meet."

"So, you didn't know what kind of legal work he was here for?"

"No, it was always personal between us." Her voice cracked. "I still can't believe this."

"Your last call was at ten-thirty, and you didn't try again until morning—why was that?"

"I'm a nurse. My shift started at eleven, twelve hours straight. Are you saying I'm a suspect or something?"

"Easy now," Dixon said gently. "No one's accusing you of anything. For now, it looks accidental, but I need the full picture. If you remember anything else, call me. And... I'm sorry for your loss."

"Thank you, Chief," she whispered. "Goodbye."

The line went dead. Dixon leaned back, staring at the cove photo on his phone—a strip of beach framed by cliffs, waves frozen in midcrash. The image looked peaceful, but he knew better.

He enlarged the image, studying the far edge of the frame where the surf met the rocks. For just a second, he thought he saw something—a faint blur, like a figure caught midturn. He blinked, and it was gone. Maybe the light. Maybe not.

Something down there wasn't finished.

He closed the photo and shut off the phone. The office lights flickered once, dimmed, and steadied again.

Chapter Sixteen

Plan B

The tide turns on borrowed time

"Got to hand it to you, Hayden," Frank said, lowering his voice. "We weren't getting anywhere until you pulled that sand dollar out of your pocket. What made you bring it all the way here?"

"I don't really know," Hayden said. "When I was packing, I kept thinking about that sand dollar Abby's spirit left behind. It felt... important. More powerful than pictures or words. I think that's why I've felt uneasy since we arrived. That thing carries some kind of energy."

"Well, whatever it is, it worked," Frank said. "Sometimes words won't cut it. Like a message in a bottle—only this one came in a shell." He patted Hayden's shoulder. "Hey, what was that all about with Diane at the beach?"

"You won't believe it," Hayden said. "Remember that attorney who booked the beach house? They found him early this morning— dead on the beach. The Haystack Beach Chief is handling it. Diane said he might try to contact one of us."

Frank shook his head. "Another mystery. Did she say accident or foul play?"

"Accident, supposedly. Maybe he slipped on the rocks. They're still investigating."

"I'll bet he saw the Tide Stalker through the window," Frank muttered. "Curiosity got the better of him. Two people now, both killed by blows to the head near the water. Coincidence?"

Hayden didn't answer. The phrase 'Tide Stalker' hung in the air like a foghorn note— low, ominous, refusing to fade.

"Chief Dixon's going to have questions when we get back," Hayden said.

"Oh, I'm sure of it. When Abby comes with us, things might get messy. He'd never believe what's really going on. Whatever we plan with her, we'd better have a Plan B. She's still fragile—mentally and emotionally. We can't pile on stress and uncertainty." Frank sighed. "Speaking of uncertainty, I need to deal with the SUV situation. Go on inside—keep the ladies company."

Hayden went back in while Frank stepped to the porch rail and checked his phone. Several missed calls and two voice messages waited. He played the first:

"Mr. Thompson, this is A-1 Car Rentals in Portland, Maine. We had a call from South Harbor that the SUV you rented was found submerged in a tidal canal this morning. Please call us back."

The second message made his stomach drop.

"This is Smithy's Dock, at the canal crossing. We pulled your SUV out of the slough— it's a mess. Come by and we'll talk. We've already contacted the rental agency."

Frank muttered, "How in the hell did that happen?" He had a sinking suspicion Hank was behind it. Maybe Abby's father had sent him to snoop around. Jim was old and housebound but still possessive and controlling—especially where his daughter was concerned.

The thought of Jim Scott watching from behind those drawn curtains made Frank's skin crawl. Some men aged into gentleness; others hardened like iron. Jim, he suspected, was the latter.

***

He called the rental agency and arranged for another vehicle to be delivered to South Harbor. They told him they'd contact the sheriff in Hancock to file a report. The replacement would arrive around noon tomorrow. Frank planned to visit Smithy's in the meantime.

Inside, Hayden and the women were already talking about what came next. The main concern was Abby's father—how to tell him and how to care for him. Everything was about to change, no matter what they said. Hayden and Frank hadn't even decided what to do once Abby returned to Oregon.

Hayden could feel the current of change moving beneath every polite sentence. It was in the way Aunt Marilyn's hands trembled as she poured coffee, in the flicker of Abby's eyes when her father's name came up. Something inevitable was approaching, like a storm seen from miles away but moving fast.

The death at Dory Cove guaranteed Chief Dixon would be waiting with more questions. And how would Abby react to hearing that her husband's spirit—the Tide Stalker—might have caused another death?

They agreed Abby's father should come to her aunt's house the next day. Whether Hayden and Frank should be there was debated, but in the end, it was decided they should—Abby might need support.

"Well," Frank said, "I guess we've got a plan. When do we do this?"

Abby looked out the window, then back at them. "Tomorrow's best. It's late already, and you two have things to sort out. Let's say ten in the morning?"

"That'd work," Frank said, "but the replacement vehicle won't arrive until noon. How about one o'clock?"

Abby nodded. "Perfect. Auntie and I will fix lunch first. Pie included."

"Deal," Frank said, smiling. "We'll return Harriet's car and run a couple of errands."

Hayden hugged Abby. "I'm just glad to finally understand what we know—and ready to face what we don't."

Abby smiled through misty eyes. "You've both done more than I can ever thank you for."

The two women followed them out to the porch. Hayden grinned and pointed at Abby's big red pickup. "Too bad we can't take that rig back to Oregon."

"Maybe we can," Abby said softly. "Maybe we can."

Something in her tone caught Hayden off guard—not quite hope, not quite fear. For an instant, he thought he saw the reflection of the sea in her eyes, as if the waves themselves were calling her home.

***

Frank turned Harriet's Taurus toward town. "Let's stop at Smithy's first. This should be interesting."

Smithy's shop was just as they remembered—the smell of salt, fuel, and damp rope. Smithy sat by a potbellied stove with another old man, both nursing coffee.

"Well, if it ain't our stranded travelers," Smithy said, grinning. "Want to see that shiny Ford Explorer? Well, not so shiny now."

"You found it in the canal this morning?" Frank asked.

"Sure did," Smithy said. "Key fob was still inside, under the dash. You boys been driving in your sleep? Maybe went for a midnight swim?" The men laughed loudly.

Frank's jaw tightened. "Nothing funny about that. Can we see it?"

"Sure. Out back. Water's drained out— mostly. Might be some seaweed or a crab or two." They cackled again.

Frank led Hayden outside. The SUV sat half-sunk in mud, doors and windows open. "Looks like they tried to drain it," he muttered. "Good thing it's not raining. Still, she's done for—too much saltwater damage."

The vehicle looked like some relic dredged from the deep—paint dulled, mirrors fogged, the smell of brine and decay thick in the air. Seaweed clung to the tires, like the ocean had tried to keep it.

Hayden leaned in the passenger side. "Craziest thing I've ever seen. Who'd do this?"

"One guess," Frank said. "And it starts with H."

"You think Hank's behind this?"

"I'd bet on it. He's working with Abby's father, trying to spook us. If he knows we're here, he'd want us gone."

"Or maybe," Hayden said quietly, "he wants us to stay."

Frank looked at him sharply, but Hayden's tone was calm, almost resigned—as if part of him already believed they'd been drawn here for reasons beyond their own choosing.

Frank frowned. "Let's just hope we're gone before he tries something else. Good thing we didn't leave anything valuable inside."

They returned to the front entry. "We've got a replacement coming tomorrow," Frank said curtly. "The agency'll take this one back to Portland."

"Maybe they'll bring you one of them cars that floats!" Smithy shouted, laughing again.

Frank didn't answer.

* * *

They drove to the same café they'd eaten at before, but the welcome was colder this time. Heads turned. Conversations stopped.

"Well, here are the men with all the questions," the server said dryly as they sat. "Find any answers yet?"

"I'll have the clam chowder and cornbread," Frank said.

"Fresh out," she replied.

Frank glanced at nearby tables with steaming bowls. "Doesn't look that way."

"Fresh out," she repeated, flatly.

"Fine. Fish and chips?"

"Out."

"What do you have then?"

"Grilled cheese."

Hayden gave a faint smile. "Two grilled cheese and two Cokes. Unless you're out of soda too."

The server turned without a word. The room fell into a low murmur.

The old clock above the counter ticked too loudly. A dog barked somewhere outside, short and sharp. Every sound seemed amplified, like the air itself had turned against them.

"Friendly place," Frank muttered.

Hayden leaned closer. "Feels like everyone knows why we're here."

"They probably do," Frank said. "A grilled cheese and a Coke—that's hospitality for you. Tonight, let's take shifts keeping watch. No telling what might happen after dark."

Hayden nodded. "Glad you've got your sidearm, but I hope you don't need it."

Their sandwiches arrived—limp bread and rubbery cheese. Hayden stared at his plate. "Abby's spirit warned me we'd face darkness on this path. Maybe this is it."

"Let's hope it doesn't get any darker," Frank said. "This cheese might already be evil enough."

They left cash on the table and walked out. Back at the B & B, they settled by the fire with hot drinks and Harriet's chocolate chip cookies. Outside, the wind picked up, rattling the shutters.

Frank explained what had happened to the SUV and thanked Harriet for lending her car.

She only nodded, expression unreadable.

"Will you need another night?" she asked.

"Yes," Frank said. "At least one more."

"No problem," she said. "You're my only guests. I was thinking of closing for a few weeks—maybe take a little vacation."

Frank raised an eyebrow. "Didn't you say you never took vacations?"

She smiled faintly. "Things change."

As she left the room, Hayden stared at the fire. "I don't like this, Frank. Something feels off."

The flames crackled low, throwing restless shadows across the walls. For a heartbeat, one of them looked like a man standing behind the chair—tall, still, watching. Hayden blinked and it was gone.

Frank sipped his coffee. "Then Plan B better be ready."

Outside, the wind shifted, and somewhere beyond the dunes, the sea began to rise.

Chapter Seventeen

Showdown

Flames reveal what darkness hid

The shutters rattled in the wind, and the old house groaned with every gust. Inside, Hayden sat in the overstuffed chair, fighting to stay awake while Frank slept. The fire's glow from the downstairs sitting room flickered faintly under the door.

The glow rose and fell like a slow breath, a lung the size of the house. Each time it dimmed, the darkness pressed closer, and Hayden's eyes fluttered, then snapped open again.

Sometime after the grandfather clock struck three, Hayden's nose caught something sharp and bitter. Smoke.

Not the sweet trace of a dying log—acrid, chemical, wrong. It hooked the back of his throat and sent a cold thread of alarm down his spine.

He sprang up, dazed, then opened the door—a blast of smoke poured in. Flames licked up the staircase below.

"Frank! Wake up—the house is on fire!"

Frank jolted awake, pulling on his pants and shoes as Hayden grabbed their bags.

Heat rolled up the stairwell with a low, animal roar. The wallpaper along the hall had begun to bubble and curl, little tongues of flame tasting the edges.

"The stairs?" Frank shouted.

"No chance—the fire's coming up fast!"

"Then we run for it. Come on!"

They bolted into the hallway, thick with smoke. At the far end, Frank spotted a window and threw it open. A porch roof stretched a few feet below. "Go!"

Hayden climbed through as fire roared behind them. They dropped onto the porch roof, crawled to the edge, and used a trellis to scramble down. Coughing, they stumbled into the yard.

Sleet stung their faces. The night was a churn of orange and black, cinders spinning like a storm of fireflies.

Behind them, the B & B was fully ablaze, flames tearing through the structure, wind feeding the inferno.

Frank and Hayden dropped their bags to the ground, breathing hard.

"Harriet," Frank said between coughs. "Her quarters were off the sitting room."

"I didn't see her," Hayden said. "You'd think a fire department would've shown up by now."

Frank pulled out his phone. "If they have one, I'm calling them." He dialed 911 and reported the fire.

His voice sounded too calm to his own ears, like it belonged to someone else reporting a stranger's life.

Hayden stared at the house collapsing in sparks. "Did we grab everything?"

"Most of it. Our jackets are gone. Didn't hear any smoke detectors, did you?"

"Not one." Hayden shook his head. "When I opened the door, it was like the fire was waiting for us."

The thought hung there, ugly and plausible, as another window blew out with a hard, bright sigh.

Frank's gaze turned toward the back. "Harriet's car—did you see it?"

"No."

"I'll check."

"Be careful!" Hayden called.

Moments later Frank returned, face grim. "Car's gone."

The words felt heavier than they should have, like a key turning in a lock somewhere far away.

Headlights appeared up the road. A truck pulled in—Smithy.

***

"Well, well," he said, stepping out. "Trouble follows you two like a bad penny. Anyone else inside?"

Frank started forward, anger flaring, but Hayden caught his arm. "As far as we know, no. Harriet wasn't home. We barely made it out."

"Don't you have a fire department?" Frank snapped.

"Volunteer outfit," Smithy said with a shrug. "But it's across the canal. Tide's in. No hydrants nearby either. Haven't had a fire like this in decades. Harriet probably bunked at Patty's—she does that when it's slow."

"Maybe you should call and make sure," Hayden said.

"She probably knows," Smithy said. "Flames like that, you can see 'em for miles."

"It's three in the morning," Hayden shot back. "How would she see them if she's asleep?"

Smithy ignored the question. "Not much I can do. Need a lift to town?"

"No thanks," Frank said coldly.

Smithy shook his head and drove off.

The two men stood in the bitter wind, the fire's heat at their backs.

"Well," Hayden said quietly, "that was quite a night."

Frank stared at the flames. "Coincidence? Harriet gone, no other guests, Smithy showing up alone... I'm not buying it. You think Hank's involved?"

"I think somebody wanted us dead," Hayden said.

Frank nodded grimly. "Our new car won't be here till noon. Let's walk to Miss Scott's. We'll thaw out there and regroup."

The mile-long walk through drizzle and cold felt endless. By the time they reached the familiar porch, dawn was still a pale smear on the horizon.

Their clothes steamed in the weak light, smoke and sea salt clinging to them like a second skin. The island was silent except for the wind and the far-off pound of the surf, steady as a heartbeat you didn't want to listen to.

Frank knocked, and Tenet's barking echoed from inside. Miss Scott's voice calmed the dog before she opened the door, gasping.

"Good heavens You look like you've been dragged through a chimney. Come in"

Frank set his bag down. "The B & B caught fire. We barely made it out."

"Oh my! Harriet?"

"She wasn't there," Frank said. "The place is gone."

"No one came to fight it?"

"Just Smithy," Frank said. "Volunteer crew was across the canal. Tide was in."

She pressed a hand to her chest. "You poor souls. You must be freezing. Showers first— I'll make a fire and hot beverages."

***

The hot water left their faces pink and raw. Clean clothes felt like a promise they weren't sure they could keep.

They followed her to the guest room, silent and exhausted. After washing the smoke from their skin and dressing, they joined her in the living room.

Miss Scott had a fire roaring and a tray of coffee, tea, and pastries waiting. Outside, gray daylight pressed against the windows.

"Coffee for you, Frank. Tea for you, Hayden," she said kindly. "Eat. You both need it." The warmth began to chase the chill away.

"I can't imagine what you've been through," she said softly. "First your car, now this. And all for Abby."

Frank nodded. "It's starting to feel like someone doesn't want us here."

"What do you mean?"

"How well do you know Hank?" Frank asked.

She blinked. "All his life. He's... troubled. My brother took him in years ago."

Frank sighed. "We think he's the one who drove our SUV into the canal—and maybe set that fire."

Her expression froze. "You can't be serious."

"Miss Scott, your brother may have known about our visit," Frank said gently. "Hank was in our room fixing a thermostat the other night. He probably saw our notes."

She sank into her chair, eyes wide. "My brother wouldn't... oh dear. Perhaps I've underestimated him. He's grown more erratic lately. If you're right, you could be in danger."

"Then we'd better bring Abby here," Frank said. "The last thing we need is a confrontation at his house."

Miss Scott nodded and hurried to the phone.

***

Hayden watched the firelight dance on the walls. "Her spirit warned us, Frank. She said we'd face darkness before we found her."

Frank gave a faint smile. "I didn't think she meant arsonists."

He didn't say which ending he was afraid they were heading toward.

"Maybe it's all connected," Hayden murmured. "Like we're walking through one of my own stories."

Miss Scott returned. "Abby's on her way. Hank left the house after midnight, hasn't come back. My brother's locked in his den, refusing to speak."

Frank frowned. "Then things are worse than I thought."

They waited. The house creaked as wind swept in off the sea. Miss Scott knitted by the fire, her needles clicking like a metronome for the storm outside.

Tenet paced once around the room and lay down with a sigh, eyes fixed on the door as if he could will it to open.

*****

A vehicle pulled up, and moments later Abby burst through the door.

"Thank heaven you're all right!" she cried, embracing her aunt, then Hayden, then Frank. "I saw the fire—there's nothing left but ashes. What's happening here?"

"We don't know," Frank said. "But someone wanted that fire."

Abby nodded, shaken. "Hank's truck was at the foundry. He wasn't in it. Father's been strange lately—distant, confused. I'm afraid he's behind this."

"Will he come here for lunch?" Frank asked.

"I doubt it. Hank's his driver, and he's gone. Father won't leave the house."

"Then we go to him," Frank said.

"First, let's stop by the B & B," Abby said. "The fire chief wanted to speak with the guests."

Frank agreed. "Then we'll sort transport and get ready to leave this island."

The B & B was a smoldering ruin. Ash drifted through the air like black snow. Abby parked near the fire truck.

The chimney stood alone like a grave marker. The air tasted of metal and wet ash.

The Fire Chief approached. "You two were inside when it started?"

Frank nodded. "We were lucky to get out."

Harriet appeared, tears streaking her soot stained face. She gripped their arms. "Thank God you're alive."

Frank gently told the Chief they suspected arson. The Chief's polite expression hardened.

"Why would anyone torch a historic home?"

Frank didn't answer. Some truths were better left unspoken.

They left for Smithy's. The new rental had just arrived—a smaller SUV replacing the ruined Explorer.

"Seems they don't trust us with the big ones anymore," Frank said dryly.

Hayden chuckled. "You know, there's a pattern here. You drove an Expedition when we started. Then we rented an Explorer. Now they've given us an Escape. Maybe it's a sign."

Frank smirked. "As long as the next one isn't a hearse."

"Where's Abby?"

"Inside with Smithy."

Hayden went to get her, returning a moment later. "All set."

Back at Miss Scott's, the kitchen was warm with the smell of tea and pastries.

"Still no word from your brother?" Frank asked.

Miss Scott shook her head. "He's not answering."

Frank turned to Abby. "You still want to go back to Oregon?"

Abby stared out the window, her reflection ghosted in the glass. "If it weren't for Father, I'd leave today. But yes… it's time. I can't live in his shadow anymore."

Hayden watched her quietly, his feelings complicated and unspoken.

He saw the same steadiness now that had been in the old photographs—not youth, exactly, but something like grace after weather.

She turned back, resolve hardening. "This ends now. I'm not afraid of him anymore. I'll go with you to Oregon—to whatever comes next."

Miss Scott nodded. "When will you leave?"

"In the morning," Frank said.

"I'll take my truck," Abby added. "We'll drive."

"Fine by me," Frank said. "Hayden can go with you, I'll fly home."

They all agreed it was best to avoid confronting Jim. Abby and Miss Scott decided to go gather her things immediately while the tide was low.

The plan felt light in the mouth, but heavy in the chest. Plans often did.

As they stepped onto the porch, Hank's truck pulled into the drive. Jim stood beside it, leaning on his cane.

Abby froze. "Father?"

"I don't know what you're planning," he said, voice shaking with anger. "But you're not leaving. There's nothing for you in Oregon."

"Let me go, Hank!" Abby shouted as Hank grabbed her arm.

Miss Scott saw it all through the window and ran for the back door, shouting for the men. "We've got trouble out front!" Frank and Hayden burst through the door.

"Let her go!" Frank barked.

Hank spun, pulling a revolver.

Frank drew his sidearm. "Put it down, Hank."

Abby froze. Jim limped closer. "You think you can just take her away? Lower your gun, mister—before Hank gets nervous."

Frank's gaze darted to Miss Scott, who stood behind her brother holding Tenet by the collar. She mouthed something—then let the dog go.

Tenet charged. Hank turned, startled, and the gun went off, shattering the porch light.

The dog clamped onto Hank's arm, dragging him down.

The fight detonated into noise—glass, a shout, the dull thud of bodies on wood.

Frank kicked the weapon away, training his gun on Hank. Jim raised his cane, shouting incoherently, until his sister snatched it from him and knocked him off balance.

"For heaven's sake, Jim!" she cried. "It's over—you can't control her anymore!"

Jim fell to his knees, gasping for breath. Abby ran to her aunt. Frank glanced toward Hayden.

"Bag in the bedroom—side pocket," he said. "Zip ties."

Hayden ran, returned, and helped secure Hank's wrists.

Hank's breath came in ragged bursts; Tenet's growl settled to a warning rumble, teeth still pinked with blood.

Jim struggled to his feet, trembling. "Don't do this, Abby. Don't go."

Abby looked at him through tears. "I have to. You've kept me prisoner long enough."

"Inside," Frank ordered. They herded everyone into the living room, Tenet still growling low, the storm building outside.

When everyone was inside and Jim and Hank were subdued, Miss Scott's composure finally broke. "Why?" she demanded. "Why burn down the B & B? Why bring a gun here and risk killing us all?"

She clutched her phone, trembling. "I have no choice, Abby. We have to report this. It won't be good news for Jim or Hank, but I can't ignore it."

Abby nodded, eyes glistening. "Do it, Auntie. Father—you're sick. I can't believe you'd do this. You need help, real help. It's out of love that I've tolerated you this long, but that ends tonight."

Miss Scott called the authorities. Within half an hour, two sheriff's cars pulled up through the storm. Jim and Hank were handcuffed and led away. Another deputy stayed to take statements from Abby, Miss Scott, Frank, and Hayden. The wind howled off the ocean as dusk fell, and the last light faded into gray.

Blue and red lights strobed across the walls, turning the room into a slow, silent tide of color. When the cars finally rolled away, the night seemed too dark by comparison. Silence filled the house.

"I'm sorry it had to come to this," Frank said quietly. "But it could have ended much worse. Your father will get help, Abby. Hank too."

"At least I don't have to worry about him being alone," Abby said softly. "But Auntie— how will you manage here?"

Miss Scott smiled gently. "Don't you fret. I've been thinking of leaving this island for a while. There's a lovely senior center near Portland that allows pets. Tenet and I could use a change of scenery. It's time we all moved on."

Hayden rose and hugged Abby. "Are you still willing to leave tomorrow?"

"Of course," she said. "It's too late to gather my things tonight, but we'll go first thing in the morning."

"Then it's settled," Miss Scott said, smoothing her apron. "Abby, take your old room upstairs. I'll fix us some dinner and open a bottle of wine."

While the women worked in the kitchen, Hayden and Frank stood by the fireplace, watching the flames dance.

"Quite a day," Frank murmured.

"Three days in one," Hayden said. "After that wine, I'll sleep like the dead. But first, I have to ask you something."

Frank smiled tiredly. "If I can manage an answer."

Abby came in with two glasses of wine. The men thanked her, and she returned to the kitchen.

Hayden took a sip. "Do you always carry zip ties around?"

Frank chuckled. "No. But something told me we might need them. Picked up a few at Smithy's the other day."

Hayden laughed softly. "And that move with the dog—how'd you know Miss Scott would let him loose?"

"I didn't," Frank said. "I saw her holding Tenet and gesturing. The dog was growling like thunder, so I guessed she was about to act. Turns out, she'd told me before that Tenet doesn't like Hank. Bit him once. Lucky for us, Tenet remembered."

"Good thing he did. That shot was close enough for me."

Frank nodded. "Hank will face justice, and Abby's father will finally get the care he needs."

"So you'll fly back alone?" Hayden asked.

"Sure. You go with Abby—it's a long drive for one person. Call when you reach Portland."

Hayden hesitated, then smiled. "You think I'm getting close to her, don't you?"

Frank raised an eyebrow. "Am I wrong?"

Hayden's cheeks reddened. "She's remarkable, Frank. I've felt drawn to her ever since I met her spirit. Now... it's different. She's fifty six, a few years younger than me, but it's like I've known her forever."

"Don't overthink it," Frank said. "If she's meant to find peace, maybe that includes you. We'll figure out the rest when the time comes."

Abby called them to the kitchen for dinner. They ate quietly, sharing warmth and relief, each knowing life had just turned a corner.

The food tasted better than it should have—not because it was perfect, but because it marked the end of something.

The next morning, Abby retrieved her belongings and packed them in the pickup. The sky hung low and gray, the air thick with salt and the hush that follows a storm.

They said their goodbyes—promises to call, to write, to meet again once Abby was safely in Oregon. Miss Scott and Frank stood on the porch, waving as Abby and Hayden left.

As they pulled away from the house, Hayden looked out the window at the distant coastline. Abby's younger spirit had warned of darkness, but he sensed something lifting now—a shadow fading.

They crossed the narrow swale while the tide was still out, the sand glistening like wet glass beneath the truck's tires. Behind them, the island sat cloaked in mist, its cottages and pine ridges fading into shadow

Still, a question lingered in the back of his mind. Had the evil truly unraveled, or merely changed its shape? He didn't want to hand the answer to the ocean. The ocean preferred its own truths.

Hayden glanced in the side mirror, watching the last of the dunes disappear. "Feels strange leaving," he murmured.

Abby nodded, eyes fixed on the winding road ahead. "It's not over yet. You can feel it too, can't you?"

He didn't answer right away. Out beyond the marsh, a ripple crossed the still water— brief, deliberate, like something alive beneath the surface. Hayden's hand tightened on the door handle. "Yeah," he said quietly. "I can feel it."

The truck climbed the rise, and the island was gone. Only the ocean remained, restless and waiting.

Somewhere far to the west, a different coast was calling—and with it, the unfinished story of a woman who had lived two lives and remembered only one.

Chapter Eighteen

Oregon or Bust

The road west carries whispers of its own

The miles slipped by in silence as Abby guided the pickup across the border into Massachusetts. The hum of tires filled the cab, steady and hypnotic. Both were bone-tired from the chaos left behind in Maine. Conversation had vanished somewhere between exhaustion and uncertainty.

The highway unspooled ahead like a ribbon of dull silver, vanishing into the gray November horizon. Each mile felt like a heartbeat receding into memory.

Hayden stared out the passenger window, the passing lights smearing into pale ribbons. He knew he had to break the silence.

He shifted forward and took a breath. "Well, here we are—heading west at last. Feels good to be on the road home. How are you holding up?"

Abby's hands tightened on the steering wheel. "I'm glad you spoke. I didn't know what to say. This past week's been... unreal. I keep trying to make sense of it, but the harder I try, the less it fits. I now know I was married once, but I can't feel it. Maybe that's what memory loss does—erases love too."

Her voice wavered like a song half-remembered, and for a second Hayden thought she might cry—but she didn't. Abby had become too practiced at holding herself together.

Hayden nodded slowly. "It's hard to imagine what that must be like. Honestly, the whole thing still blows my mind too. Meeting your spirit at the Oregon coast, living through this... it's like stepping into one of my own novels. Except this time, the mystery is real."

Abby's lips curled into the faintest smile. "I'm glad you and Frank followed the clues. I hadn't felt right for years. My father changed in ways I couldn't explain. I used to wonder who I really was, before the accident... and what I'd missed."

The road hummed under the tires, the sound filling the spaces between their words like the sea fills a shell.

She turned to him. "What was my spirit like?" she asked quietly. "What did you take away from that encounter?"

He thought for a moment. "I remember falling asleep on the couch, and a knock woke me. I thought I was dreaming until I saw the wet carpet. She stood in the doorway, wearing a raincoat—rain dripping onto the floor. I found the sand dollar she left the next morning. That's when I knew it was real."

Abby's voice softened. "What did she look like?"

"Pale, delicate... dark eyes, full of depth. She looked lost but determined. You—only younger. Her face was the same as yours, though her expression carried a kind of sorrow I can't describe."

He hesitated, remembering the strange ache of that night—the way the air had shimmered between dream and waking, the salt tang that hadn't belonged indoors.

Abby nodded slowly, eyes fixed on the highway. "Maybe that's what I've been feeling—empty. Half a person. I tried to be content on the island, but I see now that something was always missing."

Hayden smiled. "Even at twenty-six, she had your grace. You may not remember her, but she's still in you."

Abby blushed faintly. "You're kind, Hayden. Kinder than you think."

He gave a quiet laugh. "Maybe. But I get impatient sometimes. I've spent most of my life writing alone, so people are... difficult for me. Except you. You're different."

He hesitated. "I'll be honest. I find you attractive—more than I should. I've never been married, and I don't meet many kindred souls. But I also know this is complicated— your past... all of it."

The wipers hissed back and forth, marking the silence between them. Outside, snow flurried like static across the windshield.

The hum of the highway filled the silence that followed. Abby glanced sideways, her expression soft. "I don't remember what love felt like before," she said. "But right now, I know what warmth feels like."

Hayden smiled. "That's a good start."

They drove in comfortable quiet for a while until Hayden pointed to an exit. "How about a bite to eat?" Abby nodded, smiling wider now. The tension between them had softened into something gentle, uncertain, and new.

For the first time in days, the miles felt lighter—as if the ghosts in the back seat had dozed off for a while.

***

Frank had just walked in the door from the airport when his cell phone rang. He tossed his keys on the counter and answered.

"Hello, this is Frank."

"Mr. Thompson, this is Diane from the rental agency at the coast. I've been trying to reach Mr. Langsford, but his phone goes straight to voicemail. Do you know how to contact him?"

Frank frowned. "That's odd. He should have it on. Is something wrong?"

"Well, we've had quite the commotion here. Did he tell you about what happened on the beach?"

"You mean the accidental death?"

"That's the one—but it turns out it wasn't an accident. The coroner says it was a blow to the head from behind. They're calling it a homicide."

Frank straightened. "A homicide?"

"Yes, and that's not all. The man was going to Astoria to handle a legal matter—turns out, the beach house trust expires at the end of December. He was preparing to put the property up for auction."

The words hit Frank like sleet. The case, the fire, the foundry—all of it seemed to twist into the same knot.

Frank rubbed his forehead, pacing. "That's... a lot. Do the police have leads?"

"None yet. He'd been talking to an online girlfriend, but she's not a suspect. Oh—and the beach house is vacant now. No bookings until your friend's next week."

"I'll come down tomorrow," Frank said. "I want to look around before Hayden gets back."

"Of course, Mr. Thompson. I'll have it ready."

After hanging up, Frank stared out the window at the yard, leaves scattered like old letters. The call left him uneasy. The coincidence felt too sharp to ignore.

Somewhere beyond the shore pines, the ocean was probably rolling under a cold moon. The thought of it made him shiver, though the room was warm.

He tried calling Hayden, but his call went to voicemail. He called Abby's number.

"Hi, this is Abby."

"Abby, it's Frank. Is Hayden with you?"

"Yes, right here. Hang on."

Hayden's voice came through the Bluetooth. "Hey, Frank. What's going on?"

"Your phone's off, pal. Dead battery?"

Hayden laughed. "Caught me. What's up?" Frank relayed Diane's news: the murder, the trust, the looming auction.

"Sounds like we've got more trouble waiting," Hayden said.

"Exactly. I'm heading down tomorrow to look around. You two get here when you can. The clock's ticking."

"Copy that. We'll be there by late Sunday."

Abby glanced at Hayden. "A murder? And the house up for auction? Don't we still own it?"

Hayden sighed. "It's complicated. You'll understand everything once we're back."

She watched the road unwind before her, the word "murder" echoing through her like a cold wind finding an open door.

The rest of the drive passed in alternating conversation and silence, both lost in thought. As darkness fell, Abby pulled off at a small town.

Inside the roadside motel, the clerk peered over her glasses. "Sorry, folks. Holiday festival in town—only one room left. Queen bed."

Hayden looked at Abby. "Want to keep driving?"

Abby shook her head. "I'm done. One night won't hurt. You can have the couch." "Deal," Hayden said.

The room was modest but clean. A queen bed, a sagging couch, and the hum of an old air conditioner. Abby disappeared into the bathroom, and soon the sound of running water filled the room. Hayden sat on the couch, exhaustion pressing down like a weight.

The glow from the bathroom door threw a soft band of light across the carpet, trembling with the rhythm of the water. It looked like a heartbeat.

He thought about the strange turn his life had taken—from a quiet Oregon cabin to this journey across the country with a woman caught between two worlds. There was a softness to her that lingered even in silence, a warmth that pulled at him when he wasn't looking. He could still see her eyes from earlier in the evening—steady, searching, touched with something that made him forget the noise of the day. The curve of her smile, the faint shadow of a dimple when she laughed—it all stayed with him longer than it should have.

He felt something stirring in him—affection, curiosity, maybe even love—but he knew he had to move carefully.

Fate, he decided, wasn't cruel—it was simply thorough. It left nothing half-finished, not even grief.

***

The sound of water faded, replaced by the soft scrape of the door opening. Steam drifted out in a pale ribbon, curling through the thin light. Abby stepped into view, her hair damp and loose around her shoulders, her face touched by the glow from the single lamp. She looked younger that way, almost weightless, as if the years she carried had slipped away with the steam.

Hayden tried not to stare, but the sight of her caught him off guard—simple, unguarded, and achingly human. He looked down at his hands, pretending to fuss with his watch, but the image of her lingered anyway, like a reflection he couldn't quite look away from.

She wore a thin robe, her expression peaceful for the first time in days.

"I feel human again," she said with a laugh. "The bathroom's yours."

Hayden nodded, retreating with a smile. When he returned, Abby was asleep, phone in hand. He gently took it, set it on the nightstand, and pulled the covers over her.

She murmured something unintelligible in her sleep—his name, or maybe someone else's. The sound made his heart ache in a way he couldn't name. For a long moment he stood there, studying her face in the half-light. So much strength, and yet such fragility.

He turned off the lamp and lay on the couch. Outside, the hum of the interstate mingled with the steady rhythm of Abby's breathing. His mind drifted to the coast—to the beach house waiting under gray skies and the questions still buried in the sand.

Sleep came slowly, carried on the sound of the wind and the whisper of waves that only he could hear.

And far away, where the Oregon coast met the night, something listened—the same unseen current that had always bound the living to the lost.

INTERLUDE

The Tide Waits

The sea moved with the patience of something ancient and knowing. At Dory Cove, the horizon wore a band of pewter light, and the air tasted of rain and iron. Waves crept across the sand in slow, deliberate strokes, smoothing away footprints that no longer mattered. Each gust of wind carried the faint echo of laughter and cries from years gone by—human sounds thinned by distance and memory, yet still clinging to the shore like mist.

A half-buried crab pot lay rusting in the dunes, its wire bent and sea-stained. Beyond it, the remains of an old dock jutted from the surf, black timbers leaning like the ribs of a shipwreck. When the tide rose high enough, the sea licked at those timbers, tasting their salt, claiming them again and again.

A lone gull circled low, wings cutting through the silver-gray air. The bird called once—sharp, mournful—and vanished into the fog. Its cry seemed to answer the hush that followed, the kind of silence that carries both promise and warning.

Beneath the water, unseen currents shifted, winding their way through kelp and stone. Something restless moved there—ancient, waiting—drawn by the memory of a woman and a man and the unfinished tether between them.

The tide came in higher than before, whispering across the sand like a voice just waking.

It was not yet time, but the sea was listening.

Chapter Nineteen

The Ravine's Secret

Some truths hide behind the overgrowth

Frank arrived at the beach house, tossed his bags onto the bed, and went straight to the front windows facing the ocean. Below, the surf rolled quietly against the sand where the young attorney had been found. He grabbed his jacket, stepped outside, and hiked down the steep hillside toward the cove. The day was calm—sunny, a light westerly breeze pushing the smell of salt inland. Gulls circled lazily overhead, keeping watch as he made his way down the slope.

The place felt changed since the last time— emptier, as if the beach itself were holding its breath. Even the gulls sounded distant, their cries swallowed by the hush that hung between sea and sky.

On the beach, Frank stopped to take it in—the cliff face to the south, the old rusted iron brackets jutting from the rock. He crouched and studied them, wondering aloud, "How the heck did he ever launch and retrieve a dory boat through this surf? And where would he have stored it?" The logistics didn't make sense.

The salt wind bit his face, carrying the odor of rust and seaweed. The brackets, blackened with age, looked more like relics of some shipwrecked machine than a fisherman's aid.

He walked north, following faint remnants of the police investigation. Marker flags still stood in the sand, fluttering where the body had been found. Beyond that, at the northern edge of the cove, the beach narrowed beneath a rocky hillside. Between that ridge and the beach house rose a thick ravine, tangled in brush and wind-twisted pine.

Frank studied it for a moment. Something about that overgrown cut in the landscape pulled at him. He climbed toward it and tried to force his way through, but the thorns and roots were too dense to pass. He'd need heavier tools—and a plan.

The entrance to the ravine breathed cold air, as if the earth itself exhaled. Somewhere within that green-black tangle, something waited. Frank could feel it like a hum beneath his ribs.

***

Back in town, he found himself at the Haystack Beach Hardware store, scanning aisles for gear. He picked out a heavy Mackinaw jacket, a sturdy pair of gloves, and then frowned at the empty rack where machetes should've been. At the counter, an older man with gray hair and a ready smile greeted him.

"Find everything you need?"

"Almost," said Frank. "You carry machetes?"

The man chuckled. "Must be on an adventure, judging by that coat and those gloves. We haven't sold machetes in years. Nobody around here clears land by hand anymore—just power saws and brush cutters."

"Any idea where I might find one?"

"Try Trevor's Collectables. Old shack south of Dory Cove, ocean side of the highway. The fella hoards tools like gold."

"Dory Cove?" Frank looked up sharply. "You know that area?"

"Sure do," said the clerk, leaning on the counter. "Used to call it that years ago. I knew a young man who lived down there. Hard worker, always fixing up something."

Frank's pulse quickened. "You must mean Jeremy Stayton?"

"That's the one. Nice guy. Fished with a dory boat right off that little beach. Tragic business—lost his wife in a storm. After that, he just... drifted. Last I saw him, he came in for camping supplies and a road atlas—wanted one that included

British Columbia. Said he was heading north to start over. Never saw him again."

Frank took it all in. "That's helpful, thank you."

The man smiled. "You know him?"

"I've got a friend who'd sure like to."

"Well, if you find him, tell him Chuck from the hardware store says hello."

Frank nodded, and paid for his items. As he stepped out with the cold wind in his face, the conversation clung to him like the salt mist. A road atlas, British Columbia— he hadn't vanished without a plan. Maybe spirits didn't wander aimlessly after all.

A few miles later, he spotted the weathered sign: Trevor's Collectables. The building leaned with age, its paint bleached by salt air. Inside, the place smelled of pipe smoke and rust.

It was like stepping into a memory—dim light through dusty windows, the faint hiss of a distant radio, and the sweet, stale smell of tobacco that made the air thick.

Tables sagged under piles of old tools and knives. Frank found a set of machetes that looked usable, banged them together to get someone's attention, and waited.

A hunched man appeared from a back room, pipe clenched in his teeth. "What can I do for you, young man?"

Frank lifted the machetes. "How much?"

The man squinted, amused. "You look like you mean business. Ten bucks apiece."

"Deal." Frank handed him a bill, then asked, "Did you ever know Jeremy Stayton?"

The old man's eyebrows shot up. "Oh, sure. Lively kid. Bit of a scavenger, like me. Collected things nobody else wanted. Married a beautiful gal—met her once. After she died, he vanished. Never heard from him again. Probably went north, I'd guess. Folks don't come back from that kind of loss."

Frank wondered if grief could be mapped the same way as coastlines—curving, eroding, leaving behind strange new shapes that no one recognized.

***

Frank thanked him and headed back to the beach house, the two machetes gleaming faintly in the late light. Inside, he placed them on the kitchen table and put on his new jacket ready to head back down to the ravine. Just as he reached for the machetes, a firm knock sounded.

Through the peephole, he saw Chief Dixon standing on the porch. Frank hesitated, then opened the door.

"Well, Chief," he said. "Didn't expect a visit."

"I heard you were back and thought I'd stop by," said Dixon, stepping inside without waiting to be invited. "Wanted to bring you up to date about the incident here."

Frank shut the door, quickly removed his Mackinaw and tossed it atop the machetes on the kitchen table.

The Chief wandered toward the window, peering down at the beach. "You heard about the murder?"

"Murder? I thought it was an accident."

"The coroner called it cardiac arrest. but the kid was healthy as a horse. Dropped like a stone, face down. No rocks nearby, no signs of struggle, no missing property. Just walked north and fell dead. It doesn't sit right with me."

Frank kept his expression neutral. "Heart attacks happen, even in the young."

"Sure. I've seen panic stop a man's heart before. But my gut says he saw something that scared him to death."

Frank raised an eyebrow. "What could he have seen out there in the dark?"

"Hard to say," the Chief replied. "But the sheriff and state police have closed their books. I'm expected to do the same. Still..." He reached into his coat and pulled out a business card—Frank's card. "You're a private investigator, aren't you? I'd like to hire you to take another look."

Frank studied him for a moment. "I'll think about it. I've got other business for now, but once my partner gets here, maybe we'll talk."

"Don't take too long," said Dixon. "Cases go cold quick."

At the door, the Chief paused, went to the kitchen table eyeing the jacket on the table. He felt the collar. "Nice Mackinaw.

I've seen those at the hardware store. Bit pricey for me, though. Maybe I'll get one when I retire."

He turned to leave, then looked back over his shoulder. "Oh—and that girlfriend in Astoria? Said she was on the phone with the victim when he died. He told her he saw someone walking along the beach, swinging a light. Said he was going down to check. Never called her back. Makes you wonder—don't it?"

Frank forced a smile. "I'll let you know what we decide."

The Chief tipped his hat and walked to his car.

The sound of gravel under the tires lingered long after the cruiser vanished. Frank stood still, listening to the surf and the slow, unsettling rhythm of his own heart.

When the sound of the engine faded, Frank exhaled and turned to the window. The beach below was empty, washed clean by the tide. What could have terrified a man to death? And why now?

He grabbed the machetes, pulled on his jacket, and made his way back down to the ravine before dusk. The brush was dense, the air damp with decay. He swung the blades steadily, cutting through the tangle. Twenty feet in, he stopped—something dark glinted under the moss. He crouched, peering closer.

It wasn't a shadow. It was the face of an old wooden structure, sunken into the hillside, the door nearly hidden by vines.

The boards were black with rot, the iron hinges fused with rust. A faint smell of salt and something older drifted out—like water trapped for decades.

A shiver crawled down his neck. The daylight was nearly gone, and the wind whispered through the ravine like breath through hollow wood.

Frank backed away, following his narrow path out, the sound of surf guiding him. As he reached the open sand, the breeze shifted— and behind him, faint and distant, came the creak of a door.

It was a small sound, almost nothing, but it froze him mid-step. The kind of sound that could come from settling timber—or from something that had just remembered how to move.

Chapter Twenty

Together Again

Where memory meets the wraith of the sea

Frank was up early. Dawn hadn't fully broken, and the house was still shadowed in a soft gray light. The kitchen smelled of salt air and coffee. He'd set out bacon, eggs, and hash browns, ready to cook a hearty breakfast before returning to the beach. As he turned the stove on and the pans began to warm, a knock rattled the front door.

He frowned. Who on earth would be here this early?

When he opened the door—"Surprise" shouted Hayden and Abby.

They rushed inside, the chill morning air following them.

"You must have known we'd show up for breakfast," Hayden said with a grin.

"Not really," Frank laughed. "Boy, you two made some time getting here this early. I didn't expect you until tomorrow."

Abby smiled. "We took turns driving and only stopped for gas after one night at a motel. About thirty-six straight hours on the road."

"Well, it's sure good to see you both. Hungry?"

They nodded, and Abby gave him a warm hug.

"Okay then," Frank said, "I'll get things going. Hayden, show her around. We'll eat when it's ready."

The house felt different with them inside— less like a place of silence, more like a living thing rediscovering its pulse. The laughter bouncing off the walls seemed to drive the shadows back a little.

Hayden took Abby's hand and led her through the old house. They passed the bedrooms, the narrow hall to the living room, and the broad windows that looked out over the ocean. The faint light from the horizon silvered the waves. Abby moved closer to the glass, studying the framed photographs on the wall.

"That young woman there—that's you," Hayden said softly.

She laughed, brushing her fingers against the frame. "So many pictures... but I don't remember any of them." She pointed to a man's face in one photo. "Is that Jeremy?" Hayden nodded.

The man in the photo smiled from another lifetime—wind-blown hair, eyes full of mischief, the kind of face that belonged to stories that ended too soon.

The smell of breakfast drifted through the rooms. "Almost ready for you guys," Frank called from the kitchen.

Before heading into the kitchen, Hayden opened the back door and led Abby onto the deck. She walked to the railing, breathing in the cool, briny air. Seagulls wheeled above them, their wings flashing white in the dawn. A few landed on the railing one by one.

"Oh, my goodness! Are these the ones you told me about, Hayden?"

He smiled. "The same. I think they remember you."

She laughed and stepped back. "I feel like Mary Poppins."

Frank opened the door. "You two coming in or starting a bird sanctuary out here?"

They laughed and followed him inside. The three of them sat around the table, the plates piled high with bacon and eggs, the coffee and tea steaming between them. They swapped stories—Hayden and Abby's long drive, Frank's discoveries at the beach, and the unexpected visit from the police chief.

"You said you found a building down there?" Hayden asked.

"Of sorts," Frank replied. "Only the wooden front, covered in moss. Looks like it's been buried for decades."

The word "buried" seemed to hang in the air, heavy and uninvited, like a thought none of them wanted to voice.

After breakfast, they cleared the table and prepared to hike down to the beach. While Abby stood on the deck gazing at the sea, Hayden walked over to Frank, who was drying the last of the dishes.

"Frank," he said quietly, "have you thought about how Abby's spirit might show herself now that she's back?"

Frank hung the towel and leaned on the counter. "I don't know. I haven't let myself think that far. You're the one who's seen her spirit—what's your feeling?"

Hayden sighed. "I'm afraid. I've fallen in love with Abby, and if her spirit returns—if it joins her again—I could lose her. She might remember her life with Jeremy and..." He trailed off.

Frank put a reassuring hand on his shoulder. "Hey. Don't go borrowing trouble, my friend. Thirty years is a long time. People change, even spirits, I guess. She may get her memories back, but she's also lived through this journey with you. Give her time—and keep her steady. As for Jeremy..." He paused. "My hunch says he went north—maybe as far as British Columbia. But we'll talk about that later. Right now, let's see what secrets are hiding in that ravine."

***

Hayden managed a nod, though his chest felt tight. He wondered what it meant to love someone who'd already died once.

They joined Abby outside and started down the trail. The beach spread wide and bright in the morning sun, the sea calm and silver. Abby walked close beside Hayden, glancing often at the surf.

"Does any of this look familiar?" Hayden asked.

Abby shook her head slowly. "It's beautiful... but no. Nothing sparks a memory." She hesitated. "When do you think I'll meet my spirit again?"

Hayden gave a small shrug. "Maybe when it's time."

Frank led the way toward the ravine. "Here's the entrance I cleared. Watch your footing—it's tight going."

The air cooled as they entered, the light thinning to a dull green. The sound of the ocean faded until all that remained was the crackle of broken twigs underfoot and the occasional drip of water from unseen roots.

The brush swallowed them quickly. The air turned damp, filled with the scent of pine and rot. After some cutting, the moss-covered front of the structure came into view. It looked like a forgotten outbuilding from another century, half-swallowed by the hillside.

"Looks like an old double door," Frank said, scraping away moss with the machete. "Two padlocks—solid stainless." He fished the keyring from his pocket. "Only one beach house key left. Diane must have pulled the rest."

Hayden offered, "I can go ask her for the old ones."

"Doubt they'd help," said Frank. "These locks are frozen solid." He swung the blunt side of the machete against one. The metal clanged but didn't give. "Guess I need a bigger hammer."

Hayden ran back up the hillside for the axe. Abby squatted near a twisted pine trunk, running her hand over the moss. "No one would've ever found this," she said. "What do you think we'll find inside?"

Frank grinned. "Hopefully the dory—and maybe a few answers. Hopefully not the ghost that walks this beach at night." They laughed uneasily.

The sound died quickly in the ravine's hush, swallowed before it reached the trees.

Moments later, Hayden returned, breathless, carrying the axe. "Your turn, Frank."

Frank swung hard, the butt of the axe striking the first lock. It shattered after three blows, then the second followed. The doors groaned but resisted. Together, the two men forced them apart just enough to squeeze inside.

A heavy smell of salt and mildew filled the air. The beam from Frank's phone revealed a large object draped in a rotting canvas. They pulled it back and froze.

Beneath the tarp lay a dory boat—sleek, dark blue, its oak trim still gleaming faintly under layers of dust. The name was still visible on the bow.

The name shimmered faintly in the flashlight beam, the paint worn but legible—a word that belonged to another life, waiting patiently beneath the earth.

They stood in silence, absorbing the moment.

"I can't believe this," Hayden whispered.

Abby looked at it from the doorway. "It's strange—I feel like I should remember this. But it's all just out of reach."

Frank moved toward the small workbench at the back. "Let's see what else is here." He scanned the shelves and found two weathered notebooks full of sketches and notes. "Hand writing," he said quietly, slipping them into his coat pocket.

***

Then the air shifted.

It began with a faint tremor, like a breath drawn in the dark—a sense that the space had remembered it was occupied.

A deep slam shook the room as the doors clapped shut. The darkness was instant and heavy.

Abby gasped. "What was that?"

Frank and Hayden lunged for the doors, shoving their shoulders against the wood. It didn't move. Hayden banged his fists. "Hey! Who's out there?"

The only answer was the rising hiss of wind through the cracks.

"Someone's locked us in," Abby said. Her voice trembled.

"Stay calm, hand me the axe Hayden"

"It's outside," Hayden said.

Frank cursed under his breath. He fumbled toward the back wall for something—anything—to use as a lever. His flashlight beam flickered. Then something cold touched the back of his neck.

The pressure came swift and merciless, dragging at his throat like the grip of the tide itself. The smell of the sea grew stronger, brine and rot and something older—something alive. He froze. A rope—tightening.

He struggled, clawing at his collar, fighting to reach his gun under his coat. The stench in the air turned foul. He slammed back against the bow of the boat, gasping, vision dimming. Then he fired.

The gunshots cracked through the air like thunder. The pressure around his neck loosened, and he collapsed to his knees, coughing. Hayden and Abby awkwardly rushed to him, their phone lights shaking as they found him on the floor.

Frank's voice was hoarse. "Help me up. We need to get out—now."

Hayden grabbed a pickaxe from the wall and swung at the door. Splinters flew. After a dozen strikes, light burst through—a gap wide enough to crawl out.

Outside, they stumbled into the open air, gasping. Frank sank to the sand, clutching his throat. The sunlight was warm, the sea calm again, as if nothing had happened.

Abby knelt beside him. Hayden stood watch, scanning the ravine.

Frank caught his breath, voice ragged. "For a moment, I thought I was going to be the third victim."

Hayden turned toward the waves. "If the Tide Stalker really is in some other state... he's not the man we thought he was."

Frank shook his head. "Whatever he's become—it's not human. Not anymore."

* * *

The wind carried their words away like ash, scattering them across the wet sand. Somewhere deep in the ravine, the door creaked once more, almost satisfied.

They sat for a long while in silence. Then Frank rose, steadied himself, and began the slow walk back up the hill, Abby and Hayden beside him.

Behind them, the wind shifted again, whispering faintly through the pines.

By the time they returned to the beach house, night had folded over the sea. The storm that had gathered offshore now pressed against the windows, its wind a low, restless moan. Inside, the fire glowed soft and steady, casting warm light over faces pale with fatigue. They said little as they cleaned their wounds and poured cups of tea and coffee, the silence between them heavier than words. Outside, the tide hissed against the rocks—a slow, uneasy rhythm that seemed to breathe with the house itself.

The flames flickered in the hearth, reflecting in Abby's eyes like twin embers. None of them spoke it aloud, but each understood: the sea was not done with them yet.

Chapter Twenty-One

Uninvited Guest

Where love, loss, and the supernatural share the same bed

After the ordeal on the beach, exhaustion claimed them all. Frank fell asleep on the couch, his arm draped over the side, while Hayden showed Abby to the master bedroom before retreating to the smaller guest room. The house went quiet except for the wind rattling the shutters. Rain swept in from the sea, hammering the skylight above the kitchen.

The storm moved in heavy bands—rain, then a hush, then rain again—like a breath the ocean couldn't quite catch.

It was nearly dark when a shadow climbed the back deck. The storm shrouded the figure as it peered through the window, its outline distorted in the glass. The handle of the back door began to turn. The latch clicked softly, and the door creaked open, letting a gust of rain scented air and dripping wetness spill onto the rug.

The wet air crawled across the floor, cold as a cellar, carrying the clean scent of salt and the sour trace of kelp.

The intruder slipped inside, closing the door behind with a careful hand. Water pooled on the wool beneath its feet.

A thread of seaweed clung to the threshold like a signature left in haste.

The under-counter lights cast a faint glow across the kitchen and into the living room where Frank slept, unaware. His gun hung in its shoulder holster on a hook nearby. The floor moaned under the weight of each cautious step.

Somewhere in the stove, the damper ticked—metal cooling, then expanding—as if answering the steps with its own uneasy heartbeat.

The figure paused at Abby's door. The handle turned slowly, the hinges groaning. Through the narrow opening, the shape of Abby's sleeping form was visible beneath the quilt. Her breathing was soft and even. The dark shape lingered, then stepped inside, the cold of the storm trailing it like fog.

The lamp's brass knob caught a dull glint and then disappeared, swallowed by the shadow that crossed the carpet.

Piece by piece, the intruder stripped away its soaked garments, laying them over a chair. Its hair clung dark and wet against pallid skin. The air in the room dropped several degrees, frosting the mirror on the dresser.

Abby stirred, shifting to her side, unaware.

The figure moved closer, silent as mist. The wind outside gusted harder, the damper in the living room stove clanging faintly. The rain grew heavier, thundering across the skylight. The house trembled against the gale.

Then, without a sound, the figure slid beneath the quilt. The mattress sank slightly, and cold, damp arms wrapped tightly around Abby.

Her breath hitched once, then steadied— as if some old reflex remembered this embrace, even if her mind did not.

***

In the back room, Hayden stirred at the noise of the storm, his mind floating in and out of uneasy dreams. Frank woke to the rattle of the stove pipe and the shuddering windows. He rose, switched on the brass floor lamp, and wandered into the kitchen.

The floor was wet beneath his socks.

He frowned, following the glistening trail from the back door. When he opened it, a blast of cold rain slapped his face. The deck was empty, save for wind and darkness. He locked the door, muttering, "Strange... maybe Hayden went out?"

Lightning stitched the horizon and was gone, leaving the glass full of his own reflection—older, startled, small against the night.

As he passed Abby's room, he gently pushed her door closed, careful not to wake her, then stepped to the smaller bedroom.

"Hey, you awake?" he whispered.

Hayden groaned and sat up. "Barely. That storm's wild. Makes me want to stay buried under these covers."

"Were you outside just now?"

Hayden frowned. "Outside? In this weather? No way. Why?"

"The rug by the back door's soaked—like someone walked in from the rain."

Hayden sat upright. "Did you check on Abby?"

"She's asleep. I closed her door so she wouldn't wake."

Hayden's voice tightened. "Frank... the last time the rug was wet, Abby's spirit came in out of the rain."

Frank sighed. "Then maybe she paid a visit. But I didn't see or hear anyone."

"Unless," Hayden said quietly, "it wasn't her spirit. Unless it was—"

"The Tide Stalker?" Frank rubbed the scar on his throat. "If he'd shown up, trust me, we'd have known."

The memory of rope tightening flashed so hard it left a taste of metal on Frank's tongue.

He tried to shake it off and began preparing dinner, but Hayden couldn't rest. He paced the living room, watching rain streak down the back door window. A gnawing thought gripped him: what if Abby's spirit had returned—and entered her body again?

The question felt dangerous, like handling a live wire: hope on one end, terror on the other.

He ran down the hall and switched on the light, heart pounding. The door to her room creaked open. Abby lay on her side, motionless.

He reached out and touched her forehead and it was ice cold.

"Frank!" he shouted. "Get in here"

Frank hurried down the hall. "What's wrong?"

"She's freezing—she won't wake up—Frank, I think she's gone"

Frank bent close, his fingers trembling as he checked her neck for a pulse. Then he leaned down, listening for breath. Nothing.

He stood slowly, his expression stricken. "I don't feel a pulse, Hayden. I'm sorry."

The storm seemed to hush at that, as if even the weather was waiting for what came next.

Hayden's knees gave out. He sat on the bed and held her hand, his tears falling onto the quilt. The storm outside roared, lightning flashing through the skylight. Frank placed a hand on his shoulder but said nothing.

After a long silence, Frank whispered, "Come on. Let's sit out there a while."

In the living room, they sat side by side on the couch. Hayden's sobs quieted, replaced by hollow exhaustion.

"I can't believe she's gone," he said softly. "We brought her back... only for her to die here. I thought I was saving her. All I did was delay it."

"Hayden..." Frank began, but words failed him.

Hayden shook his head. "Her spirit warned me. Maybe it was too much for her. Maybe this was part of the Lookingglass resolve. Dang it, Frank, I loved her."

Frank could only squeeze his shoulder.

The stove ticked again, gentler this time, like a clock deciding to keep time after all.

***

After some time, Hayden stood. "I need to see her one more time."

He walked back to the bedroom, his heart hammering. Abby lay as before, her hand still cold in his. He lifted it gently and pressed his lips to her fingers. Her skin began to warm beneath his touch.

He blinked, staring. Her face, pale moments ago, was flushing with color. The blue of her lips faded to pink.

"Abby?" he whispered. "Abby, can you hear me?"

Her body stirred. She gasped softly, her eyelids fluttering open. "Jeremy... is that you?"

Frank, hearing the voice, rushed to the doorway and stopped, stunned.

"No," Hayden said gently, gripping her hands. "It's me—Hayden."

Abby blinked, confused, then smiled faintly. "I had the worst nightmare. I... I think

I remember everything now. Oh, my head..."

"We thought we lost you," Hayden said.

"I felt your kiss," she murmured. "It brought me back."

The word "back" rang through Hayden like a bell, clearing smoke from a room he hadn't realized he'd been living in.

Frank crossed the room, still shaken. "How do you feel?"

"I'm here," Abby said slowly. "And I remember... thirty years of it. The boat, the storm, losing Jeremy... all of it. But it feels like someone else's life." Her voice trembled. "I love you, Hayden. Please—don't leave me again."

Hayden stared at her, startled. "Leave you again? I never—"

"In my dream," she said, "you were gone. I was trapped in my body, reliving it all. The memories hit me like flashes of lightning. I couldn't move, couldn't speak. Then—your kiss. And the nightmare ended."

They helped her to the living room couch. Frank built a fire in the woodstove, and Hayden made tea. Abby shivered under a blanket as she sipped from her cup, her color returning. Frank sat opposite them, hands clasped. "Well," he said quietly, "now we know how her spirit returned. Abby, you're back—body and soul. How do you feel?" "Better," she said.

"Good," Frank said. "Because we've got hard choices ahead. Jeremy, the Tide Stalker, the house, and the trust running out. Not to mention that police chief nosing around."

Hayden frowned. "Maybe she needs time before we chase ghosts again."

Abby looked up. "Do you still have the envelope that Lookingglass gave you?" Frank nodded.

"Maybe it's time to open it," she said softly. "We've found me. Isn't that what he asked for?"

"I think we wait," Frank replied. "Lookingglass said only to open it if we reached a dead end searching for you and Jeremy. I found two notebooks in the boat shed—I think they might hold the key to where he went."

Hayden rubbed his temples. "If Jeremy's still alive, how do we find him? And what if finding him makes things worse?"

Outside, the rain softened to a hush, like a story catching its breath before the next chapter.

Frank sighed. "We'll decide tomorrow. Tonight, rest. We all need it."

***

Dinner was quiet. Frank's pasta and salad went mostly untouched. Later, he took the notebooks to his room, leaving Hayden and Abby in the master bedroom.

They lay facing each other under the soft glow of the lamp. Abby reached for his hand. "You're such a kind man, Hayden."

He smiled. "What's going through your mind right now?"

"A hundred things," she said. "It's strange, having my younger spirit back inside me. I remember so much, yet it's all... faded around the edges. I remember living here, fishing with Jeremy, feeding the gulls, tending my garden. But I don't remember his plans after that. Maybe he was always thinking of leaving."

Her eyes grew distant. "If the accident hadn't happened, would we have stayed? Or would he have gone north, like Frank thinks? I can't say. I only know he became restless. He never told me everything. After the storm... maybe he started over somewhere new. British Columbia, perhaps."

She turned to him again, voice soft. "I don't understand this Tide Stalker—why his spirit is so angry. Can love curdle into something so cruel? Can a soul stay lost that long?"

Hayden brushed her hair from her face. "Maybe you're not rambling at all," he said gently. "Maybe you're remembering."

She smiled faintly. "Let's stop for now. Hold me tight."

Outside, the storm raged on. Inside, they lay awake, hearts racing in rhythm with the wind. Neither slept until dawn.

When sleep finally came, it came on the thinnest thread, like a line cast into dark water and held very, very still.

Chapter Twenty-Two

The Ghosts we Carry

Haunted not by spirits, but by love left unfinished.

Frank spent much of the stormy night leafing through the notebooks he'd recovered from the boat shed. Jeremy's notes spoke often of fishing in the waters off British Columbia, though none mentioned the dory boat. It made sense that he would want to get far away from Haystack Beach—a dream shattered in the cove he once called home.

The loss of the most beautiful, loving woman had eroded him, leaving a hollow shell of sadness and depression. In time, he'd become a recluse, vanishing from the world. He didn't even say goodbye to Lookingglass, or anyone. His spirit, twisted by regret, seemed now to walk the beach forever, searching for the love he'd lost. Perhaps he had built another life elsewhere, but he had never been whole.

Unlike finding Abby, locating Jeremy felt like an impossible task. Frank had already run an extensive background search—nothing. No trace on social media, no property or court records, not a single lead. Until now, perhaps.

His conversation with the old men in town, along with these notebooks, might hold a clue worth following. British Columbia and Vancouver Island boasted hundreds of miles of rugged coastline, dotted with fishing villages—an overwhelming expanse to search. Time was running short.

The beach house trust would expire soon, and any hope of finding Jeremy before the legal proceedings might dissolve in futility. And when they did find him—how would he respond, knowing Abby was still alive after thirty years apart? Could love survive such distance in both time and heart?

By the early hours, the storm had softened to a drizzle. Frank rubbed his tired eyes and brewed a pot of coffee. He spread the two notebooks across the kitchen table and fed wood into the stove. In the dull gray light of morning, he sat in his sweatshirt and sweatpants, hands wrapped around a steaming mug, thinking.

He highlighted certain entries, marked possible locations, and began drafting a list of towns that made the most sense—small harbors, remote coves, isolated marinas. Between sips of the strong black brew, he traced the coastline in his mind, picturing Jeremy's escape northward.

The sound of bare feet on the wooden floor broke his concentration. Hayden wandered in, bleary eyed, hair tousled.

"You know," he said, yawning, "I love the smell of coffee but hate the taste. Guess I'll always be a tea man." He filled a mug with hot water and joined Frank at the table. "So—what did you find in those notebooks?"

Frank looked up, his gaze distant. "Sorry, I was miles away in thought. I'm trying to see where this all leads. How's Abby doing? She sleep okay?"

"I think so," Hayden said. "She's still confused. Called out Jeremy's name a few times in her sleep, had some dreams—or nightmares. It's like two people are living inside her. Her young spirit, that came back last night, and the fifty-six-year-old Abby with a thirty-year gap in between. She told me she loved me, Frank— and now I don't know what to do with that. Technically, she's still married. Maybe she has feelings for Jeremy too. I guess I'll back off a little, see where her mind settles. But I can't lie—I'm torn."

Frank sipped his coffee and nodded slowly. "I get it. But listen to me—if the Tide Stalker still walks the beach, that means Jeremy's alive. If he were gone, the spirit would've vanished. They're bound somehow, like two ends of a rope. I think when we find Jeremy, that connection will finally break."

Hayden folded his arms. "You've got it all figured out, huh?"

Frank smiled faintly. "Not even close. But I made a list of places to look. If Jeremy left these notebooks behind, maybe he was traveling light—took only what he needed and moved on."

Hayden rose and stretched. "Okay. I'll run down and talk to Diane about the house. January first is only two weeks away. Not much time if Abby—or Jeremy—want to keep it. What's your gut say about him?"

Frank drained the last of his coffee. "He probably remarried. Maybe has a family now. But I can feel it—he's still out there somewhere. Fishing, maybe retired by now. When we find him, Abby's going to face another storm—one she'll have to weather herself. But if we can give her peace, that'll be enough."

He looked up. "Oh—Hayden. You haven't seen my phone, have you? I was using it in the boat shed when that thing attacked me. Thought I picked it up."

Hayden grabbed his cell phone. "No. Let me call it." He dialed Frank's number. The phone rang in his hand, but there was no sound anywhere in the house.

Frank frowned. "Dang. That means it's still down there."

"You really want to go back there?" Hayden asked.

"Not particularly. I'd need more than my service revolver this time. Go talk to Diane. I'll keep an eye on Abby."

***

Hayden dressed, checked on Abby—still asleep—and headed out in Frank's SUV.

At the rental agency, the parking lot was empty. Diane's yellow VW bug was nowhere in sight. He leaned back in the seat, feeling his pulse race. His hands trembled on the steering wheel. Taking deep breaths, he tried to calm himself. By the time Diane's car rolled in, the morning clouds had broken into slivers of light.

She climbed out, waving. "Hey, Hayden. How are you? So much has happened lately."

"Sure has," he said, following her inside.

She hung her coat and sat at her desk. "So—what brings you by?"

"I wanted to ask about the beach house. I heard the attorney who was found on the beach was there to handle the trust?"

Diane nodded. "That's right. He came to file papers in Astoria. The trust was set to end on December thirty-first, and the property would've gone to auction. After his death, his law firm contacted me. They're extending the proceedings a couple of weeks into January. But—" she sighed—"they don't want it rented out anymore. I was going to call you and Frank. I'll need you both to vacate soon."

Hayden looked at the floor, thinking. This might be their easy exit—a way to leave without raising questions. "We can go tomorrow. Would that work?"

"That's fine," Diane said. "And don't worry about payment. I won't charge for the last few days. I'm sorry about all this, really. It's been a mess. I hate being the last to know anything."

"Don't beat yourself up," Hayden said with a gentle smile. "You've been wonderful to work with. My time here's been... life-changing."

She tilted her head. "How is it, staying there after what happened? Kind of creepy, right? I figured Frank would dig into it as a detective."

"I don't think so," Hayden said. "There's not much to investigate. We'll drop the key off on our way out tomorrow." He shook her hand and stepped out into the cold coastal wind.

***

Back at the beach house, Abby sat at the table eating toast while Frank drank his third cup of coffee. They both turned as Hayden entered.

"How'd it go?" Frank asked.

Hayden filled them in on the trust extension and the eviction notice.

"So we've got a short reprieve," Frank said. "That gives us time to search for Jeremy. I wonder where the funds from the auction would go? Maybe that's in Lookingglass's envelope."

"Then open it," Hayden said. "Let's see what he left us."

Frank chuckled. "You and your shortcuts. We've solved half the mystery already, and we'll see this through the right way. What do you think, Abby?"

She set down her cup. "I came into this story halfway through—like walking into a movie mid scene. I'm still catching up. But I'm not ready to stop. Let's keep going."

Hayden nodded, admiring her determination. "Then let's do it. Whatever it takes."

Frank stood. "Good. We'll wrap things up here today and leave for Portland in the morning. Abby, can we leave your truck at Hayden's place? We'll take my SUV."

"That's fine," she said. "And yes, I have my passport."

Frank grinned. "Then we're all set." "What about your phone?" Hayden asked.

"Oh—that's sorted. Abby picked it up when we were at the boat shed. Battery was dead, so we didn't hear it ring. I'm glad—I've got half my life in that thing."

Abby laughed. "Since we're leaving tomorrow, how about dinner out tonight? Something fun—maybe I'll remember something."

"Count me in," Frank said. "I'll also stop by and tell the chief we're heading out. He deserves a goodbye."

Abby smiled. "I'll call my aunt later, see how she's doing."

Hayden stretched. "Sounds like a plan. I'll sit on the deck for a bit while you two get ready."

Outside, the air was fresh, still tinged with salt from the storm. Hayden sat with a cup of tea and stared at the wide gray horizon. Two months ago, he'd come here for solitude—to write, to escape—and instead had fallen into a mystery that had consumed his heart.

He'd always been a loner. His parents, driven by their own ambitions, were distant. As a child, he spent hours alone, inventing stories in his head. In high school, they called him withdrawn. In truth, he found comfort in solitude—his imagination his closest friend.

College hadn't changed that. After graduation, he became a copywriter, working from a small Portland apartment, writing late into the night. His world was quiet, safe—until the day he met a woman in a bookstore. She listened to his ramblings about plot twists and characters, smiled at his awkward jokes. For the first time, he felt seen. They went for walks, coffee, laughter shared between two solitary souls.

And then, she was gone—hit by a car one morning on her way to work. The grief nearly broke him. He buried himself in fiction again, where characters didn't die without his permission. Years passed. He wrote, published, aged. Then Frank entered his life, and later—Abby. And now, impossibly, love had returned.

He smiled to himself, realizing how far he'd come from that lonely apartment.

The door opened behind him. Abby stepped out, sunlight brushing her face. "Hey there," she said softly. "You've been out here a while."

He smiled. "Just thinking. The ocean's hypnotic."

She dragged out a chair and sat beside him. "Beautiful, isn't it? Frank's in the shower. Hope there's hot water left for you."

He chuckled. "A cold shower might do me some good."

She tilted her head. "You don't really want to keep going, do you? I can tell. You always want to open that envelope, like you're looking for a way to stop."

Hayden sighed. "I don't know what's in there—maybe instructions if we failed to find you. Maybe nothing at all. But Frank's relentless. He'll chase this until the end. And I owe him that. Still... meeting you, Abby, has been the best part of all this. I just—don't know how to handle it sometimes."

She squeezed his hand. "I'm glad you came into my life. Even if everything's still a blur, I know I'm meant to be here with you. And when all this is over—you'll have one heck of a novel to write."

Hayden smiled faintly. "Maybe just the last chapter of one."

The door opened again. "Bathroom's all yours," Frank said. "And Abby's ready for town."

Hayden nodded, heading inside.

Frank sat beside Abby on the deck, both looking toward the ocean.

"How's our friend?" Frank asked.

"I think he's tired," Abby said softly. "He didn't expect any of this when he came here. But he cares about us—about you, too."

"I know," Frank said. "He's been through a lot. So have we all."

Abby studied him. "He told me he once loved someone. It ended badly."

Frank nodded. "That's why he's afraid now. He doesn't want to lose you too."

Abby was quiet for a long time. "I didn't realize. This whole thing is so strange for all of us. I can only trust that we'll find answers."

She suddenly winced, gripping her head.

"Abby!" Frank grabbed her arm as she wavered.

"I'm okay," she whispered. "Just a flash— green light—then gone."

"Let's get you inside." He helped her to the couch. "Want some ibuprofen?"

She nodded weakly. "Please—and a cold cloth."

When Hayden returned from his shower, he froze. "What happened?"

"Headache," Frank said. "Green flashes again."

Hayden lifted her legs gently onto his lap.

"You okay?"

"I'll be fine. Just need a minute."

Frank frowned. "You sure this isn't connected to last night?"

Abby managed a faint smile. "Probably just exhaustion. Oh—I spoke to my aunt this morning. My father's in a nursing home now. Hank's in prison under evaluation. Aunt's moved off the island, listing both houses. It's all being taken care of."

Hayden nodded, relieved. "That's good news."

***

Within the hour, they were on the road toward town.

At Captain's, they found a booth near the window.

"Does this place look familiar?" Hayden asked.

Abby scanned the room and shook her head. "Not at all. I don't think Jeremy and I ever went out much. He was always busy." After lunch, they drove down Main Street toward the police station. Suddenly, Abby grabbed Frank's arm. "Stop! Pull over."

"What is it?" Hayden asked.

She jumped out before answering and hurried toward a small storefront on the corner— Sea Star Bookstore.

"Let her be," Frank said, holding Hayden's arm. "Something's stirring."

Hayden watched as she stood at the door, staring up at the old sign. After a long pause, she stepped inside.

He waited, restless. "She remembers a bookstore but not a restaurant she probably ate in a hundred times?"

"Memory works in strange ways," Frank said. "Give her space."

Hayden's pulse ticked with unease. "Her spirit's part of her now, but she still barely remembers anything. It doesn't make sense."

Frank looked at him. "You fell for her spirit, Hayden. That's what scares you. You can't love a ghost."

Hayden turned, anger flashing. "You think I don't know what's real? Don't treat me like I can't tell the difference between life and fiction."

He jumped out of the SUV, leaving Frank shaking his head.

Outside, Hayden sat on a bench near the bookstore, watching holiday shoppers drift by with bags of taffy and caramel corn. The air smelled of winter salt and sweet vanilla. He waited almost an hour before finally going inside.

The store was narrow, aisles stacked high with old books, the air rich with the scent of paper and time. At the counter, he asked the clerk, "Have you seen a woman in a black jacket?"

The clerk laughed. "You and half the men in here. Oh—one woman in black went to the back to talk with Mira."

Hayden hesitated. "Mind if I join her?"

"Go ahead."

He passed through the velvet curtain—and froze. On the wall beside him were several of his own novels in the used section. Great, he thought. I'm a recycled item now.

He smiled faintly and pushed through the curtain. Abby sat across from an older woman, both deep in conversation.

"Hayden!" Abby said, lighting up. "You won't believe this."

"What is it?"

"This is Mira—the owner. She's an old friend. I used to spend hours here before the accident. She still had five books I ordered thirty years ago—wrapped with my name on them"

Mira rose and shook Hayden's hand. "Mr. Lansford. I know your work well. I have many of your books here."

Hayden blinked. "Apparently so. Nice to meet you."

Mira smiled. "Perhaps you'll come back one day for a signing?"

Caught off guard, he nodded. "Maybe next summer. I'm halfway through a new one now."

Abby grinned. "See? Everything's coming full circle."

The bell over Sea Star Bookstore gave a small, tired ring as they stepped back onto the sidewalk. Rain feathered the harbor, and lights along Main Street burned with that early-winter tenderness that makes even old storefronts look loved.

"Five books with my name on them," Abby said, laughing under her breath. "Mira said I'd prepaid. Thirty years late and she still kept them wrapped in butcher paper."

"Some debts are worth carrying," Hayden said.

They walked without speaking for a stretch, the rain turning to mist, the mist to nothing. Abby slipped her arm through his, resting her hand in the crook of his elbow as if it had always belonged there.

"What came back in there?" he asked.

"Not pictures," she said. "Shapes. The feeling of paper on my fingers, a bell that sticks, the smell of glue. I remember wanting to learn how stories end." She looked up at him. "I guess I still do."

At the corner, Frank leaned against the SUV, watching a mother wrestle a toddler into a yellow raincoat. "You two look like you stole a secret," he said.

Abby held up the paper bundle. "Borrowed, maybe."

They drove the slow river of Main Street toward the station. The Chief would have his say; Frank would have his. It all felt temporary in a way that made Hayden oddly grateful—like weather you knew would pass, even if it rattled the windows.

After the tense few minutes at the police station, they returned to the harbor road. A bicyclist in a reflective vest ghosted past them, a white ribbon of wake behind his tires. Christmas lights stitched from lamppost to lamppost blinked in soft patterns, a code the town understood and the three of them were still learning.

"Dinner?" Frank asked.

"Somewhere with chowder that isn't out," Hayden said.

"High bar," Frank replied, and Abby snorted laughter so sudden she startled herself, hand to her mouth, delighted and confused by the joy of it.

At a small seafood café, they stopped for dinner—fried halibut, chowder, and a shared bottle of wine. None of them said much. Back at the beach house later, Abby took more ibuprofen for her headache. Hayden packed his bags, uneasy but determined to see this through.

Frank lay on the couch, staring at the dark windows that faced the beach. Somewhere beyond the tide, the Stalker still walked. Tomorrow, they would leave this place behind—yet its spirits would follow.

Interlude

Jeremy's Notebook (1986–1991)

April 3, 1986—Haystack Beach

The gulls were bolder this morning. Abby fed them the heel of last night's bread, and one balanced on the rail like it had found a church steeple. She laughed, and a fog lifted in me I didn't know I was carrying. There's a way she looks at the water, as if the tide were a page and she's reading ahead. I pretended to check the weather radio, but I was watching her reflection in the window. There's a life here if we can learn the rules: wind, tide, luck, each one taking its turn at the wheel.

October 19, 1987—Dory Cove

First real blow of the season. I ran the boat too late, stubborn as always, and the shore break boxed the bow like angry hands. I told Abby I had it under control. I did not. After, we sat in the kitchen, towels around our shoulders, steam rising from tea mugs, seaweed on the mat like a confession. She said, "We're not invincible." I nodded. The truth is I've never felt more breakable than when she puts her palm to my chest and says, "This is home."

June 12, 1989—Somewhere North of Astoria

Stopped at a hardware store inland for rope and a spare plug. Clerk asked if I was "one of those dory idiots." I said yes without thinking. He laughed like he'd caught me stealing. I wanted to tell him that sometimes a man rows out because the shore is louder than the sea.

January 8, 1990—Notes on Northern Grounds

Vancouver Island keeps turning up in talk: Ucluelet, Clayoquot, Winter Harbour. A kid at the fuel dock swears there's a run that makes a living up there if you don't mind isolation and weather that teaches manners. He drew a chain of harbors on a napkin with a golf pencil and said, "If you disappear, disappear where it's normal." I folded the napkin into my wallet and felt like I'd hidden a map to my own vanishing.

October 3, 1990—The Night Before

Abby set a sand dollar on the sill and said it was for luck. I wanted to tell her I'd been dreaming of green light under black water, a lantern moving along the shore where no one walks at that hour. Superstition is a coward's way to tell the truth: I fear the sea will take what the land cannot hold.

October 4, 1990—After

If memory is a door, mine won't close. Rope burns stay when all else washes clean. When the wind hit us broadside and the pot line sang around the cleat, I thought, Hold me steady. I didn't say it. I haven't said anything right since.

March 2, 1991—Northbound

Bought an atlas with pages that smell like dust and new beginnings. Drew a line up the coast that isn't a road so much as a hope. I left the house at dawn. Didn't wake Lookingglass. Didn't write a note. A kinder man would have done both. The gulls followed me to the headland and then, smart birds, turned back.

June 25, 1991—West Coast of Vancouver Island

There's a way the fog unzips at noon and you feel forgiven. Then evening comes and says, not so fast. I mend nets with men who don't ask and don't answer. We drink from dented thermoses and talk about weather as if it were a relative. Abby's name is a tide chart I keep folded too tight. When I open it, all I can read is danger.

Chapter Twenty-Three

Memory Overload

Some memories return as blessings; others arrive like storms

Leaving the beach house the next morning was uneventful. Abby stood on the deck, talking softly to the seagulls, her hand pressed to her temple—the dull headache from the night before refused to fade. Inside, Frank, coffee mug in hand, stared through the wide ocean-facing windows, his reflection blurred against the gray surf below. Hayden loaded the SUV, shut the rear hatch with a firm click, and signaled everyone it was time to roll out.

He wanted to leave this place—and never return. It seemed like an eternity since his arrival in October. He didn't want to go to Canada, but he knew he had to follow Frank and, as Lookingglass had demanded, write the last chapter. Anxiety gripped his body, as it had for weeks, and he turned once more to the small orange bottle of Xanax in his coat pocket.

Outside, the wind had turned raw and cold, the air heavy with salt and sleet. Gray clouds bunched over the ocean, and as they pulled onto Highway 26 heading east, snowflakes began to drift from the low ceiling of sky.

By the time they reached the mountain summit, snow was falling thick and fast. Traffic slowed to a crawl, the long line of vehicles ghostly under the weight of flurries. Several cars had Christmas trees strapped to their roofs—reminders of families on holiday outings, far removed from the turmoil inside the SUV.

They were almost at a complete stop near a rest area when a silver SUV ahead lost control, skidding sideways on the packed snow. Frank jerked his wheel, but his own SUV slid into the ditch. Hayden pulled Abby's pickup onto the shoulder just behind him, hazard lights blinking in the whiteout.

He jumped out, boots crunching on snow, and ran up to Frank's window. "You okay?"

Frank rolled it down, his breath visible in the freezing air. "I'm fine—a little whiplash is all."

"Abby's got a tow chain in the truck. I'll get it, and we can pull you out."

Hayden maneuvered the pickup in front of Frank's stranded SUV, crouching in the swirling snow to fasten the chain. He motioned for Abby to ease forward. The truck strained, tires spinning, then the SUV lurched free from the ditch.

It was hard to see the road edge through the driving snow. Hayden unhooked the chain, checked on Frank again, and slid back into the pickup where Abby waited, pale and quiet in the passenger seat.

The white-knuckle drive took several more hours before the snow thinned and the landscape opened to gray hills dusted in white. By late afternoon they rolled into northeast Portland.

They spent the rest of the day preparing for the trip north to British Columbia. Abby's headache still lingered—a deep, throbbing ache she hadn't mentioned in full severity. Hayden was relieved to be home, away from the haunted beach house, yet uneasy knowing the story wasn't over.

He hadn't written a single line of his intended novel there. Instead, he'd been pulled into a mystery beyond his control. His normal life thrived on order, precision, and routine— the very structure that now felt shattered. When that structure slipped, anxiety crept in, quelled only by medication. It was a wicked dependency, but solitude had long ago eroded his ability to cope with unpredictability.

Frank was the one person who anchored him—a voice of reason and quiet discipline. But even that friendship had been tested. Hayden felt the growing distance between them, the weariness in their exchanges. His feelings for Abby, tangled and sincere, only deepened the divide.

That night, Hayden offered Abby his bedroom, but she chose the hide-a-bed in his small office. Her headaches came and went in waves, each one more intense. Even with the maximum doses of ibuprofen, the pain pressed behind her eyes like a living thing. The two spirits within her—the younger self and the woman she had become—were at war. Fragments of her past clashed with the lost decades of her life, and in the dark hours she sat on the edge of the bed, head in her hands, whispering to herself as though trying to negotiate peace between them.

Frank knocked at the door early the next morning. He and Hayden loaded the SUV while Abby stayed in the bathroom longer than usual.

Hayden tapped gently on the door. "We're ready to roll."

"I'll be out in a minute," she replied faintly.

He turned to Frank and shrugged. "We've barely spoken since we got back yesterday. I think her headaches are getting worse—she probably didn't sleep at all."

Frank adjusted his coat. "Could be stress. Or anxiety over what's ahead. Let's keep an eye on her. If she can't handle the trip, we'll stop."

Abby emerged moments later, her face drawn but determined. She forced a smile as she joined them by the door.

They headed north on Interstate 5, crossing the Columbia River into Washington. Bitter east winds buffeted the vehicle, pushing flurries of snow across the freeway. Abby leaned against the headrest, one hand gripping her temple.

Frank drove, eyes narrowed against the glare of drifting snow. Hayden sat in the back seat, watching quietly as Abby's breathing grew shallow.

"That's to be expected," Frank said gently. "You've been through a lot."

She didn't respond. After several miles she whispered, "I'm not asleep... the pain's getting worse. It's really bad."

"Sorry, Abby," Hayden said from the back seat. "We can pull off soon, find a rest stop, maybe get something to eat—"

"I can't eat," she murmured. "I'm nauseous. I need something stronger than Advil."

Frank's hands tightened on the wheel. "We'll take a detour. Bellingham's the next city—they'll have a hospital."

Her seat reclined as far back as it would go. Her breathing grew shallow, a low moan escaping every few minutes.

Frank steered toward the next exit, following signs to the hospital. Hayden jumped out before the SUV came to a full stop, opened Abby's door, and helped her inside the emergency entrance as Frank went to park.

Inside, Hayden checked her in at the front desk. Abby sat slumped beside him, eyes half closed, mumbling incoherently. The sterile brightness of the lobby made her pallor almost translucent.

When a trauma nurse called her name, Hayden guided her to the intake room. Abby couldn't answer the questions, so he explained what he could—carefully omitting any mention of spirits or supernatural causes. The nurse nodded, professional but puzzled, and led Abby through a set of swinging doors.

Hayden returned to the waiting area. Frank joined him a few minutes later, snow still clinging to his coat. "I guess we wait," Hayden said, sinking into a chair. "They won't let me back there."

"She's in good hands," Frank replied. "Maybe there's something medical we didn't know about."

Hayden stood, restless, pacing slow circles. "I told you it was her spirit—her younger self. No doctor will believe us, but that's what did this." He stopped, rubbing his temples. "Her brain just... couldn't take it."

Frank said nothing. He watched his friend, seeing the same haunted exhaustion he'd seen weeks ago at the beach house.

Several hours passed. The hospital quieted as night deepened. At last, a man in green scrubs approached. "Mr. Lansford?"

Hayden and Frank stood. "That's me," Hayden said. "This is Frank—my friend."

The doctor motioned for them to sit. "I'm Dr. Patel, neurology. I wanted to speak with you before we move Abby to a room."

He glanced between them, tone grave but calm. "How long have you known her?" "About a couple of months," Hayden said. "You told the nurse these headaches began just a few days ago?" "Yes. She seemed fine before that."

The doctor exhaled slowly. "All right. I'll get right to it. We did a brain scan—and found something highly unusual. I've been a neurologist for twenty years, and I've never seen what's happening in her hippocampus."

Frank leaned forward. "What's going on, exactly?"

"The hippocampus—that's the part of the brain that forms memories— is behaving in reverse. Instead of losing cells, it's creating new ones, fast. I've never seen anything like it." We relieved some pressure, administered sedatives and pain medication, and she's resting comfortably now. But her brain is, in essence, in overload."

Hayden's eyes widened. "Overload? You mean—too many memories?"

Dr. Patel nodded. "Precisely. Normally, short-term memories transfer gradually to long-term storage. But in her case, that process is out of control. We're admitting her for observation—maybe longer, depending on how stable things remain. I'll bring in colleagues tomorrow to consult."

Frank asked, "How serious is it? Could she have something like a seizure?"

"We're monitoring for that. She's stable, but her brain is under immense strain. I don't yet understand the cause."

The doctor rose, offering a faint, sympathetic smile. "You mentioned traveling into Canada?"

"Yes," Hayden said softly.

"Then for now, stay close. Get a motel nearby. I'll update you tomorrow. She's comfortable—that's the important thing." He handed Hayden a business card and walked away, the scent of antiseptic trailing behind him.

They sat in silence for a long while, the hum of hospital machinery faint beyond the doors.

Hayden rubbed his face. "I knew something like this would happen. I told you back in Haystack Beach."

Frank sighed. "She remembered the bookstore—and her friend. That's progress."

"You're missing the point," Hayden snapped. "That's what caused this. Her spirit dumped a lifetime of memories into her brain. The human mind can't handle that. And now we're watching it unravel."

Frank met his eyes. "So what do we do?"

"Nothing," Hayden said quietly. "Even if I told the doctor the truth, he'd never believe it. What's he supposed to do—drain memories out through a tube?" He shook his head. "We'd sound insane."

Frank stood and stretched, his own fatigue evident. "Let's get some rest. She's in good hands. I'll find a motel nearby."

Hayden stared at the linoleum floor. "You go. I'll stay here in case something happens."

"You sure?"

He nodded. "Yeah. Go on."

Frank gave him a firm pat on the shoulder and left for the night. As he reached the lobby doors, he paused, pulled out his phone, and called Miss Scott.

Her voice cracked through static on the line. "Frank? What's wrong?"

"Abby's in the hospital. Head trauma of some kind—or worse. We don't know yet."

"Oh, dear Lord."

"She's stable. I'll keep you posted. Get some rest, okay?"

"You too," she said softly. "And please... tell her I love her."

Frank pocketed the phone and stepped into the snowy night, his breath rising like smoke.

Back inside, Hayden spoke briefly with the night nurse, arranging to stay in the waiting room if needed. Then he sank into the same hard chair, exhaustion dragging him under.

Hayden leaned back in the chair, head tilted toward the sterile ceiling. For an instant, he saw her as she'd first appeared on the deck— drenching wet but radiant and beautiful, caught between two worlds. He'd thought he was saving her. Now he wondered if he'd only been keeping her from rest.

Sleep came quickly—and not kindly Dreams twisted into chaos: Abby's pale face, the tide rolling backward, Looking-glass whispering in riddles. His body jerked, murmurs spilling from his lips as he slid from the chair to the cold tile floor.

At the front desk, the attendant noticed and called for help. Two orderlies rushed over, kneeling beside him.

"Sir? Sir, can you hear me?"

No response. His body convulsed, trembling uncontrollably. They lifted him onto a gurney and rushed him through the double doors toward the emergency wing.

The next morning dawned cold and clear, sunlight glinting off the thin crust of snow along the sidewalks. Frank parked in the hospital lot and walked briskly toward the lobby, his breath fogging the air.

Inside, the waiting room was empty. The same chair where Hayden had sat the night before was pushed back from the wall, a blanket half-crumpled on the floor. Frank frowned and went to the front desk.

"Excuse me," he said. "My friend was here last night—Hayden Lansford. We brought someone in for treatment, and he stayed overnight. I don't see him here now."

The receptionist typed quickly, glancing at her monitor. "I wasn't on duty last night, sir, but it looks like he was taken into the emergency room around nine-thirty."

Frank's brow furrowed. "The emergency room? What happened? Is he all right?"

"I'm afraid I can't share medical details, but he was admitted for observation. He's in room 226"

Frank nodded, half in disbelief, half in relief. "Thank you." He turned toward the elevators, muttering under his breath, "What now, Hayden?"

On the second floor, he found the room. Hayden lay asleep, a thin oxygen tube beneath his nose and an IV-line snaking from his arm. The steady beeping of the monitor filled the otherwise quiet room. Frank stood at the foot of the bed for a long time before pulling a chair close and sitting down.

The door opened quietly behind him. The same neurologist from the night before entered, clipboard in hand. "Morning, Frank, isn't it?"

"Yes," Frank said, standing. "What happened? The nurse said he had some kind of episode."

Dr. Patel nodded and pulled up a chair beside him. "Yes, a seizure—a fairly severe one. He's stable now and resting comfortably."

Frank exhaled. "A seizure? He's never had one in his life. What caused it?"

"Well, that's what we're working out. We ran scans—no sign of tumors, no trauma, nothing structural. However, his bloodwork showed a high level of alprazolam—Xanax. At least ten milligrams."

Frank blinked. "Ten? He only takes one, maybe two at most. Are you saying he overdosed?"

"Not intentionally, perhaps. But his system was saturated. That dosage alone could have triggered the seizure. We've given him flumazenil to help clear it. He's lucky someone noticed quickly."

Frank rubbed a hand over his face. "Good grief. He must've been desperate—or just exhausted beyond reason."

The doctor nodded sympathetically. "He'll recover physically, but I can't speak for his emotional state. Sometimes the mind simply breaks down under prolonged stress."

Frank stared at Hayden's motionless hand resting on the blanket. "He's been under a lot of pressure lately—research, travel, lack of sleep. And the woman we brought in—Abby—she's not well either."

"Yes, Ms. Scott," said Dr. Patel, his tone softening. "She's in the ICU. We had to induce a controlled coma to stabilize her brain activity. Without it, the neural firing in her hippocampus might have caused irreversible damage."

Frank's head jerked up. "A coma? She was talking yesterday. You're telling me she might've—"

"She was deteriorating fast," the doctor said gently. "We had no choice. I've consulted two specialists, and we're all puzzled. Her brain is operating at a level of hyperactivity I've never seen. Imagine a supercomputer suddenly overloaded with data—something has to give."

Frank sat back, stunned. "Is she going to recover?"

"I wish I could tell you. We're monitoring her around the clock. Right now, the best we can do is let her brain rest."

Frank rubbed his temples, the exhaustion in his face deepening. "Two of them, down at once. This whole thing's turning into a nightmare."

The doctor placed a hand on his shoulder. "She's stable. He's stable. Take that as a win for today." He stood, straightened his coat, and nodded toward the window. "You can stay here until Mr. Lansford wakes. The nurses will page me when he does."

Frank nodded, murmuring his thanks as Dr. Patel left the room. He sat quietly for a long time, the steady rhythm of the heart monitor the only sound. Outside, snow flurries drifted against the windowpane like fragments of ash.

He leaned forward, elbows on his knees, and looked at Hayden. "You're supposed to be the one keeping me steady, old friend," he said quietly. "What the hell are we walking into?"

Frank stayed by Hayden's bedside until late afternoon. The fluorescent lights buzzed softly overhead, the world outside fading to a dim gray twilight. He thought of Abby—of her lost memories, her fractured mind—and of the invisible line they'd crossed somewhere back on that beach.

As he dozed in the chair, one thought kept circling through his mind, quiet and relentless:

Outside, snow thickened against the glass, erasing the world a little more each minute— as if memory itself were falling.

They had gone searching for the truth— and now the truth was consuming them.

Chapter Twenty-Four

Dark December Days

When the mind breaks open, it isn't always madness—it can be memory fighting to stay alive.

Frank sat in the shadows of Hayden's hospital room. The curtains were drawn, the lights dim, and the stillness weighed on him like a heavy coat. He tried to make sense of everything the doctor had told him. Just a few months ago, he'd been raking leaves in his yard on a lazy October afternoon, when Hayden had called with a mystery that seemed almost whimsical.

Now here they were—far from whimsical.

The faint hum of fluorescent light pulsed in rhythm with his own heartbeat. Somewhere down the corridor, a gurney wheel squealed— a thin, human sound against the mechanical silence. For a fleeting second, he could almost hear the sea again: waves collapsing, wind whispering in the pines. The hospital's hush carried the same eerie calm as the coast before a storm.

He reached into his satchel and pulled out the envelope Lookingglass had given him. The wax seal, deep wine-red with an old English crest, caught the faint lamplight. His fingers turned it over slowly, tapping it against his knee. Was this the moment Lookingglass had meant—the point of no resolve that would permit him to open it?

He remembered the man's eyes that night—clear, knowing. "Only open it when you no longer trust what you see," Lookingglass had said. Frank hadn't understood then, but now the words echoed like prophecy. The envelope seemed heavier than paper, as if holding the weight of every answer he might not want to know.

In his long career, Frank had relied on reason to decipher other people's irrationalities. He weighed motives and clues, but this situation had long since drifted outside reason.

"Frank?" came a whisper.

He startled, slipping the envelope back into his satchel. "Yeah, I'm here. You awake?"

Hayden blinked against the dim light. "I think so. Am I back in the land of the living?"

Frank laughed softly—half relief, half exhaustion. "Barely. You scared ten years off me."

Frank stood and pressed the bed control, raising Hayden's head. "Looks that way. I was shocked this morning when they said you'd been moved to the ER. You picked a fine way to avoid sharing my dingy motel room."

Hayden smiled faintly. "I don't remember anything from last night. Just... strange dreams. Someone said I had a seizure. Can you believe that?"

Frank went to the window and opened the drapes. "You've been through the wringer, that's for sure. It's dark as a tomb in here."

Hayden squinted toward the glass—and stiffened. "Close the drapes. Quickly."

Frank turned, startled. "What's the matter? Too bright?"

"No. That bird on the sill—a raven."

Frank leaned closer, catching only a glimpse before it took flight. "It was just a bird."

"Just a bird?" Hayden's voice dropped. "Ravens are bad omens."

Frank sighed and let the drapes fall shut. "You're still groggy. Try not to read too much into it." He sat back down, not wanting to argue.

Outside, something knocked faintly against the window—a loose branch, maybe—but it made Frank's shoulders tense. For a heartbeat, he thought he heard the faintest tapping, like a knuckle on glass. Then silence.

Moments later, the door opened and Dr. Patel entered with a chart. "Well, Mr. Lansford, I see you're awake. How are you feeling today?"

"Groggy. Like I've been hit by a train. What happened to me?"

The doctor glanced at Frank. "Has your friend filled you in?"

"Not yet."

"Then let's go over it. May I speak in front of him?"

"Of course," said Hayden.

"You were brought in from the waiting room last night around nine-thirty. You were unresponsive and in full seizure. We found a high level of your prescription medication—Xanax—in your blood."

Hayden's eyes widened. "That's impossible. I only took two yesterday—one before you came to talk with us and one afterward."

"Could you have taken more without realizing it? Stress can cloud the mind. The front desk staff said you collapsed from the chair and began convulsing. Two milligrams wouldn't have caused that reaction."

Hayden looked to Frank. "You know me. I've never abused it."

Frank shook his head. "Never once."

Dr. Patel nodded. "I believe you. Still, Xanax can cause amnesia. It's possible you lost track. We'll run more tests to be sure."

Hayden rubbed his temples. "All I remember is dozing off... then these horrible dreams—demons, darkness, death everywhere. That's all."

The doctor sighed. "You've been under enormous strain. We'll rule out anything physical first, then go from there. We'll run more tests later."

Hayden forced a smile. "Fine. Test away. I'm not crazy."

"Good to hear," said Patel with a faint grin. He made a note and headed for the door.

"Doctor—how's Abby?" Hayden called after him.

The neurologist paused, glanced at Frank, and nodded for him to explain later. "She's being monitored closely," he said, and left.

When the door closed, Hayden swung his legs over the side of the bed. "So? What's going on? Where is she?"

Frank told him everything—the induced coma, the neurologists' confusion, the fear that her brain might not recover.

Hayden covered his face with both hands. "It's unbelievable. Every day it gets worse. I'm losing her, Frank. And maybe losing my own mind."

Frank leaned back in his chair. "You're not losing it. You're worn out and scared, that's all. As for Abby... we have to accept she might not come back the same. But she's strong. Don't count her out yet."

A technician entered, pushing a wheelchair. "Mr. Lansford? Time for your tests."

Hayden frowned. "I'm not going anywhere."

The young man smiled. "Doctor's orders. We'll have you back by dinner, I promise."

Hayden sighed and stood, muttering, "Can't even nap in peace."

Frank chuckled. "I'll be here when you get back. I've got a thrilling view of the parking lot to keep me company."

As the technician wheeled him away, Hayden gave a half-hearted wave.

Frank rose and opened the blinds again. No ravens this time—only a gray, snow-blown sky. Tiny flakes drifted through the air like sifted frost. He decided to get coffee and some fresh air before visiting Abby.

Outside, in the hospital's small arboretum, he sat on a wooden bench, steam rising from his cup. His breath curled like smoke in the frigid air. Snowflakes tumbled through the branches of evergreen trees, the wind whispering over the patio stones. The quiet reminded him of the coast—the calm before the next storm.

Back inside, he stopped at the ICU desk and asked to visit Abby. They allowed only a short visit. Donning a protective gown and gloves, Frank followed a nurse through the ward's bright corridor.

Abby lay motionless amid a tangle of tubes and monitors. Electrodes dotted her scalp; a breathing tube fed oxygen into her lungs. Her skin was pale and luminous, almost other-worldly. One monitor traced her heartbeat steadily, but another—tracking brain waves— showed a thin, trembling line flat across the screen.

Alive, Frank thought. But not here.

Her beauty now was terrible in its stillness—a fragile echo of the woman who had once laughed under salt wind and seagull cries. For the first time, Frank understood why Hayden loved her. Even in silence, she held the room like light in glass.

He sat beside her, eyes burning. After a long silence, he reached for his satchel. The sealed envelope was there, heavy as guilt. He turned it in his hand, tracing the wax crest with his thumb. Hayden would want to be here, he thought. But if she doesn't wake—.

He took out his pocket knife and rested the blade against the wax.

The door opened. Frank jerked upright. He slipped the envelope back into his satchel. Its wax seal caught the ICU light for a moment—like a small eye watching him turn away.

A young man in a white coat entered, startled to see him. "Oh I didn't realize someone was in here," he said cheerfully. I'm a resident neurologist here at the hospital. I'm Doctor Sta—."

"How is she doing?" Frank interrupted.

"Good. Dr. Patel and I are both on this case. You must be Mr. Thompson, you have quite a pair of friends here."

Frank's tone hardened. "How is she?"

The doctor's optimism faltered. "We've tried several adjustments, but every attempt to stimulate normal brain activity spikes dangerously. Keeping her in a controlled coma is the safest course for now. We're exploring options."

"What kind of options?"

"Well…" The doctor hesitated, then brightened slightly. "I've been working on a neurochip—a micro implant designed to modulate hippocampal overactivity. It's shown promise in lab animals. If we can safely test it in her, it might reduce the overload without damaging the surrounding tissue."

Frank's expression darkened. "Lab animals. She's not one."

"I understand your hesitation," he said quickly. "We'd monitor her continuously, and if her brainwaves destabilized, we'd remove it immediately. The risks are minimal compared to doing nothing."

"The risks," Frank said, "sounds like playing God."

The young doctor stiffened. "We're trying to save her, Mr. Thompson."

Frank said nothing. The doctor left, clipboard in hand.

Frank stood over Abby again, his shadow falling across her still form. "Hang in there," he whispered, his voice breaking. He bent down and kissed her cool cheek.

In the hallway, he pulled out his phone and hesitated before dialing. "Miss Scott? It's Frank. She's here… barely, but she's here."

A long pause hummed through the line before her soft voice answered. "Tell her I never stopped believing she'd find her way home."

Frank swallowed hard. "I'll tell her," he said. Though he wasn't sure Abby would ever hear it.

Back in Hayden's room, the bed was empty. The nurse said he was still in testing and might be sedated for the evening.

Frank left a message that he'd gone to the motel and would return in the morning.

It was nearly nine that night when they wheeled Hayden back into his room. He was groggy and pale from the long rounds of testing. Outside, the snow had thickened, driven sideways by hard northeast winds spilling down from the Fraser River Canyon.

The nurse checked his vitals, drew the drapes, and dimmed the lights before leaving the door slightly ajar.

Silence settled over the room.

"Hayden," came a soft voice. "Wake up. It's me—Abby."

He stirred, eyes fluttering open. "Abby? What are you doing here? How... how are you even out of ICU?"

She smiled faintly, shadowed in the dim light. "I'm fine now. Let's get out of here."

He pushed himself up on one elbow. "Out of here? Abby, you were in a coma."

"Not anymore. The headaches are gone. We need to leave before they trap us in more tests. Hurry."

The blue light from the parking lot filtered through the blinds, washing her face in a ghostly hue. For a moment she looked translucent, her eyes deep pools of silver shadow.

Hayden hesitated. "We don't even have a car. I should call Frank—"

"No time," she whispered. "Just trust me."

He swung his legs over the bed, dizzy but obedient. She helped him dress quickly. "You're in scrubs," he muttered. "Why aren't you dressed?"

"Had to blend in," she said. "Now come on."

She peeked into the hallway. A dinner cart stood nearby. "I'll push it. You follow me."

They slipped into the corridor, shoes soft against the linoleum. The fluorescent lights hummed overhead. They were halfway to the elevator when two nurses shouted from behind, "Mr. Lansford! Please stop!"

Hayden turned toward the voice, startled, but kept walking. The cart rattled ahead of him. "Abby, hurry!" he called.

One of the nurses—a tall man—caught up, grabbing Hayden by the arm. "Sir, you can't leave"

Hayden twisted free and pointed down the hall. "Abby! Help!"

The woman in green scrubs turned. Her face was puzzled, unfamiliar. "I don't know who you think I am, sir, but I'm not Abby." The words hit him like a slap.

The nurses led him gently back to his room. "You must've been dreaming," one said kindly. "Sedation can cause sleepwalking."

Hayden shook his head as they helped him into bed. "I saw her. She woke me. I swear she was here."

Her hand had felt warm. That's what haunted him. Warm, not cold.

"She's in ICU," the nurse said. "If you're discharged tomorrow, you can see her then."

He lay back, disoriented. "I can't believe this... It felt so real."

"Would you like us to call your friend Mr. Thompson?"

Hayden hesitated, then nodded. "Yes. Tell him to come. Please."

"Of course. I'll bring you some tea while you wait. It's snowing hard out there, so it might take him a while."

Hayden smiled faintly. "He'll make it. He always does."

Frank drove through the storm an hour later, wipers dragging across the windshield.

The hospital's lights shimmered in the swirling snow ahead. As he parked and stepped into the gale, a dark shape rose from the lamplight— large wings sweeping low over the lot.

The wind howled like surf in his ears. The raven turned once above the lights, scattering flakes like black snow before vanishing into the night.

A raven.

Frank paused, heart thudding, watching it vanish into the blizzard.

Inside, somewhere above him, Hayden dreamed again of Abby standing by his bed, whispering his name—her voice echoing through a corridor that had no end.

INTERLUDE

The Raven's Omen

The raven perched on the hospital's ledge long after the storm passed. Its feathers gleamed like oil in the weak morning light, a shimmer of violet and midnight blue where the sun tried to break through. The city below was waking— car tires hissing on wet streets, the hum of generators, the faint clang of a bell from the nearby chapel—yet the bird remained motionless, a solitary sentinel against the cold glass.

Inside, the hallways smelled of antiseptic and fear. Machines hummed their mechanical lullabies, and the living clung to the edge of sleep. But beyond the windows, the raven tilted its head toward the west—toward the sea— and gave a low, rasping croak that cut through the hum of the waking hospital.

A nurse crossing the hallway shivered, glancing toward the sound. The air there felt wrong—charged, almost electric—as if a storm had entered through unseen cracks in the glass.

The bird's black eyes caught its own reflection, then blinked. For a heartbeat, its shadow lengthened across the window and rippled like dark water. In that shimmer, something stirred—not a figure, not a face, but an impression of movement, of a form bound to the tide, waiting.

The raven opened its wings, the span of them wider than seemed possible, and with a single, heavy beat it vanished into the pale sky. The reflection remained for a moment longer, then faded with the morning sun.

Far below, unnoticed, the runoff from melting snow carried down the hospital's gutters and disappeared into the storm drains— water bound for the coast.

And somewhere, far to the west, the sea began to move again.

Chapter Twenty-Five

The Winter Crossing

The search for Jeremy leads into deeper waters

The hospital staff informed Hayden that the doctor would be in shortly and he could get dressed and ready to leave. Frank had spent the night and sat by the window, watching the clouds break apart and expose ribbons of azure sky. The heavy snowfall had ceased, and the sun struggled to shine through the shadowy outlines of trees beyond the glass. The silence was deep enough to hear the ticking of the wall clock and the faint hum of machines down the hall.

"I'll be glad to get out of this place and move on," Hayden said, buttoning his shirt. "Of course, that depends on how Abby's doing. I was out of it yesterday—what do you know, Frank?"

Frank set his coffee mug down and looked at him for a long moment, weighing how much to say. He studied Hayden's tired face, thinking how much the younger man reminded him of himself years ago—too loyal, too stubborn to walk away from anyone in pain.

Before he could answer, the door swung open and the doctor entered, his breath visible from the cold draft that followed him.

"Good morning, gentlemen," he said briskly. "Mr. Lansford, we ran you through quite the gauntlet yesterday. Most of your scans are normal, though there are a few puzzling anomalies."

Hayden frowned. "In what way?"

The doctor glanced at his clipboard. "Not disease or degeneration, nothing like that. But many of your brain cells have gathered in unusual clusters. Nothing dangerous, just... unconventional. Combined with your session with our resident psychologist, it appears you're under significant stress. The story you related about your friend Abby, while heartfelt, might seem—let's say—difficult for most to accept. We recommend follow-up with your physician, neurologist, and a psychiatrist."

Hayden's jaw tightened. "So you think I'm crazy."

"Not at all," the doctor replied evenly. "We've ruled out physical causes. Now it's the mind that needs time and care."

Frank shifted in his chair but said nothing. The light from the window reflected on the floor like a pale mirror between them.

Hayden exhaled slowly. "All right then, Doctor. What about Abby? Can she leave with us?"

The doctor's tone softened. "Not yet. Her condition is stable but fragile. My assistant spoke with your friend here—we're preparing to proceed with the experimental neural implant. It may reduce the hyperactivity in her hippocampus. Frankly, it's the only chance she has."

Hayden turned sharply toward Frank. "Why didn't you tell me?"

Frank rubbed his temple. "There wasn't time, Hayden. You were in tests all day. I only got the summary."

A silence fell between them, filled by the faint hiss of the radiator. Frank could almost hear the pulse of the machines down the corridor—the steady rhythm that marked Abby's fragile hold on life. He knew this argument wasn't about secrecy; it was about fear. Neither of them wanted to admit how close they were to losing her.

After a long discussion, both men reluctantly agreed to the procedure. When the doctor left, Hayden sat quietly on the edge of the bed, elbows on his knees. "This whole thing keeps getting darker."

Frank stood near the window, watching a ray of sunlight pierce the thinning clouds. "When I first heard what they planned, I was dead set against it. But something changed overnight. Maybe I realized how much she means to you. We've come too far to give up now. If this keeps her alive, even a little longer, it's worth trying."

Hayden nodded, his voice barely above a whisper. "I appreciate that. What's next?"

"I'll head north into Canada," Frank said. "You stay here and be with her. I'll track down Jeremy. I know he's out there—and tied to what's been haunting that beach."

"British Columbia's a big place, Frank. How will you even start?"

Frank smiled faintly. "Men like Jeremy don't stray far from the sea. I'll follow the coast. He's somewhere near the water—I can feel it."

Before leaving, they visited Abby's room one last time. The machines hummed softly, their green lights blinking like beacons in a fog. She lay motionless, the rhythmic hiss of the ventilator the only sound. Hayden held her hand, his thumb tracing the faint pulse beneath her skin. Hayden leaned close and whispered something Frank couldn't hear, his forehead resting lightly against hers.

The machines hummed softly, their green lights blinking like beacons in a fog. Somewhere beneath it all, the steady hiss of her breathing kept time with the sea

***

Through the glass wall, Frank stood silently, then turned and left. As he walked the hospital corridor, the sound of his boots echoed like slow waves against tile. The automatic doors parted, letting in a wash of cold sunlight that felt almost clean after so many days of shadow.

By late morning, sunlight glimmered on the melting snow as Frank reached the border at the Peace Arch. The guard glanced at his passport and asked routine questions, but Frank's thoughts were already miles ahead. The sound of gulls followed him across the checkpoint. The ocean stretched beside him like a sheet of hammered steel. Determination kept him steady as he wound north through the coastal roads.

As the SUV labored to the ferry dock, he felt the shift from one world to another— the hum of civilization fading behind him, replaced by the hush of deep forest and distant surf.

Once aboard standing on the observation deck, he leaned into the wind as the ferry's horn blared across the Strait of Georgia. The spray hit his face like cold breath. He thought of Abby's voice, now trapped in machines, and wondered if love could travel over water. He welcomed the spray—it kept him awake, alive. Ahead, Vancouver Island rose from the mist, dark green and ancient.

Frank thought of Abby—of how her breathing had matched the rhythm of the ventilator. The sea felt like that machine now: endless inhaling, endless release. He wondered if she would ever wake to see another sunrise.

He disembarked at Nanaimo and continued northward.

***

The roads were wet and narrow, cutting through towering cedars that dripped with meltwater. In a quiet seaside village, he stopped at a small pub near a marina and ordered fish and chips. The scent of vinegar and salt hung in the air.

A man wearing a heavy sheepskin coat sat beside him at the bar, his hands rough and weathered from years on the water.

"Bit of a chill outside, eh?" the man said, smiling. "You're not from around here."

Frank smiled back. "No, up here from Oregon. Looking for someone who might've settled here years ago."

"A fisherman, I take it?"

"That's right."

The man nodded. "You've come to the right place. I'm Sam Neil. I run a fishing camp up in Campbell River."

They shook hands and talked as they ate. When Frank mentioned Jeremy Stayton, Sam frowned thoughtfully. "Never heard the name. But if he came here to disappear, this island's the place to do it. Hundreds of miles of coast, small villages tucked away where time stands still. He might've even changed his name."

Sam took a slow drink, eyes narrowing. "You ever hear of the Ghost Fisherman? Locals say he walks the tide flats when the moon's thin, carrying a lantern no wind can blow out. Folks used to think it was just stories to scare kids—but last winter, one of my crew saw a light out past Winter Harbour. No boats were out that night."

Frank hid a chill under his calm expression. "A lantern," he repeated quietly.

Sam nodded. "Yup. Out there, stories never die—they just drift with the tide."

"If you wanted solitude, where would you go?" Frank asked.

"Winter Harbour," Sam said without hesitation. "Way up on the northwest tip. Rugged country, hardly any roads. Only way in is by boat or a logging road that's half impassable most of the year."

Frank's eyes lit slightly. "Sounds like just the kind of place he'd hide."

Sam grinned. "If you're heading that far, stay the night at my place in Campbell River. I've got a few empty cabins. You'll need a good rest before that drive."

Frank accepted. That night, he slept under a handmade quilt, the air filled with the scent of cedar. But his dreams were uneasy—shards of moonlight flickering across water, a cold voice whispering from the tide.

In his dream, he saw a man on a boat, back turned, a lantern swinging from the bow. The sea around him glowed faintly green, like phosphorescence—and when the man turned, his face was his own.

At dawn, Frank drove north again. Snowbanks lined the shoulders, but the sky was clear, the sunlight sharp and cold. The road wound through towering spruce forests, then dipped toward the sea.

In Port McNeil, he parked by the marina and walked along the dock. The wooden planks creaked beneath his boots. A few fishermen worked quietly on their boats, their breath rising in the frosty air.

"Hey there," Frank called to an older man with a long white beard and a corncob pipe. "I'm looking for someone. Name's Jeremy Stayton—fisherman, from Oregon originally."

The man puffed on his pipe, squinting. "Can't say I've heard the name. Lots of folks come through, few stay. This coast eats the weak ones. Either they drown or they leave."

Frank thanked him and returned to his SUV. As he drove further north, the forest grew thicker, the road rougher. The air smelled of fir, salt, and distant rain.

By twilight, he reached the turnoff to Winter Harbour. The road narrowed to a single lane of gravel and snow, winding between ancient evergreens. The world grew darker with each mile. When he finally reached the harbor, the moon had risen, casting silver light across the quiet bay. Fishing boats rocked gently at their moorings, ropes creaking softly in the wind.

Only one house showed light on the hillside above the docks. Frank parked and climbed the slick wooden steps. He knocked, and after a moment, the door opened to reveal a man in his sixties, white-bearded, eyes bright as glass.

"Didn't expect visitors this late," the man said, voice low and rough.

Frank introduced himself, and the man stepped aside. The warmth inside was immediate—a crackling wood stove, the scent of salt and smoke. A small Christmas tree stood in the corner, decorated with shells, glass floats, and netting. The light flickered across the fisherman's face as he poured two drinks.

"I'm John Lambert," he said. "Been here most of my life. You've come a long way. Who are you looking for?"

"A man named Jeremy Stayton," Frank said. "He fished the Oregon coast thirty years ago. I think he may have come here."

John stared, his expression frozen in surprise. "That's a name I haven't heard in a long time."

Frank leaned forward. "You knew him?"

John nodded slowly. "Ya. He came here about thirty years back. Quiet man. Built himself a small cabin by the cove. Worked the boats, kept to himself. Married a native woman—Addy from the Nuu-chah-nulth tribe. Two sons. For a while, he seemed happy. Then one day, he left. No warning, no goodbye. Just gone."

John's voice softened. "Sometimes at night, Addy said she could hear him talking in his sleep—calling out a woman's name. Abby, I think it was. Said he'd wake shaking, eyes wild, like he'd seen her ghost."

Frank's chest tightened. "Did he ever speak of Oregon after that?"

"Never. But he kept an old sand dollar on the windowsill. Said it was a charm that washed up the night his world ended."

Frank's breath caught. "Do you know where he went?"

John refilled their glasses. "Probably he moved south, closer to the villages where his wife's people lived. He wanted schooling for the boys, or so he once said. But I saw something in him near the end—haunted, like he was being followed by visions he couldn't shake. Whatever drove him from your coast, it followed him here."

He met Frank's gaze. "If you find him, tread carefully. Some men bury their pasts for a reason."

Frank nodded. "I appreciate the warning— and the drink."

"You can stay the night," John said, standing. "Storm's coming. Roads will be bad till morning."

Frank accepted the offer. The old man showed him to a small bedroom that smelled of salt and wool. The mattress sagged, but it felt good to lie down. Through the window, moonlight spilled across the harbor, turning the waves into bands of silver.

Frank took out his notebook and wrote a single line: 'The living aren't the only ones who travel'. Then he closed it, set it on the nightstand, and turned out the lamp.

As he drifted toward sleep, a sound rose faintly through the wind—a distant wail, half human, half sea-born. He sat up, heart pounding, but there was only the moan of the wind through the firs.

Yet long after he lay back down, the sound came again—fainter, further out over the water this time. Three notes, rising and falling—too human for wind, too mournful for gulls.

INTERLUDE

The Crossing

Dawn came gray and trembling over the Sound. The ferry sat low in the water, its decks slick with frost, the scent of diesel mingling with the cold tang of the sea. Frank leaned on the railing, collar turned high against the wind, watching the slow churn of the engines beneath him. The waves foamed white in their wake, stretching south toward the invisible line of the border.

He felt it before he saw it—that subtle shift in the air, as though crossing not just distance but memory. Behind him lay the hospital, the sterile rooms and whispered fears, the lingering echo of Hayden's sleepless voice. Ahead waited the island, the unknown, and a man who had been lost to the sea for three decades.

The ferry horn sounded—low, mournful, almost human. The sound carried across the water and vanished into mist. Frank closed his eyes. For a moment, he saw Abby's face reflected in the ripples below him, her expression serene but watchful, as if carried within the tide itself.

He had made hundreds of crossings in his life—case files, crime scenes, confessions— but this one felt different. The air itself seemed to bend around him, thick with old grief and salt. Even the gulls flew lower, silent, as though wary of disturbing whatever ancient thing lingered just beneath the surface.

As the ferry neared the island, the mist lifted, revealing a jagged coast draped in evergreen and fog. A single shaft of light broke through the clouds, catching the sea in a brief shimmer of silver and blue. Frank tightened his grip on the railing, his reflection wavering like a shadow on water.

When the ramp dropped and the engines quieted, he drove forward, tires echoing on the steel deck. It wasn't just a new country he entered—it was the threshold of something old, something that had been waiting for him.

Behind him, the wake stretched out like a fading path, and the tide rolled in again to erase it.

Chapter Twenty-Six

Eye of the Storm

What the sea remembers

The long drive down the island gave Frank time to think and sort things out. He had explored plenty of odd and unbelievable cases in his career, but this trip would be close to the top of the list.

The more he thought about it, the more the whole story felt like a loop—spirits chasing spirits, and him caught somewhere in between faith and logic.

Several hours later, he stopped at Port Alberni for a quick lunch before continuing on to Ucluelet, about an hour and a half drive west. The weather had cleared, and the weak winter sun shone through the towering forest, throwing long shadows across the winding road.

He rolled the window down just enough to smell the sea returning on the wind—kelp, resin, and the faint sweetness of rain-soaked cedar.

He arrived in Ucluelet—a rugged, windblown harbor town clinging to the edge of Vancouver Island. His map showed two marinas: one for pleasure craft and another, farther south, where the fishing fleet tied up. The latter seemed far more likely to hold the man he was searching for. The small harbor sat tucked inland east of the lighthouse and the Wild Pacific Trail—steep, forested, and largely untouched.

Frank parked his SUV beside a faded red Ford pickup with a bed full of crab pots and walked to a small bluff overlooking the port. About half the slips were empty; the rest held old, weather-beaten boats that looked barely seaworthy. A long wooden plank led down to the floating docks. Grasping the frayed rope handrail, Frank made his careful descent, the boards slick beneath his boots.

Gulls cried overhead, their wings cutting the gray air. Somewhere deep below, the hollow thud of water against pilings echoed like a heartbeat.

The only movement came from an old man working on a white vessel near the end of the dock. Frank called out. The man straightened, emerging from the cabin—a wiry figure with a face like a crumpled chart of the sea.

"Hi there," Frank said. "Mind if I ask you a couple of questions?"

"That depends, mister," the man replied, eyes narrowing with a mix of suspicion and amusement.

"I won't take much of your time," Frank said. "I'm looking for someone, and I'm hoping you might point me in the right direction."

The old man climbed up onto the dock with deliberate movements, pipe in hand, and struck a match against a piling. "Who are you looking for?"

"A man named Jeremy Stayton. You wouldn't happen to know him?"

The man's pipe flared as he puffed thoughtfully. "And who might you be? And why are you after Jeremy?"

"I'm Frank Thompson, from Portland. I'm helping an old friend locate him," Frank said, his voice calm but firm.

"I thought maybe you were from the university," the man said with a dry chuckle. "Folks from over there drop by from time to time."

"You know Jeremy, then? You know where he lives?"

The man nodded slowly. "Yup, I know him. See that cedar-shake house across the inlet? Weathered gray with the white picket fence?" He pointed with the stem of his pipe.

Frank squinted across the still water. A thin ribbon of smoke curled from a chimney among the trees.

The man tapped his pipe against the piling, scattering ash into the water. "He left before sunrise. Out crabbing, I expect."

"I see. Is anyone else there?"

The man gave Frank a long look. "You sure do ask a lot of questions. Yep, Adurecuta would be at the house,"

"Occupational hazard," Frank said with a faint smile. "I take it that old red pickup up top is yours?"

"Sure is," the man said. Jeremy never drives over, takes his dinghy across. That one—slip number ten. He uses it to get back and forth from the house. No need to drive the long way round to get here."

Frank nodded. "Appreciate the help." He started back up the dock, then turned. "One more thing—who's Adurecuta?"

The man was already lowering himself into his boat. "His wife, of course!" he shouted, and disappeared inside.

Frank muttered to himself. "Naturally."

He could almost hear Hayden's voice teasing him: Of course she's his wife, Frank. But the idea of Jeremy remarried after all those years still sat uneasily in his chest.

Back in his SUV, he traced the route on his map: north on Peninsula Road, then a narrow gravel road running the east side of the inlet. The late afternoon sun dipped low as he wound through the forest, the trees closing around him like sentinels.

Ferns brushed the sides of the vehicle. The road curved tighter, each turn darker than the last. Frank felt the strange pull of the sea even through the trees, that old, magnetic force that always led men toward their undoing.

He parked below the hillside house and opened the gate in the sagging picket fence. Two wicker chairs sat on the porch facing the calm inlet. The place looked peaceful, almost domestic—an illusion that didn't fool him.

He knocked three times. The door opened to reveal a woman with long gray hair cascading over a magenta sweater.

A black leather hat shadowed her face, and a string of strange trinkets dangled around her neck, clicking softly in the breeze.

"Hello, Mrs. Stayton," Frank said, forcing a polite smile. "I spoke with a man at the dock who told me Jeremy was out crabbing. I've come a long way to talk with him."

She studied him in silence, her expression unreadable. The wind chimes above them sang softly. "I'm sorry," she said at last. "Have we met before?"

"No, ma'am. I'm helping an old friend. It's a long story." He handed her his business card.

She looked it over, then nodded. "Then you'd best tell it somewhere warm. Come in— let's have some tea."

The living room smelled of cedar smoke and herbs. Frank sank into an overstuffed chair by the fire, stretching his legs toward the heat. The fatigue of the long drive washed over him.

The firelight flickered over the wooden walls, reminding him of the beach house nights—Abby in her chair by the window, Hayden scribbling in his notebook. A world away, yet somehow circling back.

She returned with a tray and two steaming mugs. "You can call me Addy," she said. "My native name is Adurecuta—it means 'herb gatherer.'"

Frank took a cautious sip. The tea was bitter and sharp. "Strong flavor," he said. "Gives you a bit of a jolt."

She smiled faintly. "All natural. I gather what the forest gives."

Frank's gaze drifted to the mantel. Framed photos lined the shelf—family portraits, smiling faces. "Your sons?" he asked.

"Yes. Michael, the younger, teaches at the university in Vancouver. Thomas—he's finishing his neurosurgery residency in Bellingham."

Frank froze, his cup halfway to his lips. Bellingham. His heart thudded. The neurologist who had operated on Abby—the one eager to implant a chip—Thomas Stayton?

He set the cup down carefully. "That's... remarkable," he said, buying a moment. "Small world."

"Are you all right, Mr. Thompson?" she asked, noticing the color drain from his face.

He forced a weak smile. "Just the tea— stronger than I'm used to."

She nodded and watched him closely. "You seem like a man carrying a story. Perhaps you should tell it before Jeremy comes in."

He sat forward, elbows on his knees. "This visit is personal, not business. I assure you, nothing illegal. I just need to ask your husband about his past. Has he ever spoken of the years before he came here?"

She hesitated, about to answer, when a buzzer sounded faintly from the kitchen. She stood. "That means his dinghy's ashore. He'll be up shortly. We'll wait for him."

She switched on a few lamps, stoked the fire, and stepped out to the porch. Frank's phone vibrated in his pocket. A text from Hayden:

Abby's out of surgery. She's awake and back to normal. We're leaving in the morning. Dr. Stayton saved her life.

Frank read it twice, the words sinking in. Dr. Stayton. The son of the man he'd been chasing.

His mind spun—the circle tightening in ways he hadn't foreseen. Fate, coincidence, or something stranger, he couldn't tell. He only knew the story was folding back on itself, and he was somewhere in its eye.

Before he could gather his thoughts, footsteps sounded on the porch. Addy entered, followed by a tall, weathered man with silver streaked hair and a towel around his neck.

She said, "This is Mr. Thompson—a visitor who's come a long way to speak with you."

Frank stood, heart pounding, and extended his hand.

The fisherman's grip was strong, his gaze direct but guarded. "So," he said, lowering himself into a chair opposite the fire, "what's this about?"

Frank took a breath. "It's about the past, Mr. Stayton. A past that's not finished yet."

Jeremy leaned forward, resting his rough hands on his knees. "The past?" he said, his voice low but steady. "Most folks spend their lives trying to forget it. What's so important that dragged you up here in the middle of winter?"

Frank studied him closely—the lined face, the wary eyes, the faint tremor in his voice that betrayed the name he hadn't yet heard. "I'm working with someone who's been... searching for answers. Someone who was once close to you."

The fire cracked sharply between them, a single ember leaping to the hearth like a signal. Neither man moved. Outside, the wind rose— soft at first, then stronger, carrying the distant sound of the sea. The storm was building again.

INTERLUDE

The Letter Never Sent

The hospital lamp burned low, its weak yellow light trembling over a stack of papers and a half-empty cup of cold tea. Hayden sat at the small writing desk, the rhythmic tick of the wall clock marking each slow second. Outside, snow fell in whispering sheets, soft against the windowpane, dissolving into rivulets that traced crooked paths toward the sill.

He had been trying to write her a letter— not to the Abby resting in the ICU, sedated and breathing to the rhythm of machines, but to the part of her that lived beyond that body. The part he had met in the mirror, in dreams, in the faint shimmer of salt air that seemed to follow him since Haystack Beach.

The first line had come easily enough: 'You should have stayed at the sea'. But what followed faltered, splintering into fragments of what he couldn't quite say aloud.

He wrote of the silence between them— the silence that had grown since the storm, since the strange young spirit had returned to inhabit her. He wrote that he didn't fear losing her—he feared forgetting the version of her that had believed in him. He wrote of the way Frank's calm reason seemed to dissolve when the world no longer obeyed its own rules.

And finally, he wrote the truth he could never speak in her hospital room: If you wake, I will believe in anything—in spirits, in fate, in mercy.

The pen hovered, a drop of ink pooling into the paper's grain like a heartbeat stilled. He folded the letter, slid it into an envelope, and sealed it with the faint press of his thumb.

Morning found it untouched on the desk— no address, no stamp, no name. When Hayden left his hospital room, he paused, looking once at the envelope in the half-light, then turned and closed the door.

Chapter Twenty-Seven

The Awakening

When Spirits Rest

Hayden sat in the sterile, brightly lit surgery waiting room, his heart pounding a frantic rhythm against his ribs as worry gnawed at him. He watched the second hand sweep across the wall clock, its steady movement a hypnotic pulse that only heightened his tension.

The smell of antiseptic and coffee hung heavy in the air, a mix that always reminded him of long vigils and uncertain endings. He was adrift in the swirling chaos of his thoughts when a firm shake from the doctor snapped him back to reality.

"Mr. Lansford?"

"Oh—yes, doctor. How did it go? Is she all right?"

"She's doing great," the doctor said, his voice calm and confident. "Everything went smoothly. Her vitals are stable, and she's alert and responsive. They'll move her to a room shortly."

Hayden let out a tired sigh. "I felt like I was drifting out there. When can I see her?"

"Why don't you head to the third floor? Someone will show you to her room so you can wait there."

"Thank you so much, doctor—"

"Stayton," he said, offering a polite nod. "Doctor Stayton. I'm sorry we haven't formally met. I spoke earlier with your friend Frank Thompson. I'm a neurosurgeon in residency here and co-developed the microchip we implanted in Abby's brain to control her neural activity, along with Dr. Mylar."

"Excellent," Hayden said, the words more a sigh of relief than conversation.

Yet as the doctor turned away, a faint chill rippled through Hayden, as if the name itself carried a shadow.

As the automatic doors sighed shut behind the doctor, the name Stayton echoed in Hayden's mind, tugging at something faint but familiar. A shiver ran through him. Could it be coincidence—or connection?

He rode the elevator up and was soon shown into Abby's room. The stiff recliner creaked as he sat and collected his thoughts. Stayton. The name carried weight. Could this doctor be related to Jeremy somehow? He rubbed his temples, uneasy, then decided to text Frank. He hadn't heard from him all day.

The reply came moments later: I'm with Jeremy right now. I'll contact you tomorrow.

Hayden froze, staring at the glowing screen in disbelief.

The room seemed to tilt. He gripped the phone tighter, the words blurring as if they'd been written underwater. With Jeremy. That meant the past was no longer a ghost story—it was breathing somewhere north of here.

A nurse wheeled Abby in moments later, and the silence broke. She looked radiant— alive. Her eyes were clear, her skin warm, her expression peaceful. Hayden stood quickly, the recliner groaning in protest.

"Hey there, beautiful," he said, smiling through tears. "You look absolutely radiant."

The nurses adjusted the monitoring leads and checked her vitals, then left quietly. Hayden leaned close, kissing her cheek. "I was so worried about you. How are you feeling?"

"I feel good," she said softly. "They told me I've been in a deep sleep for days. Funny thing is, I don't remember anything after we got here. I had the worst pounding headache ever."

Hayden sat beside her and took her hand. "Did they tell you about the procedure?"

"Yes," she whispered. "They implanted a tiny microchip in my brain—cold, metallic. It's meant to calm my racing thoughts and restore my mind."

He squeezed her hand gently. "They said your spirit—trapped for years in another dimension—was consuming your strength.

These doctors saved your life. I think that wandering spirit has finally let go."

Abby touched her forehead and leaned back into the pillows. "The only thing I remember is waking in that old house in Bandon thirty years ago—the ticking clock, the creaking floors—and then going home to Maine. I have no memory of Jeremy or marriage."

The blankness in her tone unsettled him. For the first time, it wasn't what she remembered that frightened him—but what she'd lost.

Hayden's voice trembled. "I was worried sick, Abby. I love you so much. The thought of losing you terrifies me."

Abby reached for him and pulled him close. "I love you too, Hayden. That's all that matters. You had to follow Lookingglass's wishes—don't regret it. Maybe I wasn't meant to remember that life. The old spirit in me is gone now. What's left is ours."

They sat quietly for a long time, peace settling between them. By nightfall, Hayden stood and stretched. "Abby," he said softly, "I have to tell you about what happened while you were unconscious."

He told her everything—the seizure, the Xanax, the doctors' suspicion that he'd broken down, even the strange dream where she urged him to escape. Abby shook her head, disbelieving, but held his hand tightly.

"I'm looking forward to tomorrow morning," Hayden said. "Then we can leave this place."

Abby smiled, her eyes shining. "Me too."

She lowered her bed and soon drifted into a natural sleep, her breathing steady. Hayden pulled a thin blanket over himself in the recliner, his thoughts tangled between relief and unease. Frank's with Jeremy. The phrase echoed until he finally surrendered to restless sleep.

***

Morning came with its usual bustle— nurses changing shifts, doctors murmuring in hallways, the clatter of breakfast trays. Abby's nurse came in with a cheerful smile.

The dawn light filtering through the blinds painted thin golden bars across the floor— hope, but fragile as glass.

"How did you sleep, Hayden?" Abby asked.

He groaned, stretching. "If they charge me for that recliner, I'll protest. Between that and the cold air vent, I barely survived. I'm ready to check out."

"How about you?" he asked Abby.

"I was out all night. It felt good—natural."

Dr. Stayton entered, smiling. "Good morning, you two. How's our patient?"

Abby returned the smile. "Best sleep I've had in ages."

"Excellent. Any headaches?"

"No, none at all."

He did a quick neurological exam, tested reflexes, scanned the microchip data, and finally sat back, typing a few notes.

"I'd say you're doing wonderfully," he concluded. "You're healthy—physically and mentally. I see no reason to keep you here. Christmas is only hours away, so you'll be ready for the holidays. I'll schedule a follow-up after New Year's. You'll take with you a small head monitor—it'll record data and send it to me automatically. I expect a full recovery."

"Any restrictions?" Abby asked.

Dr. Stayton chuckled. "Nothing major. Maybe skip racquetball for a few days."

Abby laughed softly. "Thank you, doctor. I don't understand all of it, but I'm grateful."

He smiled. "You and Mr. Thompson were heading north when you came here, right? Where in Canada were you bound?"

Abby looked at Hayden, who took a deep breath. "Frank was leading the way. I think we were going to Vancouver Island."

Stayton's eyes brightened. "Really? That's where I'm from. My parents live there—on the west side, near Ucluelet. My father's a fisherman; he was out crabbing yesterday, actually. I'll be heading home tomorrow for Christmas."

The air seemed to thin around Hayden. The invisible threads between them were tightening fast now, knotting past and present together. Hayden's pulse quickened, but he said nothing.

"Well," the doctor said cheerfully, "I'll get your discharge papers ready. If you happen to make it to the west coast of the island, give me a call. I'll be there through New Year's."

He handed Hayden his card, smiled, and left the room.

Abby beamed. "Such a nice young man."

He slipped the card into his pocket. The card felt heavier than paper—like something dredged from the tide.

Hayden nodded, still processing everything—the coincidence, the invitation, the quiet thread linking it all.

Moments later, the nurse returned with the discharge papers. "You're all set. Call this number after the holidays to schedule your follow up." She helped Abby set up the monitor, then left them to dress.

"I can't believe we're finally leaving," Hayden said. "We'll stop by Frank's motel and go from there."

A wheelchair arrived, its wheels whispering on the linoleum. Abby smiled as they were led through the bustling lobby.

Outside, the winter sun hung low over the parking lot, cold and metallic, the kind of light that promised both endings and beginnings. A sleek black car waited in the cold sunlight. The Uber door opened, and Hayden helped her in. The motel ahead gleamed faintly through the drifting mist—a brief haven before whatever lay waiting on the island.

The sea was calling again—and this time, it would not let them go.

Addy's Private Moment

The wind had quieted after midnight, though the house still whispered with the sound of the sea. Addy sat by the window, her shawl wrapped tight, watching the faint pulse of light from the distant buoy. The rhythmic flash comforted her—a heartbeat out there in the black expanse of water.

On the table beside her sat Jeremy's old journal, the leather worn smooth by years of hands. She'd read only bits of it over the decades, respecting his privacy, but tonight her fingers lingered on the edge of the cover. The air in the room felt heavy, close. Something in her spirit told her the past was moving again.

The elders had warned her long ago that grief, when left untended, can become a living thing. It feeds quietly, breathing in the dark corners of the heart until one day it takes shape—a spirit not of death, but of sorrow. She had seen that shadow in Jeremy's eyes when she first met him all those years ago. She had loved him anyway.

She opened the journal. The first page held a sketch—a rough outline of a boat, small and half-finished. Beneath it, in careful handwriting, were three words: The sea remembers.

Addy traced the letters with her finger. "So do I," she whispered.

A log shifted in the stove, sending a brief flare of orange light through the room. On the wall, her reflection merged with the flicker of flame—one face in two worlds. For years she had wondered what ghosts carried, what he saw when he looked at the horizon and grew silent. She had accepted that some stories would never be told.

But tonight felt different. The air itself seemed restless, humming with the energy that comes before change. Somewhere out beyond the black surf, fate was rearranging its pieces.

She rose, crossed to the door, and looked toward the sleeping shape of her husband in the next room. He murmured something in his dreams—a name, faint and distant as a memory carried on the wind.

Addy pressed her hand to her heart. "Whoever you are," she whispered, "be kind when you come."

Then she turned down the lamp, leaving the room in quiet amber glow. Outside, the tide was rising again—soft, steady, inevitable.

By morning, the sea was gray and restless, the calm of the night gone. Addy's unease had deepened into certainty—something was moving toward them through the fog.

When the knock finally came at the door, she already knew whose voice would follow.

Chapter Twenty-Eight

Stormy Seas

When the past resurfaces, no one stands untouched

The fire crackled softly in the hearth, the faint scent of cedar mingling with the salt-tinged air that crept through the cracks of the old house. Frank studied Jeremy—the deep lines carved across his face spoke of years weighed down by guilt and sorrow. His rough, calloused hands still held the damp kitchen towel, as if clinging to something solid amid the swirl of disbelief.

A gust rattled the windowpanes, and for a heartbeat, the howl of the wind almost resembled a voice calling from the shore.

Addy moved quietly about the kitchen, the teapot whistling a thin, ghostly tune before she turned off the burner. The warmth of the fire offered a fragile comfort against the chill that hung in the room.

Frank watched her hands—steady, practiced, belonging to someone who had spent a lifetime holding a broken world together.

"I'm not sure where to begin," Frank said at last. "There's so much to tell. But let's start with what matters most."

He leaned forward, his eyes steady, voice low and certain. "Abby is alive."

Jeremy's head jerked up, confusion and disbelief flashing across his face. "What in God's name are you talking about?"

"I mean Abby—your wife from the Oregon coast," Frank said softly. "She survived."

"That's impossible," Jeremy whispered. His gaze dropped to the floor, his hands trembling slightly. "She drowned. I saw it with my own eyes... the sea took her." He rose slowly, walking to the fireplace, and ran his fingers along the carved wood of the mantel as though seeking truth in its texture.

The silence between words was thick, filled only by the steady ticking of the clock and the whisper of wind through the chimney.

Frank clasped his hands between his knees. "I know it's hard to believe, but by some miracle, she lived. She was found and taken to her aunt's home in Bandon. The accident stole her memories—six years of your life together wiped clean. She never remembered your home, your marriage, or you."

Addy entered, carrying a steaming mug. The fragrance of wild herbs drifted through the room as she handed the cup to Frank, her eyes moving between the two men. "Would someone please tell me what's going on here?"

The only reply was the pop and crackle of the fire. Jeremy stood motionless, the towel slipping from his fingers.

The towel hit the floor with a damp thud— a sound too small to hold the weight of what had just been said.

Frank set the tea aside and rose. "I told him something from his past—something he never expected to hear."

Addy hurried to her husband's side, gripping his arm. "What did he say, Jeremy?"

Jeremy swallowed hard, his voice rough. "He says... Abby's alive."

Addy's expression flickered between fear and disbelief. "Alive?"

Jeremy turned toward Frank, his eyes dark with turmoil. "Are you absolutely certain?"

"I am," Frank said. "She's alive—and she's safe."

"If that's true," Jeremy said, his voice hardening, "then where is she now?"

Frank hesitated. "There's a long story behind that—thirty years of it, to be honest. But the short answer is, she's in Bellingham with my friend Hayden Lansford."

Jeremy stepped closer until he was just inches away. The tension in the air was thick enough to taste. "You expect me to swallow this after three decades? That's madness."

"Then maybe we should bring your son Thomas into the conversation," Frank said quietly.

Jeremy froze mid-step. His eyes narrowed. "What about my son?"

"Dr. Stayton," Frank said. "He's the neurosurgeon who saved Abby's life today."

The words struck like thunder. Jeremy's expression twisted—shock, confusion, anger. He slammed his fist against the mantel, then turned, pacing furiously.

A gust roared down the chimney, scattering ash across the hearth as if the sea itself had heard.

Addy reached for him, but he tore away, storming toward the front door. "You can't come here and unravel my life with one conversation" he shouted, voice cracking. The door slammed open with a loud bang, letting in a blast of icy wind.

***

Addy turned to Frank, her eyes brimming. "You have no idea what you've stirred. His grief after the accident nearly consumed him. He was broken—a shell of himself. My tribe's elders gathered to help him heal, to draw out the darkness that haunted him. It took months, years, for the storm inside him to quiet."

Her voice softened, filled with sadness. "But a fragment of that darkness remained— like a shadow he could never outrun."

Frank nodded slowly, understanding dawning in his eyes. "I know that darkness. I've seen it in Abby too. She carries the same unseen scars."

The admission felt heavier than truth—it was empathy, shaped by his own ghosts.

Addy took a deep breath and wrapped her shawl tighter around her shoulders. "Stay inside, Mr. Thompson. I'm going to him. I don't know how this will end, but be ready for anything."

She slipped outside, the door closing softly behind her.

Frank stood alone, staring into the fire. The clock ticked faintly, each second stretching long. Outside, coyotes howled—a mournful, echoing cry across the cold December night. The sound prickled the back of his neck.

Somewhere beyond the trees, he thought he heard the rhythmic murmur of chanting, carried faintly on the wind.

The flames cast moving shadows across the walls, twisting into shapes that almost seemed to breathe.

He moved to the window. A flickering glow painted the horizon. When Addy returned, the night air clung to her shawl, the scent of smoke and cedar following her in.

"My uncle—the tribe's chief elder—came over. Jeremy's agreed to release the burden that's been poisoning him all these years. The elders are preparing a cleansing ceremony. He'll face the pain and let it go."

Frank met her gaze. "He needs to. That darkness inside him—it's tied to the Tidestalker. I believe if he finds peace, it will finally vanish."

Addy's eyes softened. "I've always known part of him was still lost to the sea."

"He loved deeply," Frank said. "Maybe too deeply. But it's that same love that's kept him tethered here."

Addy's expression turned reflective. "You know... the irony is almost cruel. All these years, Jeremy blamed himself for losing her, and now their son has saved her life. Maybe that's how this was meant to end—a circle closing after three long decades."

Frank thought of Lookingglass's words: 'Only when both spirits rest will the tide turn.'

She glanced toward the window where the orange glow of the fire still flickered. "I should go back out. They'll need me."

Frank watched her disappear through the doorway and then sank into a chair, the exhaustion catching up to him. He rubbed his temples, thinking of Lookingglass's sealed envelope tucked in his satchel. Perhaps it was time to open it—or perhaps it was better to wait until the final chapter of this strange odyssey unfolded.

***

Through the window, the ritual had begun. A great bonfire roared, sending sparks spiraling into the indigo sky. About twenty figures stood around it, chanting softly. Jeremy was in the center, supported by two men. Addy stood at the edge of the circle, her cloak billowing in the wind. The chants grew stronger—haunting, rhythmic, old as the seas themselves.

The sound vibrated through the glass like distant thunder rolling off the water, low and tidal. Frank's breath caught. The pulse of it seemed to press against his chest with the slow force of a receding wave. Whatever clung to Jeremy wasn't only guilt—it was something older, darker, and now, perhaps, finally slipping free like a shadow pulled back into the sea.

Hours passed. When Addy came back inside, the first light of dawn was streaking the sky. Frank had dozed off in the chair. She touched his arm gently.

He startled awake. "Addy—what's happening?"

"It's nearly over," she said softly. "The darkness in him was deeper than we knew, but he's fighting through it. The elders will stay with him until sunrise."

Frank exhaled slowly. "Then maybe... at last... the curse is breaking."

Addy nodded, her eyes weary but hopeful. "You should rest, Frank. There's a guest room down the hall. It's warmer there."

He started to protest, but she smiled faintly. "Despite that tough exterior, you're freezing. Get some rest. The road ahead isn't finished yet."

He followed her down the hall, the wooden floor creaking beneath their feet. She opened a small room—a bed neatly made, a single lamp glowing softly.

"You'll be cozy here," she said. "I'll bring you coffee—and maybe a sandwich. You'll need your strength."

Frank managed a tired smile. "Thank you, Addy. For everything."

She gave a quiet nod and left him there, her footsteps fading down the hall.

He sat on the edge of the bed, the night's voices still echoing faintly outside—the wind, the chanting, the crackle of the dying fire. His thoughts drifted between the living and the lost. Abby, Jeremy, the Tidestalker... the threads were finally converging.

Somewhere beyond the trees, the first gull cried, its lonely call threading through the dawn—a promise or a warning, he couldn't tell.

INTERLUDE

The Last Light

Night was fading from the island. The bonfire had long since burned to embers, leaving only a faint red pulse beneath the ash. Smoke curled low along the ground, mingling with fog that rolled in from the sea.

Frank stood alone on the porch, a blanket draped over his shoulders, watching the first light of morning creep across the horizon. The air smelled of cedar and salt—clean, cold, and alive. Behind him, the house was quiet; the chanting had ceased, and Jeremy slept at last, his breath slow and even. The elders had gone before dawn, leaving the faint echo of drums in the still air, as if the rhythm still lingered somewhere just beyond hearing.

The tide was retreating, whispering softly over the stones below. Each pull of water seemed to draw away a little more of the weight that had pressed on this place—on all of them.

Frank closed his eyes and felt the calm rise within him, a peace edged with sadness.

He thought of Abby—of the storm that had taken her, of the decades she'd lost, of the long road that had brought them all to this fragile quiet. Somewhere, far inland, she was waking to snow and morning light, her pulse strong again.

The horizon brightened, the sea reflecting a pale strip of gold. For an instant, the light touched the roof of the house, glinting off the frost, and the island seemed to breathe.

Frank exhaled, long and slow. The last light of the old storm had passed. What remained was only daybreak.

Chapter Twenty-Nine

High Tide

When peace arrives, it never comes alone

Frank woke to the sound of gulls crying somewhere beyond the fog. For a long moment he lay still, disoriented, watching a pale stripe of dawn slip across the ceiling. The air in the small guest room smelled faintly of sea salt and burned cedar. Outside, the wind had stilled; the storm had passed.

A faint creak echoed through the rafters, as though the house itself exhaled after holding its breath all night.

He sat up slowly, his shoulders heavy with the ache of too many nights without rest. Pulling on his boots, he caught sight of himself in the mirror—eyes red, jaw unshaven, the weary look of a man who'd seen too much and slept too little.

The house was quiet when he stepped into the hallway. Only the steady tick of a clock broke the silence. The faint glow of the fireplace cast amber light across the walls, where shadows of last night's ceremony still seemed to move.

He half-expected to see shapes dancing in the embers, the remnants of old spirits reluctant to depart. He walked to the window and looked toward the shoreline. The bonfire had burned to ash, and smoke rose in thin, ghostly tendrils that wavered above the blackened stones. Addy stood near the waterline, her shawl drawn tight against the morning chill, watching the horizon where gray light met the sea.

Frank joined her outside. Frost glazed the steps, crunching under his boots. "Morning," he said softly.

She didn't turn right away. "You slept?"

"A little."

Addy nodded, her breath forming clouds in the air. "He's inside, resting. They finished the ceremony just before dawn. My uncle says the darkness left him quietly—like a tide pulling away from shore."

Frank searched her face. "What does that mean, exactly?"

Her gaze drifted toward the waves. "He's alive, but changed. When the elders drove the spirit out, it didn't fight. It... surrendered. But something went with it. I can't say what."

Frank looked past her to the sea. The water was calm now, reflecting a thin band of silver light. "He's free then," he said, though his voice lacked conviction.

"Free," she echoed. "But peace always asks a price."

They stood for a while in silence, listening to the surf. The tide hissed over the pebbles, each retreating wave whispering secrets neither could decipher.

At last Frank said, "I need to get back to Bellingham. Abby's awake now, and Hayden's waiting. They both deserve to know the truth."

Addy turned to him with a faint, knowing smile. "Then go. But don't expect truth to bring comfort," she said. "The ocean never gives without taking something back. The path that began at the sea must end there. Join us for dinner on Christmas Day."

Frank nodded, glancing one last time at the house. Through the frosted window he could see Jeremy in a chair near the fire, head bowed, his silhouette still as driftwood. Addy's words lingered in his ears as he climbed into his SUV and started down the narrow gravel road.

The tires hissed over frozen puddles, and the forest closed in around him like a dim cathedral of evergreens. A crow flitted across the road ahead, vanishing into mist—a dark punctuation mark on his leaving.

***

Across the border, dawn light spilled through the motel window. Abby sat at the small table, dressed in soft gray and sipping tea, her color returning. Hayden leaned against the wall, studying her like someone relearning the contours of sunlight after a long night.

"You slept?" he asked

"I dreamed," she said simply. "Not of the beach... not of before. Just of water—calm water."

Her voice carried a trace of wonder, as though calm itself were a forgotten language.

A small smile touched his lips. "That's progress."

Her gaze drifted to the snowy street outside. "Frank hasn't called yet, has he?"

"No," Hayden said. "But I've got a feeling he will soon."

Her voice trembled at the edge of relief, as though speaking the words might call it back.

Then the motel phone rang.

Hayden hesitated, then picked it up. "Hello?"

Static filled the line, then a voice—steady, familiar, but strained. "It's Frank."

"Where are you?" Hayden asked.

"On the road. Heading back. Last night at Jeremy's house, I had a frightening experience, though we're close to resolving this whole matter. I expect to arrive this evening, maybe late. Get some rest and a meal or two— you'll feel better. The restaurant next door serves a fine breakfast."

"Okay, what's the plan?" said Hayden.

"You can tell Abby however you see fit, but we're all going to Jeremy's place tomorrow. There'll be a reunion of sorts—on Christmas Day."

Hayden walked back and forth, his mind turning over the idea. "Christmas Day?"

Abby lifted her head and walked toward him, her eyes wide with astonishment.

"Yes," said Frank. "It can't wait a day longer."

"We were invited to their house for Christmas dinner. I've got a suite at the hotel in Ucluelet. I'll lose signal in a minute—dense forest between here and the coast. I'll check in again at the border. Take care and give my love to Abby." The call went dead.

***

Hayden stared at the silent phone, the low hum of the line fading into nothing. He turned to Abby and pulled her into his arms.

"All right," she whispered, "what now?"

"The plan's simple," he said softly. "Tomorrow we go. We'll face it—together."

His voice wavered slightly, not from doubt, but from the weight of what together truly meant now.

A nervous laugh escaped her as she sank into the couch. "It's almost too surreal. Christmas... and I'll be with my husband—a man I haven't seen in thirty years. I don't even know what I'm supposed to feel." Her brow furrowed. "His wife will be there. His son, too. How does anyone prepare for that?"

Hayden rubbed his temples. "We can't prepare, Abby. We can only show up. Whatever happens, happens. You're not alone anymore."

She looked down, then clapped her hands softly. "Well, I guess we have no choice but to face the music. Watching his reaction will be the hardest part. I can only imagine."

Hayden forced a smile. "Let's get breakfast, then maybe some rest. Big day ahead."

"Breakfast?" She shook her head, half amused. "How can you think about food?"

"Because," he said gently, "sometimes you need a little normal to get through the impossible."

They stepped outside into the December chill, their breath mingling in the frosty air as they headed to the restaurant next door.

Behind them, the motel sign flickered once and went dark, as if the world itself were holding its breath for what came next.

***

The weak December sunshine danced on the choppy waters as Frank waited at the ferry dock. He'd accomplished his mission and found Jeremy. Bits and pieces of the journey had begun to fall into place, the end now within sight.

As he watched the gulls wheel over the gray sea, Frank's thoughts drifted. How would Jeremy react when he saw Abby? And what would Abby feel when she looked at him—thirty years older, with another life behind him? He remembered the night before, glancing through the window at the brightest star in the sky. Could it have been a sign? In his imagination, he saw old Mr. Lookingglass grinning up there, his wrinkled face glowing like the moon, eyebrows arched in cosmic mischief.

Frank almost heard the man's echo: 'Stories end where they began—by the water.'

The ferry horn sounded, low and resonant. Frank boarded and moved to the rear deck, watching the wake churn white beneath the propellers. Gulls followed the ferry, hovering in its path like patient sentinels of the sea.

By the time he crossed the U.S. border, the sun had slipped behind the horizon, painting the sky in streaks of orange and violet. It was dark when he pulled into the motel parking lot.

With a weary sigh, he climbed out, already picturing the comfort of hot coffee. Inside the diner next door, the warmth and scent of fried potatoes and coffee grounds wrapped around him like a blanket.

At a booth in the back, Hayden and Abby sat together, their quiet laughter blending with the hum of conversation. Hayden spotted him first and waved. "Over here, weary traveler."

Frank joined them, shrugging off his coat. He gulped his coffee and, between breaths, began recounting his long night at Jeremy's house—the fire light, the ceremony, and Addy's warning about the cost of peace. It was clear the end of their long, strange journey was near.

By the next morning—Christmas Eve— they were packed and ready. The skies hung gray and heavy with moisture, snow flurries drifting through the air.

They crossed into Canada as a brisk northerly wind swept the inlet with delicate snowflakes falling. The world seemed hushed, suspended between anticipation and memory.

At last, they checked into the seaside hotel Frank had arranged, the lobby bright with Christmas lights and the faint scent of pine. Tomorrow would bring closure—or something close to it.

Outside, the tide whispered against the rocks, steady and patient, as if counting down the hours until truth surfaced.

Chapter Thirty

Christmas by the Sea

When the tide turns to calm

The house perched on the bluff of Vancouver Island glowed in the soft Christmas light. Snow dusted the cedar roof and the jagged rocks below, and the Pacific stretched silver and restless, waves rolling endlessly against the cliffs. Inside, the smell of pine and cedar mingled with roasted salmon, baked bread, and the faint sweetness of cinnamon pudding. The soft clinking of dishes and low murmurs of conversation gave the room a warm, domestic rhythm, contrasting the sharp winter wind that pressed against the windows.

A string of tiny white lights framed the windowpanes, their glow trembling whenever the wind pushed against the glass, as if the house itself were breathing with the sea.

Abby stood at the driveway edge, Hayden beside her, Frank a careful step behind. The sweater Hayden had lent her wrapped snugly around her shoulders. Thirty years had passed since she was swept from Jermey's boat in Oregon at twenty-six, lost to the merciless ocean. Memories of the Oregon house—the creaking floorboards, the scent of cedar, the Pacific spray— surfaced now, framed by awe and gratitude. Though Jeremy did not know it, the house still stood, preserved in trust for him and Abby. A quiet gift from the past, a tether connecting what had been to what remained.

Her pulse quickened; even the air seemed charged, as though the years between them were a living thing shrinking with every breath. The last two months had been relentless. Hayden and Frank had chased rumors, pieced together clues, and navigated dead ends with unwavering focus. Their friendship, forged in sleepless nights and frigid coastal mornings, had become a firm anchor. Abby felt their loyalty holding her now, steadying her as she approached the impossible.

She had imagined this moment countless times, yet standing here, it felt quieter—more human—than any dream could have prepared her for.

***

Before they could knock, the door opened. Jermey appeared first, older, gray threading his hair, eyes wide with disbelief and tentative hope. Addy followed, poised, calm, a tray of steaming tea in her hands. Behind them, Jeremy's sons lingered in the hallway, expressions taut with awe, curiosity, and uncertainty—young men caught between astonishment and reverence for the woman who had shaped their father's past.

"Abby?" Jeremy's voice trembled, heavy with the weight of thirty years.

Abby stepped inside, calm, deliberate. "Hello," she said softly, her voice carrying the quiet authority of someone who had been lost long enough to understand the gravity of return. Hayden and Frank followed, staying close but letting her lead.

The room's warmth met her like a tide— every color and sound too vivid, every heartbeat impossibly loud.

Addy guided Abby to a chair by the hearth, smiling gently. The eldest son, the brain surgeon, stared, awe-struck. Only days ago, he had stabilized her memory center, saving her from the overload that had threatened to fracture her mind. Now she was here—alive, whole, breathing.

For the first time since the surgery, Abby sensed calm inside her own thoughts—a silence that felt earned rather than empty.

Conversation began cautiously. they talked about the boys; Abby asked about the house; the sons offered careful words, tentative and measured. The ocean pressed through the windows, waves cresting in silver arcs, an ancient rhythm and patient. Hayden squeezed Abby's hand; Frank scanned the room, protective but calm, a silent guardian. Addy adjusted a chair subtly, her gaze lingering on Abby with quiet curiosity, as if measuring the reality of her presence.

The dialogue carried the fragility of glass— every word placed carefully, afraid to break the spell.

***

By mid-afternoon, the table was set for Christmas dinner. Roasted salmon, butter glazed vegetables, warm bread, and pudding waited. Addy orchestrated quietly, sons carrying dishes with reverence. Abby moved among them, gestures carrying echoes of her younger self, the tilt of her shoulders, the curve of her smile, the graceful lift of her hands. Hayden brushed her hand under the table; Frank remained close, vigilant yet unobtrusive.

It felt like watching two timelines overlap—past and present sharing the same breath for the first time.

The meal began tentatively.

"It's... it's hard to believe," said Dr. Stayton quietly, eyes lingering on Abby.

"I know," Abby replied softly, glancing at the eldest son. "You saved me."

He shook his head. "I didn't know who I was saving... only that I had to."

Small smiles flickered across the sons' faces as they passed the dishes. The youngest, noticing a familiar scent of rosemary, murmured to Abby, "It smells just like Mom's cooking." Abby's smile softened, her eyes flicking briefly toward Addy, who gave a small, polite nod.

Abby's glance lingered a moment longer— she sensed Addy's quiet acceptance as something closer to grace than rivalry.

The conversation warmed gradually.

Laughter threaded lightly, fragile at first, then more genuine. Hayden and Frank exchanged a brief glance—half relief, half awe—at how naturally Abby was moving through the room. The eldest son caught himself reaching for a serving dish and paused, unsure if he should speak; instead, he let the silence linger, reverent.

Abby smiled, her voice carrying warmth and the faint trace of the woman she had been thirty years ago. She marveled that ordinary laughter could feel more miraculous than the supernatural itself.

***

Dessert arrived, conversation became intimate, teasing, playful. Small jokes about the last two months of the search, Hayden and Frank's tireless persistence, the improbable reunion wove through the room. Abby caught the eldest son's fascination, the way he shook his head, slowly comprehending the miracle that had returned her life.

Addy quietly refilled Hayden's glass and gave Abby a brief, appraising glance; the youngest son subtly nudged his brother with a quiet, wide-eyed expression, a mix of awe and disbelief.

After the meal, Abby rose. "I need to see the sea," she whispered.

Hayden offered his hand; Frank stepped close. followed cautiously, Jeremy with Addy at his side, the sons trailing. Outside, the wind tugged at coats and hair, carrying the brine of the Pacific and the faint drift of snow. Abby approached the bluff's edge, the silver waves stretching endlessly below. She closed her eyes, letting the ocean's rhythm center her. Memories of the Oregon house flickered—its cedar walls, the creak of the floorboards, the boat accident— but it remained untouched, preserved in trust, a silent guardian for Jeremy and Addy.

The salt in the air stung her lips; she tasted both grief and renewal in the same breath.

Jeremy stepped closer, hesitation written in his face. "You look... like yourself," he said quietly, as if surprised the words even existed after all these years.

Abby gave a small nod. "I feel more like myself than I ever thought I would again."

He swallowed, emotions tightening briefly in his throat. "We lost a lifetime, Abby. But I never stopped hoping you'd find solid ground."

A soft breath escaped her — not quite a sigh, more like relief uncoiling. "I think I finally have."

Jeremy managed a gentle smile. "Good. That's all I ever wanted for you."

She touched his arm lightly, a gesture of gratitude rather than nostalgia. "Thank you... for saying that."

He nodded once, stepped back, and let her go.

Exhaled, sorrow and acceptance threading through his shoulders. Jeremy's soul found peace, and his mind was satisfied. The Tide Stalker on the Oregon coast would exist no longer.

The sea below sighed as though agreeing, pulling the last shadow of that name into its depths.

The moments shimmered with quiet awe. Hayden squeezed her hand; Frank remained watchful, protective, letting the miracle breathe.

Seagulls calling overhead, their voices like punctuation marks in the silence.

Finally, Abby turned to Hayden, her gaze luminous with certainty. Hayden grasped her hand firmly. Frank stepped forward, keys in hand—the old Ford Expedition waiting at the driveway. The three of them would leave, carrying the miracle of a life reclaimed.

Addy, Jeremy and the sons watched silently as Abby, Hayden, and Frank drove away. The cliffs and crashing ocean receded behind them. Snow drifted lightly across the shoreline. Abby leaned into Hayden, hand brushing his, Frank driving steadily, calm and vigilant.

The headlights carved twin paths through the snow—two lines of light leading away from the sea, unbroken.

As the road stretched along the coast, Frank spoke gently. "You know... the trust on your Oregon house expires in January. After that... it's gone."

Abby pressed her forehead lightly to the window, letting the wind tug at her hair. The house remained in her mind—cedar walls, creak of the floorboards, the Pacific spray—silent, honored, preserved long enough to remind her that the past had survived, even if it would never return.

"I'll remember it," she murmured. "That's enough. It's part of me now, even if no one else sees it."

Frank nodded. "Some things are meant to stay in memory."

Hayden reached over, brushing her hand. "And we'll carry you forward from here," he said.

Abby smiled faintly, the ocean endless beside them. The past had survived. The present was hers to live. And the future—luminous, unbroken, and vast—stretched ahead, as eternal as the sea.

Somewhere far below, a single wave struck the rocks and withdrew, leaving only stillness—a final heartbeat of the sea.

* ~ *

Epilogue

A Whisper of the Past

A few days later, Abby stood alone on the deck of the beach house. The wind tugged at her hair and the Pacific stretched endless beneath a pale winter sky. The Oregon house loomed on the bluff, silent and still, the cedar walls catching the last rays of afternoon light. It had waited patiently for her all these years, preserved in trust, a tether to a life she had lost but never truly forgotten.

She closed her eyes and breathed in the cold, briny air, letting memories drift—her laughter echoing in the empty rooms, Jeremy's hands on the railing, the boat rocking in the rough water, the soft creak of floorboards beneath her bare feet. She felt the pulse of the place, a rhythm of love, loss, and survival, and smiled. It belonged to her now, if only in memory, and that was enough.

Opening her eyes, she stepped back toward the waiting Ford Expedition. Hayden's hand brushed hers as she slid into the passenger seat, a small, grounding gesture. Frank leaned against the hood, a quiet grin tugging at the corner of his mouth, eyes scanning the horizon.

"Ready?" Hayden asked softly, glancing at her.

Abby nodded, letting the corners of her lips curve into a small, contented smile. One last glance at the house—the sun reflecting on its cedar walls, the faint shimmer of the Pacific below—and she whispered to herself, "Goodbye... and thank you."

The engine hummed as Frank steered the Expedition onto the coastal highway. Abby leaned her forehead lightly against the window watching the waves stretch endlessly alongside them. Hayden's hand found hers again, their fingers intertwining in quiet, steady companionship. Frank's eyes flicked briefly to the rearview mirror, protective, vigilant, yet serene.

The sun dipped lower, streaking the water with gold, and Abby felt the rhythm of the ocean seep into her bones, steady and eternal. She exhaled slowly, letting go of decades of fear, loss, and uncertainty. The Oregon house, preserved and waiting, would remain with her in memory, even as the road carried them forward.

Hayden squeezed her hand lightly. "We're here, Abby. Wherever we go, we take it with us."

She turned to him, her eyes shimmering faintly with gratitude and love. "Yes. With you, and Frank... we're home."

The wind shifted, carrying the scent of salt and cedar, mingling with the soft hum of the engine. Abby leaned back in her seat, letting the car, the ocean, and the horizon remind her that the past had survived. The present was hers to live. And the future—luminous, unbroken, and vast—stretched ahead, as eternal and limitless as the sea beside them.

As Frank turned onto Highway 26 to Portland he glanced in the rearview mirror at Hayden and Abby and then down to the seat beside him and smiled with one hand firmly on the sealed envelope that Lookingglass gave him.

Abby's Final Reflection

The wind never forgets where it's been.

The morning light spilled through the clouds in soft ribbons, brushing the waves with pale gold. Abby stood alone on the bluff, the sea breathing below her—eternal, familiar, and impossibly wide. The tide was high again, folding and unfolding against the rocks, the same rhythm that had carried her away once and returned her to herself decades later.

She closed her eyes and listened—to the distant cry of gulls, the rhythmic roll of surf, and the sigh of wind combing through the coastal evergreens. A soft drizzle hung in the air, cool and clean, beading along her eyelashes and darkening her hair. Each sound, each scent, felt like an echo from another lifetime: cedar floors creaking under bare feet, the crackle of a fire in the Oregon house, the low hum of Jeremy's voice calling her name. The memories were no longer sharp or painful; they drifted now like sea glass, softened by time and tide.

For years, the ocean had been her keeper— wild, unpredictable, filled with unanswered questions. Now it was only a companion. It asked nothing of her. It forgave everything. The storm that had haunted her had at last gone out with the tide.

She thought of him and Addy, of their quiet courage and the peace that had come to them at last. She thought of Frank—steady and loyal, still chasing truth like a fisherman chasing light—and of Hayden, whose steadfast heart had brought her safely through every storm.

She pressed her palm to her chest, feeling the faint beat beneath. We all crossed the same waters, she thought. Each of us just trying to find our way home.

The wind lifted her hair and sent it streaming behind her like a small banner of light. She smiled—softly, almost to herself. Turning from the sea, she took one last look at the horizon, at the endless silver-blue that had shaped her life.

"Goodbye," she whispered, not to the past this time, but to the weight of it.

And as she walked back toward the waiting SUV where Hayden and Frank stood talking, the horizon brightened, the sea calm and endless, carrying her story forward—no longer lost, but free.

The tide rolled in and out, unbroken and eternal, carrying their footprints away but leaving their story behind.

About the Author

Patrick Timm is a freelance writer and columnist well known in Southwest Washington for his long-running weather column in The Columbian newspaper. A lifelong observer of the Pacific Northwest's skies and shorelines, he brings that same attention to atmosphere and mood into his fiction.

TIDE STALKER is his debut mystery novel

The Tide Stalker Saga continues ...

Discover what the sea left behind in

The Lookingglass Papers — Coming 2026

www.ingramcontent.com/pod-product-compliance
Lightning Source LLC
Chambersburg PA
CBHW030514120726
47904CB00005B/1457